Relationship Killer

Flenardo

Publisher's Note: This is a work of fiction. Names, characters,
places, and incidents are products of the author's imagination.
Locale and public names are sometimes used for atmospheric
purposes. Any resemblance to actual people, living or dead, or
to businesses, companies, events, or institutions is completely
coincidental.

Published by
Creolistic Ink Publishing
Hahnville, LA 70057

Edited by Marsha Dickson

Graphic Designed by Pbimbola (Fiverr)

ISBN: 979-8-218-54644-1

DEDICATION

To all the ones who love infidelity,
Cherish your last orgasm because mine comes
from watching you take your final breath.

Yours Truly,

The Relationship Killer

BOOKS BY FLENARDO

THE POETIC WHORE

MARRIED TO THE PEN

FORBIDDEN FORGIVENESS

DEVASTATION

Thank You

CHAPTER 1

Dominic has been thinking about his latest mark nonstop since they have been chatting online for the past two months. He never knew guys to send six to eight dick pics daily until he met Viktor Henderson, a bi-sexual construction foreman from Phenix City, AL.

Is this what females go through when they first meet a guy? he deliberates while sliding his arms out of his coat and handing it over to the attendant for the evening.

He nods his head and walks over to the illustrious check-in counter. "Sherlock Homes," Dominic announces as the shirtless guy at the counter taps some keys on the tablet in search of his name.

"Mr. Holmes, your verification is good to go. Please enjoy the party."

It has taken persistence and the proper connections to gain access to this masquerade party. Dominic loves the secrecy of using book characters and bank account routing numbers for entry.

Dominic smiles and parts his lips slowly. He rolls out his three-inch tongue and flips it back in. "Oh, it'll be a party to die for," he responds in his deep baritone voice while winking one of his gray eyes through the mask's eyelid.

He strolls into the banquet room and sees the men drinking and dancing to Sylvester's, *You Make Me Feel* disco song. Luckily, he loves that song as well. He vogues his way to the bar and requests a drink from the bartender.

"Can you please make me a color-changing martini?"

"Great selection," the bartender concurs and spins around to prepare the drink.

Dominic snaps his fingers and bobs his head to the song while waiting for Viktor to notice him sitting at the bar.

Dominic texts Viktor a selfie of him wearing a black rooster feather shawl and a black Ancient Roman Greek mask.

Viktor's response was another dick picture with the caption, *We can't wait to meet you.*

The bartender sets the martini on the counter and serves the other guests.

Dominic takes a sip. "Ahh, this is soothing to my mouth."

He continues listening to the music, and after the third song, he wonders what is taking this guy so long to meet him.

His phone vibrates in his pocket as he orders another drink.

He pulls it out and unlocks the screen. The message reads, *Take the elevator in the lobby and meet me on the rooftop. I have something special for the two of us.*

"This guy is fucking extra," he mumbles.

He orders another drink to go, thanks the bartender, and leaves the banquet room, searching for the elevator.

Walking down the hallway, he finds the elevator on the right side and presses the button. The doors open, and he steps inside and thinks to himself as he rides, *Let's get this shit over with, so I can watch Netflix.*

The doors open, and he steps onto the rooftop terrace with the stars shining above and a cool breeze. He finds Viktor fully nude, wearing an LGBTQ mask with crystals and rhinestones. He is drinking a bottle of Koval Barreled Gin while rubbing his thumb around the head of his dick.

He waves his hand, signaling Dominic to join their intimate party. Dominic takes a small sigh and saunters over. He's unsure what to expect from Viktor.

"Aren't you cold out here without your clothes on?" Dominic asks.

"Real men drink and fuck," Viktor replies. "Come on, don't be a stranger. Get undressed. You know you want to suck on this," Viktor insists while stroking his cock.

"I think I'll keep my clothes on. Anyways, all you need is my mouth."

"Damn, the thought of watching you suck my cock through your mask is turning me on. Pucker up, buttercup. I have been waiting for you to taste me forever. I'm going to assault the fuck out of your throat. Do you mind if I drink while you serve me some hot head?" Viktor asks.

"Do you, boo," Dominic replies.

Dominic squats down and places his hands on his knees. He does the Kappa shimmy shake.

"Hell yeah! Dance on this dick," he growls and drinks another mouthful from the bottle.

Dominic rolls his tongue out of his mouth and flicks it in the air as he continues to dance.

"Viktor, are you ready for the best head you have ever experienced? It's to die for, I promise."

Viktor scoots his butt cheeks across the ledge. "Please show me that magic mouth," he implores.

Dominic crouches lower, ensuring his stance is precise before launching himself upwards. With a swift motion, he unleashes a roundhouse kick that connects with Viktor's temple, the resounding thud resonating through the air. The force of the impact causes Viktor to scream as he falls backwards off the edge of the ledge.

Dominic strides confidently towards the elevator, not bothering to look back. He takes the elevator down to the bustling party on the lower level and seamlessly blends in as if nothing out of the ordinary has occurred.

He usually kills people without them ever knowing he was there, but Viktor's dick pics were annoying as fuck. He wanted this kill to be personal, and Viktor's wife would soon reap the benefits of his cheating ways.

He heads back to the bar and confidently orders another martini, fully aware of the chaos that is about to unfold. It's only a matter of time before someone goes outside for a cigarette or vape break and stumbles upon Viktor's body, inciting panic and completely altering the mood of this clubhouse.

He eagerly awaits as the Djay plays a few more dance hits before suddenly, half of the guests rush out the door. He takes a sip of his drink, stands up, does a quick two-step across the dance floor and then joins the crowd in exiting the venue.

"It's beginning to look a lot like Christmas," he sings to himself as he enters the hallway and walks out the door.

Navigating through the crowd, he spots Viktor's lifeless form splayed across the unforgiving concrete. His body is contorted in ways that defy nature, and the crimson splatter surrounding him resembles a spilled drink on the ground. Fragments of brain matter peek out from his fractured skull, adding to the gruesome scene.

A commotion breaks out and you can sense the stirring of gossip in the air. Dominic catches a man whispering, "Who will break the news to his wife about what happened here? The clubhouse is meant to be a sanctuary."

Tonight's events left him feeling exhilarated. He had accomplished his mission of posing as a gay man to get close enough to kill Viktor, and it was quite the spectacle. Dominic takes one more sip of his drink before heading back inside to retrieve his coat.

The clubhouse is akin to an exclusive group, and they are unable to seek assistance until a strategy is devised to cover up the killing. He fully expects that by tomorrow, the media will be buzzing about the unfortunate passing of a well-regarded husband at their gathering.

In a different part of the city, Dominic's mission tonight would have been much more difficult. However, during his planning, he discovered that this specific location had never utilized surveillance cameras during their events. This was likely due to the attendance of some of Columbus's most prestigious lawyers at these parties.

Dominic enters a code on his phone, and his trusted hacker removes his fake banking profile along with his membership page, erasing any trace of his existence from their network

It was unimaginable to Dominic that he would ever work in Columbus, GA. Despite its small size, he enjoys the adventurous nature of this place and the company of beautiful women. Additionally, the high level of diversity at Fort Moore, an Army base, is a significant plus.

He has the ability to charm a successful woman, or he could cruise down Victory Drive in pursuit of a hood chick like Sexyy Redd and some ratchet pussy.

When operations require out-of-state missions, Atlanta International Airport is accessible via I-85, which is 98 miles away.

Dominic is a small-town guy who made the mistake of falling for the wrong girl at the right moment. The most insane part? He still finds himself missing her occasionally, but he understands that once someone is gone, they can't be brought back to life.

Her memories are carried within the essence of every life he has ended and every future life he will ruin.

He gazes up at the glittering stars, takes a deep breath, and strides towards his 718 Cayman Green Metallic Porsche. A few individuals leave the club like Cinderella, escaping before midnight strikes. Before sunrise, they must hurry home and transform into devoted husbands, respectable deacons, and responsible schoolteachers.

Dominic starts his car and drives away from the clubhouse parking lot. Before heading home, he tosses his mask onto the back seat and looks for a nearby Waffle House. He knows two things will likely happen at the restaurant: he'll get some scrambled eggs with cheese and watch a fight between the staff and an intoxicated customer.

The image of Viktor's lifeless form on the pavement ignites a sudden craving for salty bacon. He convinces himself that he can work it off tomorrow with a run along the Riverwalk.

Flenardo

"IN MY REALITY, HAVING A HELTER-SKELTER MIND AND SCRAMBLED EGGS IS BETTER THAN BUSTING A NUT IN A BEAUTIFUL WOMAN."

CHAPTER 2

Tiana shakes hands with the prosecutor. "Great case. For a moment, I thought you had me beat until your witness recanted their story."

"Yeah, I'm sure you tampered with the case. I don't know how to prove it. I won't be a sore loser, though. Congratulations on allowing another guilty felon to walk the streets free, Ms. Henley."

She releases her hand from inside of his and whispers in his ear, "Come on, Mark. Justice isn't blind, and facts will always prevail. How about you allow me to buy you a drink at our favorite bar?"

"Thanks, but I have to rush home, change clothes, and meet my wife at the kid's soccer game. Raincheck, perhaps?" he suggests.

"Indeed," she responds. "Please tell Julia I said hello."

They exchange hugs, gather their personal belongings, and exit the courtroom. Outside are reporters, social media influencers, and protestors eagerly waiting to speak to Tiana's client about the dropped charges.

Tiana weaves her way through the bustling crowd and raises two fingers, a signal to her client that they have a limited amount of time left to pay their debt or face the repercussions.

Tiana is renowned in Charlotte as a fierce and unfeeling defense lawyer. Her usual clients are famous athletes or underworld figures. However, she occasionally takes on more minor cases in a less prosperous area to improve her public image.

She crosses the street, retrieves her car from the parking garage, turns on her phone, and receives a flurry of missed calls and text notifications for the next few minutes. She deletes messages from family and shopping stores.

She plays the voicemail and hears Michael's voice, her long-term boyfriend whom she met while secretly dancing through law school at Uptown Cabaret.

Michael Oliver Patterson was a prosperous real estate agent with a limitless bank account. He would grant her any request, especially after learning she wanted to become a lawyer.

Once they became an item, she soon realized the real estate gig was just a front for Michael's actual business. He was using his job to sell houses in upscale neighborhoods to low-income couples, who would then use them as covers for his drug dealing operations. But it didn't stop there - some of these homes were also used as hubs for illegal gambling and swinger's events.

As Tiana's feelings for Michael grew stronger, he became even more insistent on her pursuing a career in law. Her main focus now is keeping his colleagues out of legal trouble so it won't disrupt their daily operations.

Over the past year, she has been in an on-again, off-again relationship with Michael. She made a conscious decision to better her life, but it has caused strain between them. The man who charmed her with his tough guy persona ten years ago is no longer the same man. Marriage hasn't been a topic of conversation for some time now, and she hasn't worn her engagement ring in a month; instead, it sits inside its box on her dresser.

Her mind is flooded with thoughts about her relationship as she listens to the voice message again. "Tiana, I hope you were able to keep Tyeisha from going to jail. I swear this will be the final time. If you want to come out tonight, my clients are hosting a party at their house."

As she reads the message on her phone, she rolls her eyes in exasperation at Michael's constant let-downs. She swiftly scrolls through her text conversations to find the address and time of their meet-up.

Despite Michael's attempts to reach her, she never responds to him. Instead, she prefers to call Catalina, her wild-ass Gemini friend who has been begging her to move to Columbus for a fresh start.

"Hey girl, you have perfect timing. I have been anticipating your call. What juicy stories do you have from the courtroom today?"

"I emerged victorious, as usual, and now Michael wants to celebrate our success. But it feels like ages since we've gone on vacation or had a nice dinner at a fancy restaurant."

"Damn, that's fucked up," Catalina interjects.

"I hear you, but I have no interest in attending the party. However, I'll pretend to be the perfect girlfriend just for appearances. Tell me what's happening in Columbus. How's the family?"

"Everyone is doing well, but the real question is, when are you coming to visit? It has been too long since we partied together. You can hit the dance floor and bring out your alter ego, Mercedes Chanel."

"Catalina, my days of twerking on a pole are over. Plus, my name is legendary, and I can't afford to ruin my legacy. The only pole I need is the one that comes with balls."

They laugh together before Catalina mentions, "Tiana, hold on for a second."

Tiana starts the car and patiently waits for Catalina to come back, while the call switches over to Bluetooth. Then, she pulls out of the parking garage and begins her drive home, thinking about whether or not she wants to go to the party.

Catalina beeps in. "I'm sorry, girl. That was work. Looks like they need me to come in a little earlier. I need to see you, so bring your ass down here next weekend so we can go to the island, drink until we throw up, and chase dicks."

Tiana laughs. "You almost made me choke from your foolishness. Okay, you win. I'll take some vacation days and drive down there."

"Drive down? Are you serious? I can get you a free airline ticket from my job. You can be here in about forty-five minutes or less."

"Catalina, the drive is only five hours, plus it will give me time to think about my relationship with Michael."

"Okay, have it your way. Just know the offer is on the table. I have to get my night started. Te quiero," Catalina says.

"I love you, too. Get ready for work, and I'll see you soon," Tiana promises.

Tiana rides home in silence and slips through the front door, making a beeline for her walk-in closet. She sifts through the racks of clothes, trying to find something appropriate for the party tonight. Sometimes, she enjoys dressing up like a glamorous model, but other times, she just wants to be comfortable in yoga pants, an oversized t-shirt, and a pair of running shoes.

She talks to herself as she slides the hangers back across the rail. "What does a woman wear when they don't want to be there but still wants to look and feel sexy?"

Her hands come to a sudden halt when she spots Michael's Arctic Ice-colored dress shirt amongst her wardrobe. "How did you get in here?" she asks the shirt curiously, before deciding to wear it for the evening.

She removes it from the hanger and smooths out any remaining wrinkles with an iron. Next, she selects a pair of sky-high heels, a shiny silver belt, and a matching white lace bra and thong to wear underneath the shirt.

She tries to call Michael before taking a shower, but he doesn't answer and it goes straight to voicemail. She shrugs it off and continues with her pre-shower routine. Once she finishes her much-needed shower, she applies makeup and gets dressed for the evening with a refreshed feeling.

She picks up her silver wristlet bag, places her phone inside, and walks out the door.

Even though she tries to call him multiple times, Michael's phone keeps going to voicemail as she makes her way to the party. Growing increasingly frustrated, she decides to just go without any further efforts to contact him.

She sings to escape reality as she cruises out of the city towards the Old Foxcroft neighborhood, where homes start at five million dollars. Arriving at the estate, she is momentarily speechless, realizing that Michael's party is nothing more than a display of wealth and power, with a manipulative couple at its core. Taking a deep breath, she twirls a lock of her hair around her finger before driving her car into the circular driveway, where Bugattis, Mercedes, and Bentleys are parked in pristine rows. As she steps out of the car, she berates Michael silently. *Michael, these wild parties always end up causing a scene. It's getting out of control.*

As she nears the door, she can hear loud music coming from inside. A stranger opens the door without questioning her identity and invites her in. She mutters to herself, "Everyone is too caught up in partying and drinking. They wouldn't even notice if I were an undercover officer."

She starts her quest to find Michael, ignoring the thirsty hoes and their lap dances, as well as the girls drinking from champagne bottles. She makes her way towards the kitchen and sees Devontae, one of Michael's long-time friends from school. She never liked Devontae and believes he is the reason for Michael's recent shift in demeanor.

"Mercedes Chanel has finally arrived. You're always so fashionably late," he teases, popping a green grape into his mouth.

She holds her tongue and maintains a polite facade towards his repulsive demeanor. "Would you mind addressing me as Tiana? I know you've always been envious because I chose Michael as my VIP guest instead of your small-dick ass. The other dancers returned with stories of your inability to perform, but they still slept with you for the money you were throwing around.

"Now, address me as Tiana, and kindly let me know Michael's whereabouts," she says with a scowl on her face.

He casually pops another grape into his mouth and gazes deeply into her eyes. "To me, you'll always be an ass-shaker," he repeats playfully. "But don't worry, your man is upstairs waiting for you with a surprise," he hints mischievously.

"Devontae, keep popping those grapes because, as I said, nothing is popping in your pants."

She walks away in search of Michael.

She heads upstairs to find Michael. She can't help but wonder why he's hiding up here instead of being a good host to his guests. As she walks down the hallway, curiosity fuels her search for him.

As she passes by the bathroom, she hears what sounds like a woman moaning in ecstasy. She pays it no mind, knowing that hookups are a common occurrence at Michael's parties. But as the moans grow louder and more distinct, she realizes that the man's voice sounds eerily similar to Michael's.

A muffled voice can be heard from behind the door, saying, "Take this dick, bitch. I told you not to wear that slutty ass dress tonight."

She mutters a quick prayer, hoping it isn't Michael behind the door. She turns the doorknob, but it wouldn't budge. "I should have worn my running shoes," she scolds herself.

In a last-ditch effort, she steps back and charges at the door, using her shoulder as a battering ram. The adrenaline kicks in, dulling the impact against her body. She knows she'll be sore later, but right now, all that matters is getting through that door.

As she steps into the room, her eyes immediately land on Michael in a frenzy, trying to gather his scattered clothes with a blonde woman clinging onto his pant leg.

"I didn't think you'd come," he says, guilt written all over his face.

"If you had bothered to answer your phone instead of being busy cumming on her face, you would have known," she responds irritably.

"It's not what it looks like. She doesn't mean anything to me. Can we discuss this later, after the party?"

"Fuck you and this party!" she yells.

She fidgets with her engagement ring until she is able to slip it off. With a burst of frustration, she throws it at him, and it bounces off his chest. "I thought maybe wearing my ring tonight and trying to work through our issues would make a difference, but it's obvious that you're still on that bullshit.

"Michael, it's over. Please do not call or text me again." She steps out of the bathroom and quickly goes downstairs, only to find Devontae laughing with his friends.

He asks eagerly, "Did you receive the surprise I left for you?"

She slaps his cheek with force and grits her teeth. "Fuck you!" she screams.

Not looking back, she marches towards the door, exits the house and heads straight to her car. She curses to herself as she reverses out of the driveway. "I'm done with this relationship. Michael and this city can go to hell."

"WHEN A WOMAN IS FED UP, THERE'S NOT ENOUGH DICK AND MONEY IN THE WORLD TO MAKE HER GIVE THAT MAN A SECOND CHANCE."

CHAPTER 3

Dominic's next target is scheduled in two weeks, and since he doesn't have a woman, he can fuck. He spends his time thinking of ways to kill people.

He has converted his basement into a gym with weights and training equipment, a shooting range, and a laboratory for conducting chemical tests. Tonight, he plans to participate in ax-throwing activities. However, he understands that the likelihood of throwing an ax at a live person is extremely low.

He grips the ax firmly, stands, and faces the target of his ex-wife and battle buddy. He raises the ax over his head, swings then releases, and the ax sails through the air. The sharp edge of the blades sticks in the taped photo on the center of the log.

He walks over to the log, grips the ax handle, and yanks it out of the wood. He then returns to the throwing lane and repeats this technique multiple times.

His eyes remain fixated on the tattered photo as he unleashes a bloodcurdling scream, "I hate you, Jennifer! I'll never forgive you for turning me into this monster!" He storms away from his target and flicks the lights off as he ascends the stairs. Making his way to his sanctuary, he approaches the bar and pours himself a shot of vodka.

In between kills is the only time he allows himself to drink until he eventually passes out on the floor rather than in his bed.

The pain of taking his ex-wife's life and that of his best friend's, still weighs heavily on him. Every time he takes a sip of alcohol, his mind is consumed by thoughts of that fateful night. A part of him regrets pulling the trigger, but simultaneously, the beast inside him enjoys the memory. He pours himself another drink and raises the glass in the air. "Here's to the dead," he toasts.

He grips the bottle tightly, quickly snatching it from the bar before going to the reclining chair. Crashing down into the seat, he presses the button and reclines with his feet in the air. With his eyes shut tight, he continues to drink and dwells on his cheating ass ex-wife. "Bitch got what she deserved," he babbles.

Dominic wished he could have stayed in Afghanistan, ignored Jennifer's behavior, and divorced her when he came home.

Amidst the chaos of war, his thoughts were jumbled and unclear, but he knew that protecting his troops was his top priority. He believed that killing his wife was the only viable option to achieve mental clarity and ensure the safety of those under his command.

Known for his exceptional skills as a soldier, he was held in high regard by powerful individuals. But even now, only a small group of people deemed trustworthy had been aware of the bold choice he made to construct and trigger an improvised explosive device while driving down the road. As a result of this action, he ended up traveling to Ramstein to plan out his next move.

His mind was clouded during the war, and he had troops to protect. The only way for him to clear his mind and guarantee the safety of his soldiers was to eliminate the enemy.

With the help of a General who owed him a favor, Dominic caught a secret flight back to Fort Moore.

He recalled the crisp chill of the night air and the perfect glow of the moon as he ventured into the woods behind his house. After setting up a tree stand, he patiently waited for Jennifer and Tyrese to arrive at his doorstep.

As the bedroom lit up, he peered through his binoculars and witnessed Jennifer wrapping her arms around Tyrese in a tight embrace, followed by a passionate kiss.

Tyrese had been his battle buddy for seven years, and he couldn't believe he was seeing his wife about to fuck someone he considered to be family.

He observed as they undressed, revealing their bare bodies. Jennifer lifted her legs into the air while Tyrese eagerly started to pleasure her between her thighs.

"Jennifer, I'm not going to cry over you, but the world will know you were the one that awakened the beast inside of me. I gave you everything, and this is how you repay me? I'm going to make sure everyone feels my pain," he said to himself while putting the binoculars away.

He sung an Army cadence to motivate himself to take another life.

"Your baby was lonely, as lonely could be /

Til Tyrese provided the company

Ain't it great to have a pal /

Who will fuck your gal?

Sound off! / 1,2

Sound off! / 3,4

Cadence count now! / 1,2,3,4,1,2...3,4!"

He lifted his sniper rifle and peered through the scope, adjusting it to his desired target. In the room, Tyrese laid on the bed as Jennifer straddled him. Tyrese's hands gripped her hips as she rode up and down.

Dominic carefully calculated the dimensions and distance needed to fire a bullet from his location. Pressing his cheek against the butt stock of the rifle, he gently caressed the trigger and took slow, steady breaths to steady himself for the perfect shot. As he aimed at Tyrese, he thought to himself about how little had changed since they first met - Tyrese still loved having sex with the lights on, a fatal vulnerability that was perfect for Dominic's plans.

With calm determination, he squeezed the trigger and watched as the bullet soared through the air. Time seemed to slow down as he reflected on the memories of happier times with Jennifer and how much he loved her until she broke his heart.

But now, everything has changed. The bullet pierced through the bedroom window and hit Jennifer in the head while she rode Tyrese's dick with her toes pointed.

Dominic originally planned to kill Jennifer, frame Tyrese, and watch him suffer in jail. It was a vicious idea, but Tyrese's wife Sasha deserved his Servicemember's Life Insurance.

Inside the crossbeam, Dominic watched Tyrese push Jennifer's lifeless body off him and attempt to seek cover.

"Muthafucker didn't even care for my wife. All she was to him was another side chick."

Dominic clenched his teeth and pulled the trigger, aiming at his former best friend. The bullet pierced the side of Tyrese's forehead, causing him to collapse onto the floor as he tried to flee toward the master closet.

Dominic descended from his tree stand, quickly and efficiently stowed away his gun, and dismantled his sniper position. By sunrise, he was already on a plane back to Germany, pretending to be shocked when he received news of his wife's and best friend's deaths.

He opens his eyes back to reality, tilts the bottle to his mouth, and downs the vodka in one go. He wipes the back of his hand across his mouth and drops the bottle on the floor. He chuckles and says, "I should have won an Oscar or a Grammy for my performance in the hospital."

He grabs the remote and turns on the TV to an episode of *Cheaters*. He loves watching this show and wishes he could kill everyone on the show when they fuck up.

He once wanted to be known as the Joey Greco Killer, but that wasn't original. The more he thought about his marriage and how fucked up the relationship caused him to spiral out of control, he knew the Relationship Killer would be a formidable alias.

CHAPTER 4

Michael escorts a potential buyer out the door and stands in the doorway, waving as they enter their car. He delivered a great sales pitch, but it wasn't his best work. He has been distracted since Tiana caught a bitch giving him head in the bathroom.

He has dialed her number numerous times, and every call goes straight to voicemail. He checks with some of her relatives and closest friends, but everyone's lips are sealed on her whereabouts.

He knows they are lying, especially since they always felt he was a bad influence. *Hell, I'm the one that made it possible for Tiana to get off the stripper pole and go to law school. They should be thanking me with their ungrateful asses,* he thinks to himself.

His phone rings, and he swipes to answer without looking at the number. "Tiana, I'm sorry, baby. I'm so glad you finally called me back."

Devontae chuckles over the phone before criticizing Michael's situation. "You can have any woman you want, but you'd rather mope around crying over Tiana. Come on, Mike, let's go out tonight. My treat and I'll show you some of the finest ladies I know."

"I'm not in the mood to go out. I have to make things right. I might fuck other women, but Tiana has a special place in my life.

"Devontae, I meant to ask you this for a minute, but it slipped my mind a few times. How did Tiana know I was upstairs during the party, and why didn't you or anyone else give me a heads up that she was in the house?"

"There was a lot of celebration going on that night. I was drinking and getting my dick sucked as well. You can't blame me for this one," Devontae responds.

"With friends like you all, who needs enemies?" Michael retorts. "As I mentioned before, I don't want to go out and meet any of your gold-digging bitches. I'm heading home to drink and relax for the evening."

"Enjoy your drink. I'm going to take my ass to see the thirsty gold-diggers and see who's throat I can spend the night in," Devontae boasts.

Michael presses the button to terminate the call and fixates on the screensaver, which displays a photo of him and Tiana. He admits that he has made mistakes and cannot guarantee immediate faithfulness, but he promises to be more careful in avoiding getting caught in the future.

He shuts the door, turns the combination dial, and places the key into the lockbox. As he strolls towards his sleek silver and black all-electric Escalade, he takes a moment to appreciate the vibrant blue of the sky above.

He takes the scenic route out of the suburbs, admiring the typical sight of American soccer moms jogging through their perfectly manicured neighborhood. Each house has meticulously trimmed hedges and a lush green lawn with sharp edges that stop right before the curb and driveway.

He has made significant progress since his days shining shoes in Wadesboro, North Carolina - a city so impoverished that they couldn't even sustain a Walmart store.

Despite the fact that he could easily abandon his side job and focus solely on his real estate career, his thirst for wealth always outweighs his desire for a simple life.

He leaves the suburban neighborhood and merges onto I-85, joining the busy rush-hour traffic. He never complains about the long drive home; he uses the time to return business calls he missed during the day.

As the last call ends, he turns on the radio, allowing the soothing melodies of jazz and neo-soul to calm his mind until he arrives at his extravagant mansion, which boasts seven bedrooms and ten bathrooms.

His dream home was carefully chosen for its distance from the city, and he was actively involved in its design and construction. It serves as his sanctuary, a retreat from the hectic drama of his double life. Only Tiana and Devontae know about this private location.

He grabs his suit jacket and laptop bag before stepping into his home. As he enters the foyer, he sets down his belongings and slips off his shoes. He had notified the housekeepers earlier to prepare the usual before leaving for the evening, so everything should be in order.

On the coffee table sits a tray with a glass, a bucket of ice, and an exquisitely blended Louis Latour red wine. Michael pours himself a drink and raises it to his lips for a sip, only to be interrupted by the chirping sound of his security system.

"Damn, can't a man just have a moment to himself?" he mutters as he grabs his phone.

He opens the app and sees Tiana's car on the screen. "Oh shit, there's a God after all!" he screams as he jumps from his seat, accidentally spilling his drink.

He ignores the mess, sets the glass down, and hurries to press the button to open the gate. He swings the front door open, leaps on the porch, and waits on his Queen.

He watches as Tiana's car glides up the driveway and waves his hand in the air, signaling her to come over. But as the car approaches, he realizes it isn't hers.

He steps into the house and enters a code on the wall behind the door. A hidden compartment opens, and he quickly retrieves his gun before stepping onto the porch.

As the car arrives, he shifts the lever from safe to shoot and raises the gun toward the front windshield. His finger gently depresses the trigger but releases it before the gun fires, allowing him to catch a glimpse of a figure in the car's window, though he can't make out all her features.

The woman turns off her engine and exits her car. Her hair is a vibrant shade of candy apple red, mirroring the color on her full lips. Concealing her eyes behind a pair of sunglasses, she rises to her full height and approaches the porch, strutting confidently in high heels, red lace panties, and a matching bra lingerie set.

Standing at five ten, she radiates grace and confidence, resembling a regal chocolate goddess.

He notices her phat and curvaceous ass by the way her hips sashay up the walkway.

She stops before reaching the first step, bends over, and slides her thong to her ankles. She steps out of them one foot at a time, starting with the left heel and then the right.

The wind seems almost like a woman, carrying the scent of her perfume and pussy directly to his nose. She crumples up the thong in her hand and tosses it in his direction. He eagerly catches it with teeth as it sails through the air.

She unclasps her bra and tosses it on the stairs. Michael's eyes hungrily follow her as she reveals her perky breasts adorned with nipple rings.

She saunters past him, making her way to the couch, where she leans over to pour herself a drink. He sees her butterfly tattoo with wings spread across each ass cheek.

He snaps out of his trance, closes the door, and puts the gun away. He hasn't asked her name, who she works for, or why she is here.

He loves her mysterious act of seduction, and he's not thinking clearly because all of his blood is racing to his hardening dick. He needs a stress release, and this beautiful woman will serve that very purpose.

He creeps over and grinds his crotch over her cheeks. She reaches her hand behind and pats the bulge in his pants.

"You sure you ready for all of this?" he asks.

She turns her head to the side, looks out the corner of her eye, and speaks, "Are you sure you ready for this juicy phat pussy?"

He steps back, removes his shirt, unbuckles his pants, and slides them, along with his underwear, to the floor.

"Put those sexy lips to work and suck on this dick," he commands.

She shrugs her shoulder. "My lips are lethal. I'll have you stuttering and cumming in less than five minutes. It would be best if you kicked your pants off before you trip backwards."

Who's this bitch think she is? I'm going to murder her throat, he thinks to himself.

He yanks a fist full of her hair. "Open your mouth," he demands.

She slaps his arm away. "Let me go. There's no need to be violent. I know how to suck a dick. That's what's wrong with you men—always trying to be aggressive and shit."

He releases her hair. "My apologies, little lady. Please show me your magical mouth."

She tenderly massages the tip of his dick, gliding her hands down the shaft and unleashing her tongue. She takes her time licking around the head, then opens her mouth wider and stretches her head down until her nose brushes against his pelvis.

She cuffs his balls and massages them in her hands. Shifting her eyes upwards, she sees Michael gasping and moaning for more.

She bobs faster, palms his ass cheeks, and manually forces him to thrust down her throat. She stops momentarily, scoots backwards, and leans upside down off the sofa arm.

She points her fingers inside her mouth. "Fuck this mouth as hard as you can."

He shakes his pant legs off and rams his dick down her throat, resting his balls against her nose. He fucks her face hard, grunting gibberish words and slipping a finger in her pussy.

"Oh, I need this nut. Suck me good. This is why you came over; so I can flush my kids down your throat."

As she takes short, sharp breaths, she lets out a soft moan. He responds by thrusting harder and adding another finger inside her pussy. Then, he leans over to lick his tongue over her sensitive clit.

He can't help but think of Tiana and lets out a frustrated growl as she still hasn't called him back. He redirects his anger towards the redhead in front of him. He increases his pace, demanding, "Look at me while I'm fucking your mouth."

She rolls her eyes, and that pisses him off. He musters all his strength and slides his dick in and out until his muscles clench.

"Ooh, ooh," he grunts as cum shoots from his dick and flushes her mouth.

He empties his tank, falls over on top of her, and attempts to catch his breath.

"You're heavy, baby. You have to get up."

"Excuse me, pretty lady." He rises and allows her a moment to reposition herself.

She pours herself another drink and guzzles it down her throat. "Your kids are going to become alcoholics in my stomach."

"What is your name?" he asks

"They call me Thanos," she replies.

"The Marvel character? You are fucking with me, right?" he jokes.

She laughs and then gives him a stern look. "Not at all. My throat is the destroyer, my pussy is the savior, my asshole is the chosen one, and my looks are eternal. If you combine all those elements simultaneously, I'll snap my fingers and make any man evaporate."

"Damn, tonight is going to be incredible. Finish your drink so I can serve you this Black Panther dick," he taunts.

They laugh, drink some more, and make small conversation before they engage in their orgasmic conquests.

CHAPTER 5

Lying on her back, Tiana listens to the soothing ocean waves playing from the speakers. A male masseuse gently rubs her temples and massages her feet, bringing her a sense of calm and relaxation.

Catalina suggested trying the Adonis healing experience, and Tiana was in a state of bliss. Laying there, she couldn't help but imagine the pleasure his skilled hands would bring to her pussy and ass.

It has been so long since a man has touched her body in a way that sends chills down her spine. Michael used to be attentive to her needs until slanging extra dick with clients shifted his attention away.

The Adonis brothers are a popular draw in Jamaica, known for their chocolate-colored skin, dazzling white smiles, and flowing locks that cascade down their backs. Their dicks appear to hang along the sides of their legs, and the inches keep going like the Energizer Bunny.

Tiana's ears pick up moans streaming from the adjacent table. She turns and catches sight of the Jamaican's head disappearing underneath Catalina's sheet.

"Catalina," Tiana whispers to get her attention.

Catalina ignores her and continues moaning.

"Catalina, I know you hear me!" she yells.

Catalina stops and chuckles with the Jamaican as he pulls his head from beneath the sheet. "Were we too loud? I'm sorry. I came here to catch a nut, and you should do the same."

"Can you all give us a minute?" Tiana asks.

The Jamaicans stop the services, slip on their clothes, and exit the room.

"Tiana, I know you are going through things with Michael, but do not interrupt my nut because you are pouting over his cheating ass."

"I'm not pouting."

"Yes, you are, and it's becoming pathetic."

Tiana frowns, snatches the sheet away, and jumps off the table. "Catalina, if you weren't my best friend, I swear I would bust your ass. You want to see the Mercedes Chanel you remember? Just wait until tonight."

Tiana wraps the towel around her waist, slips on her sandals, and heads towards the door. As she walks, she turns her head and says, "Go ahead and call your Jamaican back in so you can jerk his chicken."

Catalina laughs and claps her hands. "That's a good one, Tiana. Thanks for the tip. I'll make sure to do it for you."

Tiana hurries out of the room, slamming the door as she retreats to her room.

"Fuck you, Catalina. I'm going to become the most desirable woman on the island. I might find me someone's son to eat my pussy tonight."

She stomps up the hall until she reaches the elevator. She presses the button multiple times before the doors open. Once inside, she pushes the twelfth-floor button and leans against the corner wall.

As the door was closing, a hand slides in between them, followed by a seductive male voice. "Excuse me, do you mind if I catch a ride with you?" he asks.

"It's a free country," she says with a quick roll of her eyes and an exasperated huff.

She hates that she was rude because this man standing in front of her was fine as hell.

She is about to apologize when she catches a whiff of the gentleman's cologne. She can't help but notice his muscular physique, adorned with tattoos, his curly hair, and mesmerizing gray eyes.

She can tell he is biracial, usually not her type. Maybe it's her pussy talking because she reaches out and grabs his hand.

"I want to say I'm sorry. It has been a long day."

"It's OK, Ms...."

"Again, I'm sorry. My name is T-." She quickly erases her government name from her mind. "I meant to say Mercedes. Tea is what I was sipping earlier."

"Yes, I understand. You are on vacation, so it's okay to unwind. Where are you from?" he asks.

Here's another lie coming his way, she thinks. "Columbus, GA," she answers.

"What a small world; me too. What are the chances of two people from Columbus being here at the same time?" he responds.

"By the way, I didn't get your name," she reminds him.

"Pardon my manners. My name is Dominic."

"So, are you here for business or pleasure?" she inquires.

"It's always business, but I receive pleasure while I'm handling business," he answers.

"Where is the woman giving you this pleasure?" she asks.

"I don't have any female companions on this island. I prefer to travel alone. You're the first woman I've flirted with in a long time."

"Bullshit! I'm sure you have used that line with so many women."

"Maybe, but I never test-drove a Mercedes," he responds.

She grins and releases his hand when the elevator chimes for the eleventh floor.

"Ms. Mercedes, this is my stop. Have a great day. I'm sure we'll cross paths again." He adds with a smile, "Faith is on my side."

The door closes, and she sinks deeper into her corner. She pulls out her phone to call Catalina, but she's probably jerking a Jamaican cock for real.

"I'll call her ass later," she insists.

As soon as she enters her room, she heads to the closet to find something alluring to wear, scanning through the hangers. She takes a step backwards and lets out a long breath. "In Jamaica, less is more," she mutters.

She reveals a stunning sky-blue two-piece skirt set with a crop top that shows off her shoulders and high heels with ankle straps. She knows her tiger paw prints will draw attention to her toned right thigh. As her phone rings, she notices it's Catalina. Before she can say hello, Catalina explodes about her encounter with the Jamaican masseuse.

"Girl, you should have seen his impressive dick," she brags. "I couldn't help but count the bulging veins on that dark, king-sized Snickers bar. I wanted to taste it, but I don't think I've had enough to drink yet."

"Catalina, you need mental help."

"Maybe, but I was a good girl. Nothing happened, except I masturbated while he stroked his dick to some Jamaican music."

"At least you saw some dick," Tiana mutters quietly. "When do you think you'll be ready for the courtyard?" she asks Catalina, admiring herself in the mirror and flaunting her outfit for the evening.

"I'll be ready around eight or eight thirty," Catalina confirms.

"OK, I'll see you later on," Tiana answers.

Tiana hangs up the phone and thinks of the sexy man she met in the elevator. She meant to tell Catalina about her encounter but was distracted by the dick-stroking story. She will bring it up during the party, and they can share a laugh.

She practices her good knees by dropping low to the ground and twerking her ass in front of the mirror. She envisions a handsome man sneaking up behind her, grinding his dick on her ass while she dances.

She springs back to her feet, skips over to the refrigerator, and pops open a few miniature bottles of alcohol. Not only will she be amped up for dancing, but she'll also have a bit of liquid courage before the party officially begins. "Mercedes Chanel is back, bitches!" she proclaims with a laugh.

CHAPTER 6

Dominic sits in the corner, sipping on water and watching Larry and Maria tongue-kiss each other as the music plays. Larry thrusts and gyrates his pelvis against her butt as she leans over and whines her hips. He enjoys the show and gives them more time to appreciate each other before they meet their fate. It's not the affair that bothers him. It's how they are in public, knowing his wife is at home seven months pregnant. Maria isn't innocent. She has been their babysitter for five years and has already raised their other son successfully.

Dominic has thoughts of skipping this kill and sending the file back to the dark web. He ponders why people can't stay committed or start a polyamorous lifestyle, since those relationships are popular these days.

He has been following the couple all day and has had plenty of chances to take them out. It would have been a perfect opportunity during lunch if it hadn't been for the encounter with Mercedes in the elevator. He replays the moment in his mind when she slips her tender hand into his, tracing her thumb along his knuckles.

He knows she's trouble but he cannot stop thinking about her. He desires to learn more, especially since she's living in Columbus.

The DJ switches songs, and everyone seated rushes to the dance floor to dance. Dominic sets his glass down and weaves through the bustling crowd, determined to reach the couple. He plans to inject Larry with a deadly mix of three substances, quickly ending his life. Then, before Maria can even process what has happened, he will swiftly slice her throat as she collapses into Larry's arms. By the time anyone realizes what has occurred, he will have vanished into the sea of people before the DJ plays the third song.

The ambiance in the courtyard is perfectly dim, with the scent of marijuana drifting through the air. The crowd is shoulder to shoulder, and everyone out here is too high or drunk to give a shit. His watch beeps, signaling it's time to birth his thoughts into reality. He continues walking through the crowd, pulling out the needle.

This is the moment he's been waiting for. Adrenaline pumps through his veins as he carries out the killings, a grin forming on his face like a proud parent watching their child take their first steps. As he walks towards Larry and Maria, Mercedes spins before him. "Well, hello there," she greets him cheerfully before sipping her Jamaican rum. "I never thought I would run into you tonight," she says, with a hint of surprise in her voice.

He quickly covers the needle with its cap and discreetly hides it behind his back, hoping Mercedes won't notice what he's doing.

"Yeah, I figured I could use some fresh air, but the weed smoke is too much for me. I'm going to the beach to count the stars in the sky."

"I can't believe you came to Jamacia alone. Is being out in the courtyard, listening to music, part of your business?" she asks.

"You can say that, but right now, I'll catch up with that part of my life later on tonight."

"Would you like to dance?" she asks.

"Not right now, but you can join me for a walk on the beach."

Tiana pulls out her phone, texts Catalina about her whereabouts, and shares her location.

They exit through the crowd, and he finds an outside porta-potty on his way to the beach. "Before we go, please give me a moment." He steps into the porta-potty, pulls out a plastic bag to secure the needle, and throws it in the hole. *Damn Mercedes, your beautiful self might have spared them for a few more hours.* He steps out, washes his hands, and they continue to their destination.

As they reach the shore, a lively bonfire party catches their attention. He turns to Tiana, silently inviting her to join in with his eyes. She smiles and nods her head. "Sure. I haven't been to one of these parties in years."

They interlock hands and walk to a section of the beach to talk and listen to music. He descends to the ground, takes his shirt off, and uses it like a towel so she can sit down. Tiana stares at his ripped abs, colorful sleeve tattoos, and kissable pecs. She hasn't been interested in guys, but if Dominic would just hint about fucking her, she knows he can have all of this good pussy.

She sits and says, "Looks like someone loves working out."

"In my line of work, you have to stay in shape," he replies.

"What is it that you do?"

"If I tell you, then I would have to kill you."

She laughs at his jokes but notices he doesn't smile at all. He senses her discomfort and playfully taps her shoulder while grinning widely.

"I'm just fucking with you," he responds.

The awkward moment has passed, and she removes her shoes, placing her bare feet in the sand and wiggling her toes. He wraps his arm around her shoulders and gently pulls her closer. "Mercedes, there's something unique about you. I want to get to know more about you. You don't have to say anything tonight. Allow me to earn those conversations."

She pauses, takes a slight breath, and thinks, *this man is smooth with his conversations.*

"It's vital I become one with a woman I am interested in," he says. "I love taking my time and making her happy is my priority."

Tiana's phone rings and she isn't going to answer the call, but she notices that it's Catalina. "Girl, I need you to come back to the courtyard. I think I had a little too much to drink. A bitch needs her friend so I can make it home safely. I love partying, but I like to know who I'm fucking, if you know what I mean."

"No worries, girl. I'm on my way."

Tiana ends the call and turns to Dominic. "I'm sorry, but I have to check on my friend."

"I'll walk you back and I look forward to seeing you in Columbus."

He leans in, softly pressing his lips against her cheek before standing up and extending his hands to help her rise from the sandy ground.

"Don't forget your shirt. There are too many thirsty women out there for you to be out here tempting them," she mentions.

"Am I tempting you?" he asks.

"That's a story for another day," she responds.

He walks her back to the courtyard to reunite with Catalina and allows them to converse in their moment.

"Mercedes, please be safe. I'll see you soon."

"Would you like my number?" she asks.

"Not yet. I need to earn it. Columbus is small. I'll find you and work it off."

"Are you serious?"

"Trust me, I can find anyone when the time is right."

"Dominic, you are too secretive. Fuck that! Give me your phone."

He hands her the phone, and she inputs her contact information for him to save and use for the future. She gives him the phone back, and they exchange hugs; the embrace is well-needed, and neither wants to let go.

"My head is spinning," Catalina interrupts.

Dominic's lips brush against Tiana's skin just behind her ear, his breath warm and his words enticing. "This is only the beginning," he whispers before releasing her.

"Call me, and don't take forever," Tiana speaks.

"I promise."

He turns around, slowly slips through the crowd, and disappears from Tiana's eyesight. Once Mercedes is out of the picture, his mind rushes back to his mission. He truly enjoys her company, but killing is what he gets paid to do, and he loves it. Disappointed that he had to throw away a perfectly good needle, he realizes he needs to execute Plan B before the night ends.

He returns to his room, drags his suitcases out of the closet, and flops it onto the bed. He stares at a wrinkle-free latex older man mask, but that's for an advanced kill. Instead, he goes with the rasta hat with the seventeen-inch black rasta dreadlock look, accompanied by some sunglasses and sandals.

He snatches his phone and quickly taps the words *Plan B* to the hacker, then waits for the signal to proceed with his backup plan. Two days earlier, Dominic had set up hidden cameras in the couple's room, and now he observes them preparing to indulge in each other's touch and desire in the jacuzzi.

A notification on his phone jolts him out of his thoughts as he sees a message from the hacker confirming that everything is clear, meaning the cameras on his floor and the cheaters' floor have been successfully disrupted. He slips on some overalls and gloves, grabs one of his killing kits, and exits the door, taking the stairwell eight flights up to the couple's floor.

He pulls out a second phone containing Larry's passwords, bank accounts, and keyless smart lock access. Dominic enjoys technology but knows it is the downfall of humanity. Holding the smartphone up to the pad, it beeps, signaling that the door is now unlocked. He slips inside quietly, carefully shutting the door behind him. Pulling out a gun from his killing kit, along with a knife, he walks into the bathroom and finds Larry fucking Maria from behind.

Dominic greets them with a sly smile and taps the gun against the wall. "Well, well, well… Look at you two love birds."

Larry pushes and slides from inside of her as he scoots towards the rear of the jacuzzi. Maria instinctively shields her chest with her arms and stays quiet.

"There's no need to be shy now. You two are despicable humans and don't deserve to breathe after today. Your wife is at home pregnant, and you are fucking the babysitter."

"No, it's not what it seems," Larry states.

"That's the line everyone uses when they get caught," Dominic informs him.

"Listen, I'm not going to be here all night. You want to live? Then drown that bitch in the jacuzzi," Dominic orders.

"What? That's crazy," Larry responds.

"Do you want your wife to find out and take the kids, the money, and the house? Time is ticking. Right now, you can do as I ask, or I'll have your wife murdered while you are here in Jamacia. As I stated before, I don't have all night. What's it going to be?"

The husband stares at Maria and then looks at Dominic.

"Larry, you can't possibly think about killing me?" Maria asks with fearful eyes.

"I'm sorry, Maria, but I love my wife," Larry confesses.

With a firm grip, Larry pushes Maria's head beneath the water's surface, not letting go even as she struggles and desperately tries to take in precious breaths. The fight continues until her body lies motionless, floating face down in the water.

"Good job, Larry. Damn good job. I didn't even have to get my hands dirty."

"What about the body?" Larry asks.

"No worries, I'll take care of it," Dominic guarantees.

"Am I free to go?" Larry asks.

"Sure, you are free to go. Go to hell," Dominic answers. "Larry, your son will still meet his end, and I'll cut open your wife and remove the unborn child from her womb. She will be left to bleed out before I silence her screams with a swift slash to her throat."

"No, you can't do that," Larry pleads.

"Why not? This is the consequence of cheating. Plus, you were fucking the babysitter right under your wife's nose. You don't care about her because if you did, I wouldn't be here.

"I'll give you a way out once again. You made one choice tonight. You already killed the babysitter. Let's make another choice. What is your family worth?"

Dominic shows Larry a video of his wife gagged and tied up.

Larry clenches his fist and slams his hand against the wall.

"Okay, I'll do whatever you ask, but how can I trust you won't kill her?"

"The same trust you placed in your vows. It's a faith journey."

"You are sadistic!" Larry yells.

"I've heard that line before, Larry. The clock is ticking, and you have a choice to make. You can either let your wife die to save yourself, but how can you explain the dead babysitter floating in the jacuzzi with your DNA all over her body? Prison or your wife's death? Someone is going to lose tonight."

"Okay, I'll do it!" Larry screams.

Dominic tosses the gun in the jacuzzi. "Please put it in your mouth and take this night away, Larry."

Tears stream down Larry's face as he places the gun in his mouth. He stares at Maria's lifeless body and can't help but think about his family, especially his wife and children. He wouldn't be in this situation if only he had been faithful. But it's too late to change course now. With a squeeze of the trigger, the bullet tears through his open mouth and exits through the back of his head. Blood spurts onto the wall behind him. His body collapses, and the gun slips out of his hand and lands in the bubbling jacuzzi below.

Dominic stares at the scene and smiles. He thinks Plan B is way more beautiful than his initial plan. With his back facing the room, he strides away from the bathroom and begins to gather his tools for killing. Once everything is neatly packed, he leaves the room without a second glance.

The hallway is empty as he returns to the stairwell and descends to his floor. He enters his room, undresses, and tosses his clothes into a disposal kit. After taking a shower, he returns to the bedroom and lies down on the bed, completely naked.

Tonight was a blessing, and he reminisces over the two memorable moments. His mind is on Mercedes, but his dick is stiff and throbbing from the two bodies upstairs.

His lips curve into a satisfied smile as he feels the warm sensation of precum dripping from his dick. He lays still, relishing the moment until it's time to catch his flight home in a few hours.

CHAPTER 7

Special Agent Thomas strolls through the cubicle area, balancing a cup of coffee in one hand and a doughnut in her mouth. The other officers attempt to catch her attention, asking if she has heard any updates on the Jamaica case. She enters her office, kicking the door shut with her foot, and sits to examine the crime scene board, hoping to find a connection between the babysitter and the husband. Taking a bite of her doughnut and a sip her coffee, the recent murders bring back memories of her ex-husband and her friend Jennifer's tragic crime scene photos.

As a young Specialist in the Army, she had been married to Sergeant Tyrese Hall. But after his untimely death, she wasted no time in changing her last name back to her maiden name to avoid any potential drama. After declining to reenlist, she left her position as a military police officer and swiftly advanced through the ranks of the FBI, ultimately becoming the agent in charge of their Atlanta office.

This year alone, there have been two murders each month, and it seems the killer is exclusively targeting individuals involved in infidelity. She has a particular interest in this case, even as the public dismisses the murders as a joke. TikTok is currently flooded with viral videos of people seeking revenge on their partners, eagerly anticipating the intervention of the Relationship Killer.

During the past two weeks, she has met with surviving partners and spouses of those who have passed away. Every single one of them claims to have been unaware of their significant other's extramarital affairs. She knows how to spot a liar based on their nonverbal cues and eye contact. Having personally experienced loss herself, she can relate to the emotional toll it takes and empathize with others going through similar situations. It is worth noting that the beneficiaries of the deceased's life insurance policies exhibit peculiar spending patterns after receiving the payout. They seem to maintain a modest lifestyle, almost as if they are being coached on how to avoid any suspicion in a potential murder case. Furthermore, these beneficiaries do not seem eager to start dating again anytime soon; instead, their focus remains solely on their education and career pursuits.

A light knock on the door shakes her out of her thoughts. She swivels in her chair and places her coffee cup back on the table, motioning for the agent to come in. "The conference room is ready, and everyone is waiting for the briefing."

"Thank you, Agent Sanchez. Tell everyone I'll be there shortly."

Agent Sanchez closes the door to deliver the message as requested.

She drinks the last sip of her coffee, gathers her notes and laptop, and marches to the briefing room. Walking in, she takes her seat at the head of the table. "Good morning, everyone. As you have heard, there was another murder last week involving infidelity. It's time we get ahead of the local authorities and assist with these unsolved cases.

"It appears no one knows if the Unsub is a male or female. We have gathered that the killer is flawless in tracing their steps—no DNA is left at the crime scene, camera footage is being erased, and there are no possible witnesses. I know cheating is wrong, but the Relationship Killer has no right to decide someone's fate. The Unsub is cruel and demonic. The killer needs to be stopped.

"I hate to say it, but until a high-profile figure experiences the destruction of the Relationship Killer, authorities will continue to prioritize cases related to terrorism and public corruption."

She plugs her laptop cord into the server, projecting images onto the screen. "Look at this shit!" she yells as the slideshow reveals crime scenes with multiple victims, making attendees sick to their stomachs. "In 2024, my mission is to locate the Relationship Killer and shove his balls down his fucking throat," she declares with determination. "Unless someone brings in a lead, it'll be a long day. You're all dismissed."

She disconnects her laptop and departs, leaving the disgruntled agents to argue among themselves. As she heads to her office, she gazes out of the top-floor window, observing people walking on the street; during her most stressful times at work, she finds solace in watching others. "It must be nice to rush to your next destination with no concern for the danger out there," she whispers. Returning to her desk, she logs into her fake Facebook profile and searches for drama-filled videos and messy comments.

She belongs to a Facebook group called The G-Spot of Georgia, where all the messy tea is spilled without holding back— raw and unfiltered. One user recently shared a post alleging a conspiracy to cover up a suicide at the Columbus Country Club. According to her, her cousin, a regular at their events, is convinced that the man who died did not jump off the roof as authorities claim, but was instead murdered.

As Special Agent Thomas delves deeper into the comments, she discovers that the wife was set to receive a million-dollar life insurance payout. She jots down some notes, takes screenshots of several Facebook users' profiles, and then closes her laptop for the day.

It has been a long time since she and her kids escaped Columbus, Georgia, a place she despises returning to due to the pain and sorrow it brought her. However, she needs answers and believes someone at the country club knows the truth. Ready to kick in some doors, her first stop will be Facebook user Keisha Miller, who has posted more comments than anyone else and might be willing to sell her story for the right price.

Special Agent Thomas takes her keys, exits her office, and waves to her team. "Keep working on my responses; I'm going to follow up on a lead and I'll be back in a few days." Confidently descending the stairs, she makes her way toward the parking lot, presses the button to start her car, and calls an old friend to see if he's still in town. The phone rings and rings, going to voicemail as her anxiety about going to Columbus mounts. In her haste, she realizes she mistakenly used the wrong phone to place her call, switches devices, and redials. This time, her friend answers without hesitation.

"Good afternoon, Sasha. What do I owe the pleasure of this call? We haven't chatted in years and the last time we did talk, you wished that I would burn in hell."

She takes her time to respond, speaking carefully. "In the past, I was a different version of myself. But with time, I've found ways to cope with losing my ex-husband. I didn't call to talk about that though. I'll be in Columbus for work and was hoping we could catch up over lunch or dinner."

"Once you arrive, name the place and time. I'll be there. Do you need a place to stay?"

"No, I'll be fine. Thanks for the offer."

"You're welcome. Please drive safely while coming down here. See you soon!"

"Thanks. I'll call you when I arrive," she says and ends the call.

She presses the play button on her phone, syncing the music to her car, providing her with lovely tunes to accompany her as she prepares for I-85 traffic. As the bustling cars surround her, she contemplates how to make amends with Dominic, recalling how much younger she was when she falsely accused him of murdering Tyese and Jennifer. Her doubts about him stemmed from his absence at the funeral and his decision not to claim Jennifer's life insurance payout, which instead went to her mother.

She recalls the time Dominic voluntarily admitted himself into the VA mental ward, where he remained for three long years, claiming to suffer from survivor's guilt. He held the Army responsible for forcing him to defend another nation while leaving his own country vulnerable. His dramatic story captivated the public; they hung on his every word and tear during his speeches. But then, without warning, he disappeared from the public eye, citing a relapse due to his struggles with PTSD and the need to distance himself from loved ones. While she didn't fully believe his story, she was willing to listen and be more open-minded this time, understanding that Dominic was alone and had lost his wife, just as she had lost her ex-husband.

CHAPTER 8

Michael is jolted awake by the sound of his phone ringing. He quickly moves the two women he brought home last night to the side as he searches for his phone. Groggily rolling over, he reaches towards the floor until he finally finds it. The clock reads three in the morning, and the caller ID displays an unknown number. "This call better be necessary, or I'm going to fuck you up," he threatens the caller on the other end.

"Mr. Patterson, this is Angela. The police raided the house and took Devontae to jail. He said to call you as they were putting him in the police car."

He exhales, rolls to his feet, and walks across the room. "What do you mean they raided the house? What did they take?"

"They confiscated the money and arrested some of the men for buying pussy. One of the female dancers was an undercover officer who had been in and out of the house for weeks."

"The money can be replaced. At least the police didn't find the drugs. I'll make some phone calls and have Devontae out in an hour," he says.

"Make sure you switch out everyone's burner phone. Pay the renters some extra money to keep their mouths shut, and we will meet later this week," he updates her and presses the end button on the phone.

"Shit!" he yells.

He paces back and forth across the floor while dialing Tiana's number, cursing under his breath, "I need you to answer the damn phone." After the call goes to voicemail, he hangs up and quickly sends a text message, including their designated emergency code for urgent situations—a signal they had agreed upon for times of great importance. Within seconds of sending the text, his phone buzzes in his hand. He looks at the two women laying in his bed, then silently exits the room to answer the call.

Despite the sounds of her labored breathing over the phone, she responds, "I'm here, Michael. What do you need?"

"To start, I want you to come back home so we can focus on mending our relationship."

"As I mentioned earlier, what do you want, Michael?" she asks for a second time.

"Devontae is in jail, and the police raided one of my houses. They're saying it was an undercover cop or dancer that set us up."

She was on the brink of revealing that Devontae had purposely directed her upstairs, fully aware that Michael was getting his dick sucked from someone else. She pushes this thought aside and focuses on the fact that it would be effortless to end her relationship with Michael, all thanks to Devontae's manipulation.

"Tiana. Tiana! Do you hear me?" Michael yells through the phone.

"Yes, I'm here. I was thinking to myself, but I understand what's going on. Go ahead and bail him out, and I'll catch the next flight up there to have the case thrown out. And, Michael," she calmly says.

"Yes, Tiana?"

"After I do this favor for you, please don't call me anymore and don't ask for my help. I'm done with you, your shady business, and your cheating ways."

He questions incredulously, "Are you really going to waste all the time we've invested?"

"The same way you were stuffing your dick down that bitch's throat?" she snaps back and hangs up the phone.

He shakes his head in disgust and returns to his bedroom, realizing he has some time to spare before bailing Devontae out of jail. Ever since Tiana left town, he has been engaging in reckless behavior with multiple women, unable to control his sexual desires as he spirals downward. Using women to distract himself from the pain of Tiana's absence provides him with a fleeting sense of pleasure, but deep down, he knows it's a hollow substitute for the love he once had.

He crawls back into the bed and lies on his back. "Wake y'all asses up. I want to fuck," he demands.

The first woman rolls over and positions herself on top of Michael, easing his hardened dick into her dripping wet pussy. Meanwhile, the second woman sits on his face and smears her pussy across his mouth and nose. She moans as he sucks on her lips and playfully smacks her butt. She holds onto the headboard for support, enjoying the sensation. She twirls and changes position, moving into reverse cowgirl on top of his face. She keeps her eyes fixed on her friend as she rides Michael's manhood, flexing her pelvic muscles and grinning. The two women lock lips while Michael's skilled tongue works her clit with increasing speed.

The woman riding Michael intensifies her pace. Her moans grow louder until she screams, "Thrust that dick back! Make me cum!"

Michael drives his dick deep into her pussy, producing a moan of pleasure. He spreads the other woman's ass cheeks apart, and the two ladies high-five as if they're a wrestling tag team.

The woman riding him grinds up and down while the other one dismounts from his face. They both get on all fours, eagerly anticipating the intense thrusts he will provide them with.

He springs up from his prone position on the bed, grabs the shoulder of the first woman, and thrusts himself deep inside her. He pounds her with more force and intensity until he's ready to give the other woman the same treatment. The sound of his balls hitting her ass echoes in the room as the second woman changes position on the bed, spreading her legs open.

Michael guides the other woman's face towards her friend's thighs, urging her to pleasure her friend while he takes her from behind. The woman slides her fingers inside her friend's pussy, evoking moans of pure ecstasy.

"Aah, I'm about to cum," the woman on the bed moans.

With a fierce determination, Michaels slides his dick in and out, leaving just the tip before plunging back in with all his might.

The woman meets his thrusts with equal enthusiasm, her booty bouncing against his groin. Leaning over her body, he continues to move back and forth, feeling his load building inside him. Sweat drips down his chest and onto her skin as he reaches his peak.

Meanwhile, the woman uses her fingers to stimulate her friend's pleasure points while their bodies tremble together. With an earth-shattering yell, the friend experiences the ultimate release, exclaiming, "Oh my God!"

Michael fucks the other woman until he releases his seed inside of her. As he shoots his power, his body trembles, and saliva drools from his mouth. He pulls out of her and flips her over. Running his tongue between her legs, he slurps until she cums. He deepens the flickering of his tongue and explores her even more as her friends join in, devouring the sweet taste of her fruit. They add more fingers into the mix as their tongues duel for dominance. Michaels pulls his face away from between her legs and kisses her deeply, allowing her to taste herself on his lips while her friend continues to feast on her wetness.

"Oh, oh, oh, baby. Don't stop!" she screams.

Mike leans up to her face, stuffs his dick in her mouth, and she takes her morning medicine with enjoyment while her friend slaps her clit and spits on her pussy lips.

The woman giving Michael head closes her eyes and experiences a powerful climax that covers her friend's face.

Michael slides his dick from her mouth and grins. "Thanks for making my morning great."

The two women shift in bed, snuggling closer to one another as he reflects on the fulfilling experience they provided. Feeling rejuvenated, he leaves them in a calm and relaxed state, but he knows it's time to switch to business mode and get Devontae out of jail. He turns on the shower, the water running as he prepares for the day ahead, aware that no matter how many women he sleeps with, none can replace the love he has for Tiana.

CHAPTER 9

On this uneventful Saturday, Dominic steps into the sunlit yard, shirtless in loose-fitting jeans, a bandana tied around his head, gloves on his hands, and worn brown Timberland boots on his feet as he prepares to chop firewood for the evening's fire. His mind drifts to Mercedes—he likes her, maybe more than he's willing to admit, but fear lingers; the fear that he'll end up hurting her before she can hurt him. With a determined look, he raises the ax high, pauses briefly, then brings it down with force, his thoughts momentarily silenced by the sharp, rhythmic motion.

He smiles at the victory of that one blow, replaces the wood with another stump, and swings again. After removing the stump, he eagerly grabs another piece, continuing to chop with precision. Just as the rhythmic motion becomes second nature, the sound of a car engine catches his attention. He glances up and spots a purple-tinted Mustang driving up the road towards his house.

Despite the neighborhood's decline over the years due to past murders, it's still the perfect place for Dominic. After all, he dislikes people these days. With each swing of the ax, his force gradually diminishes, letting the blade sink easily into the wood. Finally done chopping, he removes his gloves and wipes his hands on his jeans.

He exhales and thinks to himself, *I wish she would leave me the fuck alone, but she's here now. I did her a favor by murdering her cheating ass husband. I'm the one she should be thanking, especially since she was able to cash out a half-million-dollar life insurance policy.*

He makes his way towards the edge of the road and uses his hands to push open the gate, giving her permission to enter his estate.

Sasha drives her vehicle through the gate with Dominic walking behind it. Glancing in her rearview mirror, she notices how well he's kept himself in shape over the years—still as handsome as ever. She parks at the front of his driveway, cuts the engine, and steps out to greet her old friend. In a spontaneous moment, she pulls him into a tight embrace, and he graciously returns the hug before asking if she'd like to come inside.

He notices her hesitation and tries to comfort her nervousness. "Sasha, stop acting like you haven't seen death in combat. There are no ghosts inside of my home."

He takes her hand and guides her up the stairs and into the den. "Please, take a seat," he says as he points towards a comfortable chair. "I'll be back with your coffee, just how you prefer it."

As she sits and looks around, Sasha feels like she's in an Egyptian museum, surrounded by memories of her best friend captured in photographs. She gasps when her gaze lands on Dominic's wedding picture, and beside it is the first group photo taken at the reception.

It has been years since she last saw a picture of Tyrese, and there he is—the cheating bastard—right before her eyes. With a mix of anger and disbelief, she places the picture frame face down and waits for Dominic to return from the kitchen. "Are you okay?" she hollers from inside the den.

"Yes, I'm fine. I'll be out in a sec," he yells back.

As promised, he quickly returns with a cup of coffee and sets it on the toaster before sitting across from her.

He didn't even let her savor the first sip before igniting a conversation that could quickly turn into an argument. "Sasha, I know you're in town to check on me, but I'm the happiest I've been in a long time," he proclaims.

She crosses one leg over the other, sips her coffee, and challenges his statement. "Define the level of happiness, because I notice you have photos of your deceased wife everywhere." Reaching over, she grabs a frame and turns it face down. "And this group photo right here? I'm going to throw it in the trash when I leave," she confirms.

He laughs and responds, "Oh, you mad because Tyrese was fucking my wife the whole time. I'm sure they fucked the morning of my wedding too."

She cringes on the outside but refuses to allow Dominic to get to her. She slightly remembers that Jennifer was acting strange at the bachelorette party, and Tyrese confessed he was too drunk to come home that night. She never put two and two together until Dominic made that statement.

"Dominic, I don't want to talk about them. I'm here because we were close friends once, and my pride wouldn't allow me to remain friends with you throughout the years. I was hurt, and it took me a long time to get over the pain."

"Pain is weakness leaving the body," he interrupts her before standing and walking out of the room. "I'll be right back. Allow me to run in the other room and grab a shirt."

As he rounds the corner, he reaches for a book on the shelf and reveals a hidden keypad. He enters his wife's birthdate, then adds the year that he killed her ass. Two blinks of the keypad light confirms to him that the underground kill room is locked and impenetrable. After returning the book, he quickly goes to his workout room closet and grabs a shirt. He puts it on and rushes back to the living room to entertain Sasha.

"Do you need another cup of coffee before I sit down?"

"I believe this will do for now. Thanks anyway."

"How long are you in town?" he asks.

"A few days, maybe longer."

"You are welcome to stay here or does the FBI pay for you to stay in those extravagant hotels?"

"Shit, I wish. Tent City overseas is better than some of the places I have stayed," she jokes.

"I have plenty of room and haven't had company in years. You are welcome to stay here," he offers.

"Sure, we can joke and laugh about the old days. I need to freshen up, and you can take me out to eat tonight," she mentions.

"You already know where we are going," he states.

"Uptown!" they shout together.

"You've been gone for a while, but there's a great Italian restaurant named Mabella's. The food is magnificent. We can eat and then go to the jazz spot down the street."

"Okay, let me get my suitcases out of the car," she adds.

"Just pop the trunk. I'll get them," he offers.

They walk outside, she presses the key fob, and the trunk pops open. Dominic runs down the steps and grabs her suitcases.

He carries her suitcases into the house and asks her to follow him to the guest room. She trails closely behind as he guides her down the hallway into a recently renovated bedroom designed for comfort. The room boasts a wall-mounted TV, a temperature-controlled bed adorned with plush, vibrant pillows, and a cozy comforter, while an intricately patterned Italian rug accents the hardwood floors. To top it off, there are vanity mirrors with a personal makeup counter for added luxury. Sasha is thoroughly impressed with the upgrade, eagerly anticipating a restful night in this beautiful room.

"Dominic, I love this room and can't wait to return and sleep."

"You are the first to sleep in this room, so feel free to break it in. Just don't bring any guys home from the restaurant with you."

She punches him in the shoulder. "Whatever, you know I have never been that type of woman."

He laughs and playfully rubs his shoulder. "Someone is still boxing at the local gym.

"Go ahead and get ready. I'll let you explore the bathroom yourself. I'm sure you will find everything you need and more."

He turns around and walks out of the room. He knows she has to adjust to coming to a place where her husband was killed.

He whistles an Army cadence and marches to his room to find something to wear for the evening.

He is in a good mood, and once they get to the restaurant, he will speak to Sasha about Mercedes. He hasn't even called her since returning from Jamacia but he thinks about her often.

He has fucked a few random bitches but hasn't dated or involved his feelings with a woman since his wife died. He knows there are women out there that are worse than men. They can suck a man's dick at the club and go home and kiss their man in the mouth. He shakes his head in disgust. His inner conscience speaks, *That's why your life has a purpose. Kill everyone who loves OPP.*

CHAPTER 10

As soon as they step into the room, the enticing aroma of food hits their noses. The restaurant exudes a romantic ambiance, with soft saxophone music playing. Vibrant Italian paintings decorate the walls while busy servers weave through the tables, taking orders and delivering plates of delicious cuisine.

Sasha is pleasantly surprised by the atmosphere and can't remember the last time she has had an enjoyable evening without thoughts of solving cold cases looming in her mind. She eagerly looks over the menu, excited to try new dishes and enjoy drinks at the jazz venue.

The host checks their reservation and leads them to a table near the window, offering a view of downtown.

Sasha sits down, smiling at Dominic as she takes his hand. "Thank you for bringing me here tonight," she tells him. "I'm starving. Can you recommend something from the menu?"

He smiles and replies, "Before we eat, let's order some drinks and toast to our reunion after all these years."

He signals for a server and seamlessly speaks Italian, surprising Sasha, since she had never known he could speak another language besides his country's grammar.

"What did you order for us?" she asks curiously.

"I remembered you love crisp and refreshing cocktails with a hint of sweetness, so I ordered a Mabella Bellini. It has one of your favorite flavors," he answers knowingly.

"Better be peach," she interrupts.

"Don't worry. I remember my battle buddy. You can take your time and browse the menu to decide what you want. But as for me, I'm going to devour these delicious grilled New Zealand Lamb Chops."

"Sounds delicious, but you know I can't be eating all that meat. I'll go with the spicy honey-glazed salmon and a salad instead."

"No worries. I'll order a double portion so you can try it anyway," he offers.

"Thanks, because the way you're describing them makes them hard to resist," she admits. "How often do you visit this restaurant, and when did you start speaking Italian?"

He chuckles. "Babbel. You pick up some impressive skills when you spend a lot of time alone."

"You could be dating, you know. You've always been attractive. So why haven't you had at least one girlfriend since...?" she pauses, hesitating before saying Jennifer's name at the table.

"It's okay to say their names," he reassures her. "Tyrese and Jennifer didn't deserve to go out like that, but life moves on. You moved on. The kids are happy, and you have a wonderful husband who supports you while you fight crime."

"Do you feel like you've moved on?" she asks him.

Before he could respond, the waiter returns with their drinks.

"Here's to new beginnings!" he exclaims, lifting his glass in a toast. Sasha joins in with her glass, and they clink them together before taking a sip.

Dominic sets down his glass and resumes their conversation with Sasha. "In case you're curious, I have met someone recently. If things continue to develop, I will bring her to Atlanta so you can perform a detailed background check for me."

"What's her name?"

"I said, someone. I'm not telling you her name yet. Just know, I'm interested in her."

"Okay, live with your secrets. Just don't fuck her in the same bed Tyrese and Jennifer were fucking in."

"That's the old Sasha I miss. The emotionless MP that would pull cars over for going half a mile over the speed limit on base," he reminds her as he sips his wine.

"I was a young specialist who was serious about my career, plus that's why I made Sergeant before you all," she proclaims.

The waiter brings the food, and Sasha looks up and says, "Finally. I was starving. This better be the best salmon in Georgia."

"I'm sure you'll love it. Excuse me, I need to go to the restroom. Please feel free to bite into my lamb chops and let me know what you think when I return."

"Okay, I'll let you know," she answers as she continues eating her salmon.

He strolls to the restroom, stops at the women's door, and looks over his shoulder before entering. Ambushing a woman who is applying lipstick, he quickly injects a needle into her neck. She falls to the ground, and he drags her into one of the stalls.

"I've been wanting to use a needle since I left Jamaica," he mutters, propping her up on the toilet.

The woman slumps over and weakly asks, "Who are you?"

"I was your executioner yesterday, but tonight, consider me your savior, especially since my nosy friend is at my table."

He takes out a marker from his pocket and writes the words "STOP CHEATING" on her forehead. As he steps back to admire his handiwork, he even chuckles at the thought of not killing this woman as she sways incoherently.

He leaves her locked in the stall, stowing away his syringe and marker. Exiting the restroom quietly, he slips into the men's room. After washing his hands and adjusting his appearance, he checks the time on his watch — only three minutes have passed since he left Sasha at the table. Not bad for a warning.

Returning to the table, he finds that Sasha has devoured not one but two of his lamb chops. "I told you they were delicious," he says with a smirk. "Are you glad I ordered extra?"

He grabs a lamb chop and bites into it while keeping an eye on the gentleman the woman in the bathroom has been chatting with. He knows the man will eventually check on her if she doesn't return soon.

Mid-bite, Dominic suddenly stops and blurts out, "Her name is Mercedes." He continues, "She's absolutely stunning. I could say more, but I've been too afraid to contact her."

"What a Pussy. Hand me your phone," Sasha demands.

He dials Mercedes' number and slides the phone to Sasha as the gentleman makes his way to the restroom.

He overhears Mercedes' voice on the other end of the line but can't make out her words. He smiles and lets Sasha take over, introducing herself and chatting with Mercedes on his behalf.

The man returns to the table, pays his bill, and goes back to the restroom. After a short time, he emerges with the woman leaning on his shoulder, trying to cover her head.

The effects of the drug were starting to wear off, giving the impression that she has simply had too much to drink and he was helping her out of the restaurant.

Just as he was lost in thoughts about the unfaithful woman, Sasha calls his name, breaking his train of thought. He turns toward her, and she hands him back the phone.

"Hello, Mercedes. It's nice that you all are chatting like besties. One day, I will introduce you all in person. If you are available, I would love to meet you tomorrow."

Dominic's face lights up with a huge smile, and Sasha knew that Mercedes has accepted his proposal. "I'll call you tomorrow with all the details," he says before ending the call.

"See, that wasn't hard at all. Sometimes, you have to push your way through and be spontaneous."

He shrugs his shoulders. "I guess you're right."

"Now, are you going to eat all those lamb chops?" she asks.

"I think I have enough to share, and after we eat, let's go to the jazz club."

"I regret not coming down earlier; instead, I was being stubborn," she apologizes.

"We're both alive and healthy. We can always make up for lost time. Who knows? Maybe I'll surprise you by visiting Atlanta this month."

"My doors are always open. I'm sure the kids would love to see you."

"They're probably taller than me now and won't even recognize me," he remarks.

"There's only one way to find out," she replies.

He gazes into her eyes and sincerely thanks her for checking on him, and they raise their glasses once more. "Here's to good friends today and always." They toast, drink, and savor the rest of their meal.

CHAPTER 11

Devontae storms into Michael's office, seething with frustration and anger. "How much longer do I have to stay low and miss out on all this money?" he demands.

Michael looks up from his work, disappointment etched on his face. "You're not going broke, you're just too damn greedy," he responds sternly. "Go beat some pussy up or take a vacation. I can't have my name or reputation ruined because you want to throw another party.

"I hired another lawyer, but she's not Tiana. I have to see if she can work well with our clients and the police."

"Are you going to allow Tiana to walk away freely, knowing she knows all of our illegal activities and stash houses?" Devontae inquires.

Michael's face hardens at the mention of Tiana. "She will never be free," he says firmly. "But I'm giving her some space and time to get her head straight.

"I do need a favor from you. I need you to go to Georgia and make sure she isn't feeding my pussy to some country-ass bumpkin."

Devontae raises an eyebrow. "So, this is the 'vacation' you want me to take?"

"You are catching on quickly. Take one of your lady friends or meet someone there. I heard the women are super thick down there," Michael suggests with a sly smile.

"Now, if you'll excuse me, I must prepare myself for a potential client. She isn't like the usual ones; she has money and seems street-smart."

"Okay, Mike. I'll chill out for a while, but we need to return to business when I return from Georgia."

Michael stands and gathers his laptop and paperwork. "Come on. I'll walk you out."

They dab each other's fists, exit the office, and get into their respective cars, with Michael allowing Devontae time to leave before starting his own and trailing down the road.

There are moments he can hear Tiana's voice: *Why are you always fooling with Devontae? You are so much more incredible than him. I'm sure he will bring you down one day.*

He brushes off his thoughts of Tiana and heads downtown to meet Ms. Gwendolyn Price, a wealthy sixty-year-old white woman known as Sugar Cougar, who has the means to sponsor any project in the city. Her grandfather was one of the city's earliest real estate tycoons, amassing a fortune back in the day, and her father inherited that wealth, passing both money and knowledge down to her.

She requested he meet her inside the library at The Ivey Hotel to discuss some properties she would like his opinion on, a place he had heard of but wouldn't typically hang out at. He knew it attracted too many snobbish and uppity muthafuckers for his taste.

He pulls up to the hotel's entrance, parks his car, and hands his information and keys to the valet attendant. As he enters the lobby, he notes the elegant artwork and marble floors, along with the abundance of stockbrokers and business executives mingling. At the front desk, he provides his name and is quickly escorted by two men who appear to be bodyguards to the library lounge, where he sees Gwendolyn for the first time; she has a perfectly crafted Botox face, perky breasts, and long legs.

Michael usually doesn't go for 'vanilla' women, but the combination of her wealth and former heartbreaker status piques his interest. He might not fuck her today, but he knows he is going to sample that pussy sooner or later.

"Welcome, Mr. Patterson," she greets him with a smile.

He embraces her and kisses her cheek. "You look stunning," he compliments her. "It's my privilege to be in your presence."

"Flattery will get you everywhere," she teases with a wink, "and I do mean everywhere."

She invites him to sit in the lounge and informs him that she had the server bring out their favorite champagne before his arrival. "Would you be so kind as to pour us a glass?" she requests sweetly.

As he pours the drinks, he can't help but think, *Who does this woman think she is? Do I look like a butler to her?* However, he forces a smile onto his face and continues with their conversation.

"Please tell me the properties you would like to know more about," Michael says.

Gwendolyn sits on the sofa, her jet-black hair cascading over her shoulders as she pulls it out of its tight bun. "I want to be a silent partner on your real estate team," she announces boldly.

Michael addresses her formally, "Ms. Price..."

But she cuts him off, "Call me Gwendolyn and cut the bullshit, Michael." She mentions the rumors of his wild parties and how he uses them to launder money. "I'm not asking for your acceptance. I am telling you; I will be your silent partner and together we can make a fortune," she asserts.

Michael hands her a glass of champagne. "You drive a hard bargain, and I have little say in this matter, correct? Gwendolyn, I appreciate your boldness. When do we start?" he asks eagerly.

"I'm talking about bringing in millions of dollars and attracting clients beyond your wildest imagination. But there is a catch," she warns.

"What's that?"

When Michael asks what it is, Gwendolyn brings up Tiana and how she is getting cases thrown out of court.

"She's around, but our relationship is strained at the moment," he says. He asks, "Is there a way to proceed without her involvement?"

"Correct me if I'm wrong, but you all used to fuck, date, or something like that, right?" she hints.

"I guess you can say we had an amicable relationship once," Michael clarifies.

"I figured you would say those things. See if she's willing to come and work with us again."

"And if she declines?"

"Then I will get rid of her. She knows too much information, and I can't have my family fortune getting disrupted over some pussy you broke up with."

Taking a sip of his champagne, Michael sets the glass down. "Your request doesn't seem unreasonable. I'll speak to her this week."

Gwendolyn crosses her legs, revealing a glimpse of her inner thigh and the lace of her panties, catching Michael's attention.

"Why did you choose me?"

"I've had my eye on you for a while now, and you seem like someone focused on their business. Your operations could use a bit of fine-tuning, which is where my team and I come in. Now, I need another favor, and you have the right to say no this time," she says.

"You are requesting a lot for a woman that doesn't usually fuck with people like me."

"It's funny you chose that word," Gwendolyn smirks. "I'm throwing a party tonight, and you are the guest of honor."

Without hesitation, Michael agrees to attend the party and asks for the location.

Gwendolyn crosses her legs again, giving Michael another quick glimpse of her panties.

"I'm pleased that you're captivated by the space between my thighs because that's where all the fun is happening."

Michael laughs before taking another deep sip of champagne. He stands up and gathers his belongings, knowing that this business deal will be highly lucrative.

"Michael, I've been in this game for a while now, and there are two rules when it comes to my money: don't lie to me, and don't fuck me over," she says sternly. "Do we have an understanding?"

"Don't worry," he replies confidently. "I'll handle everything on my end, but if I encounter any problems, I know your connections will be useful."

"Now you're thinking like a wealthy man," she responds with a smirk.

He leans in and kisses her on the cheek. "I'll see you tonight," he says before leaving the library and exiting through the hotel lobby.

He can't help but think about Tiana and how she better come home soon so they can make some serious money together.

CHAPTER 12

Dominic arrives early at the Toast of the Town wine-tasting event at the Columbus Convention and Trade Center. Mercedes suggested it as a perfect opportunity for them to connect, inspired by a recommendation from her friend, Catalina. The event's website promises an array of wine vendors, gourmet food, and artisanal beers.

Though Dominic has attended similar gatherings before, they often end in chaos, leaving him with memories more reminiscent of a crime scene than a celebration. Still, he is eager to dress up for the occasion and impress Mercedes in his Maya blue linen suit, paired with a button-down shirt and white Stella tassel loafers.

He had offered to pick her up, but she insisted on driving herself to the venue. Not wanting to push the issue, he followed her lead.

As he patiently waits near the valet booth, Dominic's attention is caught by a sleek green electric Taycan Porsche pulling up. Being a car enthusiast, he can't help but wonder who in Columbus could afford such a luxurious vehicle worth 99,000 dollars.

Out of nowhere, Mercedes emerges from the driver's side and captures his attention. She could have been a character straight out of a movie; her outfit was flawless. A long red halter top hugs her figure, with a fitted black skirt that accentuates her curves and stops just above her calves. She completes the look with crystal studded ankle strap pumps.

Her locs fall in a mohawk style that extends down her back, and her makeup adds to her ethereal radiance. Dominic eagerly embraces her, hoping to make up for every missed phone call by kissing her soft lips.

He knows this event will give him the perfect opportunity to make amends. "You look stunning," he says, wishing he had a ring in his pocket. If he did, he would marry her right now.

She smiles and thanks him, returning the compliment by saying he looks handsome when he cleans up.

"Are you trying to say I didn't catch your eye in Jamaica?" he teases.

"No, you definitely caught my eye and a few other things," she responds playfully before adding, "but I'll plead the fifth."

He offers his hand and asks if she wants to go inside and have a glass of wine. She happily accepts, intertwining her fingers with his as they enter the convention center.

The crowd is buzzing with excitement, especially around the wine-tasting booths.

Dominic's gaze falls upon the Country Club of Columbus vendor booth, triggering memories of the night he kicked Viktor off the roof.

"What are you thinking about, Dominic?" she asks as they approach the booth.

"Please forgive me. The selection of wine here is quite extensive, and I must admit, my mind was lost in contemplation. So, where would you like to start?" he inquires politely.

"So, are you more of a wine, beer, or spirits kind of person?" she asks.

"I've always wanted to try Gin Mare. Let's head over to their booth," he suggests excitedly.

"Sounds like a great idea," she agrees with a smile as they hold hands and approach the booth.

"Excuse me, do you have any samples of your finest gin?" he asks the server. The server quickly pours a sample glass of each of them and hands it to them with a smile.

Dominic takes a whiff of the gin and nods his head. "This is going to go down my throat so smoothly," he comments.

Tiana's pussy tingles when he mentions the word throat. She hasn't had any dick since she has been staying in Columbus. She shifts her movement to the side and crosses her ankles to stop the moisture from running down her leg. *This muthafucker is sexy as shit. He better know how to fuck*, she ponders.

He takes a sip and nods approvingly. "Yes, ma'am. This is delightful. I'll come back before we leave and buy two bottles."

They finish their samples while walking, and Tiana pulls him along, eager for him to try something else. "Come on, I want you to try something. They have one of my favorite appetizers here," she says enthusiastically.

She takes a toothpick topped with a strange-looking meatball and urges him to open his mouth. Like an idiot, he complies and lets her slide the meatball between his lips. To his surprise, it is a delightful mix of spicy and sweet flavors. He finishes chewing and then inquires about the dish.

"It's covered in orange marmalade sauce," she explains. "I fell in love with these meatballs the first time I tried them."

"Shit would be even better over some white rice," he adds.

"All country boys love to think white rice goes with everything," she jokes.

They laugh before she pops two more meatballs into her mouth. She grins at the lady behind the counter and whispers, "Save me a to-go box, and don't give too many out."

Dominic is drawn to Mercedes' sense of humor, and he hasn't enjoyed the company of listening to and observing a woman since his dead wife.

As they walk through the convention center, Mercedes teases him and flirts playfully. She even licks the rim of a wine sample and jokes that it could be someone's son tonight.

Dominic knows she's teasing him but feels compelled to warn her against playing games. He offers to take her for dessert before she falls somewhere she shouldn't.

With a smile, she leads him to a quiet area. Looking into his eyes, she takes a deep breath and prepares to reveal something important.

"I need to share something with you because I believe you are decent, and I don't want to deceive you."

"You asked me out on a romantic date just to reject me? We could have gone to Burger King instead," he quips with a teasing smile.

"No, we're fine," she reassures him. "Maybe too fine."

She couldn't get involved without confessing the truth. She says, "My real name is Tiana, but I used to go by Mercedes when I was younger. I would use that name to flirt with attractive guys but never intended to form deeper connections with them."

"What sparked the change with me?" Dominic questions.

"Your eyes had a particular look that day, which made me feel so alive at that moment. Are you upset?" she asks.

"I have done worse things. I'm sure we can overlook the fake name you gave me," he assures.

"Baby, that name isn't fake at all," she promises with a sneaky smile. "It comes with a lot of excitement and wealth. I'll show you what it can do one day."

"As long as we're being open with each other, there's something I want to share with you," he says.

She shakes her head and tells him, "Nope, let's go back to having fun. You can tell me later. Tonight, we're going to have a good time. I wanted to be honest, but if you prefer, you can be naughty," she adds.

He laughs and shakes his head. "You're something else. Tell me, which personality is flirting with me? Tiana or Mercedes?"

"Always Mercedes, baby," she replies confidently. "Tiana is all business."

"I know a thing or two about business myself. But tonight, I don't plan on working at all. So, if it's alright with you, I'll keep calling you Mercedes."

"I don't have a problem with that at all."

He leans over her five-foot-four frame and kisses the lips he has been fantasizing about since meeting her in Jamacia. Their tongues dance together, exploring every inch of each other's mouths.

He wraps his strong hands around her waist, kissing her with such intensity that he doesn't care who sees their public display of affection.

The kiss lasts for what feels like an eternity, and she is impressed by how excellent a kisser Dominic is. Tiana's mind drifts to his lips, sucking on her swollen clit.

She breaks the kiss. "Ooh, shit. Your ass is in trouble now," she teases. "Would you like to follow me back to my place tonight?"

"I thought you'd never ask."

She boldly touches the bulge in his pants and feels his throbbing erection. "I'm going to suck and fuck every drop of cum out of you," she whispers seductively in his ear.

"Yes, now you're speaking my language. I'll grab my two bottles of Gin, and we can leave."

"Just make sure you keep that same energy when we're together. Oh, you will feel the Mercedes Experience," she flirts and growls.

"A SIMPLE KISS COULD IGNITE A PASSIONATE NIGHT OF FOREPLAY, OR IT COULD BE THE START OF A PAINFUL HEARTBREAK. NEVERTHELESS, I WILL SAVOR EVERY MOMENT, DANCING IN HER MOUTH FOR ETERNITY."

CHAPTER 13

Tiana stands patiently as Dominic purchases his bottles of Gin, her body aches and craves for a good fuck. It's been several months since she and Michael went their separate ways, leaving her without any sexual satisfaction.

Her phone rings, "Speaking of the devil," she mumbles under her breath as she answers the call in an aggravated tone. "What the hell do you want?"

"Is that any way to talk to the man who will pour millions into your bank account?" he asks.

Tiana's voice drips with sarcasm and anger as she accuses Michael of yet another illegal venture that could get her arrested or killed.

He brushes off her concerns and insists that this is just another side of the business, promising to introduce her to Gwendolyn Price when she flies back up to see him.

"I have no interest in your drama, Michael. Why don't you go find the girl who was sucking your dick."

"Damn, you are cold tonight. It sounds like you need more than money. I know you miss this dick."

Tiana can't help but laugh at his arrogance, reminding him, "Yeah, I miss seeing your dick going down another bitch's throat."

"I have apologized over and over for that mistake."

"Cheating is not a mistake. Men think they can do whatever they want because they have good dick, and a woman will forgive them immediately."

"What about us?" he asks.

"There is no us. As a matter of fact, I'm about to give my pussy to a man that knows how to worship a woman," she reveals and hangs up the phone.

"I'm tired of Michael's bullshit and lies," she confesses as she places the phone into her purse.

She stares at Dominic and becomes wetter. Her pussy speaks by twitching and says, *I need Dominic to fuck me into another universe tonight.*

She takes a deep breath and strides over to pull him away from the vendor. He glances up with a smile, holding up a finger to signal he'll be done shortly.

After grabbing the Gin, he holds her hand and leads her outside. "The night is perfect, and I'm grateful to share it with you."

"Yes, and I can't wait until you take me home," she admits with a playful smile.

"Where do you live?" he asks, curiously.

"The Grand Rapids," she replies.

"That's right around the corner from here. I love those apartments and always wanted to check them out," he admits, his eyes lighting up with enthusiasm.

"Would you like to walk there?" he asks.

She curses silently as she knows he sees her in these expensive shoes.

He laughs and says playfully, "I can tell from your face that you're not down for that. Don't worry, it's less than a mile away," he assures her with a smile.

He crouches down and pats her legs. "Hop on, baby. I'll carry you home on my back," he says.

"How are you going to carry me and hold the bottles at the same time?" she asks.

"You have a point," he admits, handing her the bottles. "Please bless someone else with these."

She looks over her shoulder and rushes to a couple. "Please take these two bottles and enjoy your evening," she insists, shoving the bag into the man's chest before he can refuse. Quickly sprinting back to where Dominic is waiting, she hops onto his back. "Don't drop me," she whispers in his ear.

"I know how to handle precious cargo," he replies confidently.

"Giddyup!" she yells.

Gripping her calves tightly with his arms, Dominic rises from the ground and gallops along the sidewalk like a horse. As they pass people on the street, Tiana's ass and titties bounce up and down.

As they approach the riverwalk, he slows down and begins walking normally. He glances over his shoulder at her. "Are you okay?"

She takes a moment to reply, savoring the scent of his cologne and gently kissing his neck. He feels her lips against his skin and smiles before turning back around.

He carries her as they admire the stars and the half-moon shining above them. The sound of the fast-moving waves enhances the calming atmosphere.

As he carries her to her apartment, he asks her what qualities she looks for in a man.

"I'm not hard to please. I am looking for someone loyal to my heart, unselfish, and willing to build our future together. Maybe someone to have a child with one day. I have to throw that in my life as well," she responds.

"Those are beautiful qualities," he says, turning his head to look at her. "I'm sure that man is already waiting for you at the altar, dressed in anticipation of your arrival."

She giggles and jokes that she thought he was that man. "Well, I guess I need to send you back where you came from," she playfully says.

He laughs along with her and affirms that he possesses those qualities and more, but he never wants to invest his emotions into someone who isn't ready to drink in his love.

"That sounds incredible. I love how you think. You might be more than just a good fuck. I'm sorry. Did I say that out loud?" she replies.

"You sure did, and I promise not to disappoint you," he responds.

As they continue talking, they reach the gates of her apartment complex. He bends down and lets her slide off his back.

She compliments his strength and endurance; after all, he carried her almost a mile while they had a great conversation. She confesses that she had a lovely time with him.

He responds with a smile, causing them both to blush and continue gazing into each other's eyes.

"Aren't you going to invite me in?" he asks with a smile.

"Of course," she replies apologetically. "Forgive my manners." She swipes her key over the gate pad, and the entrance swings open.

They step inside and walk through the courtyard towards the apartment buildings.

"This place doesn't even feel like Columbus," he marvels.

"That's why I chose to live here for a while," she responds.

They ride the elevator up to the fifth floor, still holding hands, before finally arriving at her door.

As they step inside, Dominic is taken aback by the size of her condominium, but what catches his eye most is the balcony overlooking the Riverwalk. Excitedly, he rushes past her and opens the sliding door, stepping outside to feel the cool breeze.

"Damn, it's a good thing Mother Nature hasn't transformed into a woman. You would have left me alone tonight," she jokes.

He grins and walks back inside, taking her hand and leading her onto the balcony. "This view is beautiful, but you are lightyears beyond anything in this universe."

He kisses her deeply, his tongue gliding over her lipstick and entering her mouth. He grips her ass, lifting her in the air as she wraps her legs around him.

He sets her down gently and turns her around, telling her to focus on the breathtaking view before them. She follows his instructions and gazes at a star she deems to be the one as his tongue traces a path up her leg.

Suddenly, she feels his hand between her thighs, spreading them apart. He pulls down her thong and lifts each foot to remove it altogether.

With one finger inside of her pussy, he teases and pleases her until she can hardly catch her breath. As she turns towards him, he demands that she face the stars again.

She's never been with a man who combines aggression with sensuality in his touch. Her body responds eagerly, yearning for the moment he inserts his dick.

Moaning his name in ecstasy, she begs him to skip the foreplay and just fuck her. With quick movements, he unbuckles his belt and sheds his pants. Returning to her body, he hikes up her skirt and leaves kisses along her neck.

Stroking his fist over his dick, he whispers in her ear, "Are you ready?"

She doesn't even have time to respond before she feels him entering her, his hardness filling her inner walls. She tightens her grip around him, pulling him in deeper as he wraps his hands around her neck.

"Is this what you want?" he growls, his anger evident in his tone.

She can only respond with a moan, unable to form words while being choked.

"Harder," she gasps, begging for more.

As he grasps her throat tightly, he thrusts his hips forward. His dick penetrates deeper inside of her, causing her to scream out in pleasure and pain. He covers her mouth with his hand and continues to thrust harder, squeezing her neck and driving his dick into her with force.

Tiana worries that he might push her over the balcony with the intensity of his movements. She clinches her muscles onto his dick and matches his rhythm, biting down on his fist as they both reach a feverish pace.

"Damn, this dick is good. Fuck me, Dominic. I need to cum. I wanna cum with you." She yells, "Oh my God. Get this pussy!"

Together, they move faster and harder, lost in their pleasure. Tiana doesn't care who hears or sees them as she experiences an intense orgasm on the balcony, gripping the rails for support as she fucks him back.

"Give me that nut, Dominic. Don't be gentle with it."

He grabs onto her shoulders and plunges deeply, feeling himself close to climaxing.

"Cum with me. Cum with me, Dominic," she commands.

"I am. I'm about to bust through your pussy."

Her legs tremble, her heart races and her toes pop. Her orgasm shoots like lightning, and she yells, "Muthafucker!" from her balcony.

He follows closely behind and eagerly prepares to climax but holds back just in time. He pulls out of her and takes a few steps back towards the bed. "Sit on my face," he begs. "I need to taste you while I beat my dick."

She wants him to cum inside her, but who can resist the opportunity to have their pussy eaten by someone as sexy as him? She straddles his face, and his tongue burrows deep inside her. They both moan as he sucks on her sensitive clit.

She leans to the side, stretches out her arm, and strokes his dick. As she continues moving her hips in circles, she strokes him faster and faster with her hand. She makes sure he's swallowing every drop of her juices as she rides his face with intensity.

He thrusts his hips up off the bed while devouring her delicious lips. His excitement builds, his dick grows even harder, and hot cum explodes onto her hand.

She moves away from his face, and they lock their eyes together, smiling at each other after their lustful encounter. He catches his breath and chuckles, saying, "One down, many more to go."

CHAPTER 14

Devontae can't wait to leave Columbus and return to Charlotte to report everything he has seen between Tiana and her new flame for the past week.

He now knows where Tiana lives and how she spends her mornings, walking along the Riverwalk and having breakfast at Hotel Indigo Denim & Oak Restaurant.

He admits the food is good because he has stayed at the same hotel. At this moment, he wishes he had left his side-chick at home. Her pussy is good, but the bitch is nerve-racking.

As he walks towards the valet to retrieve his car, he realizes he left something in his room and asks Shoutel to wait for him while he quickly goes back to get it. On his way back in, he sees Tiana entering through a side door with her man. Their eyes meet briefly, and Devontae smiles while Tiana seems to pierce his soul with her gaze.

She leans over and whispers to her companion. He leaves and sits at a table in the restaurant while she storms in Devontae's direction.

If this hoe starts talking shit, I'm going to slap her ass in this lobby. I'm only playing it cool because Michael asked me to, he thinks while preparing for the confrontation.

She strides up to him, her voice heavy with irritation. "Why are you following me? It's always the same old story with you," she accuses.

"Not at all, stripper chick. I was exploring the city with my woman." He nods at Shoutel, who has been patiently waiting for him, before turning back to face Tiana.

"Why are you acting like you're too good for us? You left us in jail and you haven't been doing your job as our lawyer. Are you going to introduce me to your new partner?"

"Fuck no! You're lucky I don't slap the shit out of you right now. This is my peace away from everything. I can't wait to call Michael and cuss his ass out."

"Michael has big plans for us involving a lot of money," he claims.

"Yeah, I heard all about that bullshit. I'll believe it when I see it," she says. "You need to go check on your woman before she causes a scene. You only date hood rats, so I'm sure her jealous monster will appear soon."

"And you left Michael behind to fuck around with this country ass nigga. Without us, you'd still be stripping on that pole. We did you a favor, now do your damn job!" he yells at her.

"Fuck you, Devontae," she fires back.

Shoutel walks over and interrupts their argument. "Devontae, can we please leave? I can't believe you're making a scene in the lobby over this bitch."

"Devontae, control your hoe before I drag her outside and throw her in the river. Don't forget who I am," she warns as she gets into a fighting stance.

Dominic pretends to read the menu but is eavesdropping on the loud argument nearby. As he debates what type of omelet to order, he mentally reminds himself not to get involved with Tiana's personal drama. However, as the shouting escalates, he can't help but feel uncomfortable.

He calmly sets down the menu and tells the server that he will return soon. Walking towards Tiana, Dominic swiftly moves to place her behind him. He's had enough and decides the conversation is finished.

"I'm taking Tiana with me, and you can go your own way," he states firmly. "Tiana, please take a seat at the table. I will join you shortly," he instructs.

Devontae lifts his shirt to reveal a gun tucked in his waistband and retorts, "Nigga, who do you think you are? This ends when I say it does."

Shoutel pulls on Devontae's arm, urging him to leave. "Let's go," she says urgently. "I'm not trying to end up in jail because of some stupid shit."

Dominic moves closer to Devontae and speaks in a low voice. "Don't reveal anything unless you plan on using it," he warns.

He scans the room, aware of the cameras in every corner. Dominic shakes his head with confidence. "I'm not afraid of death. I've faced it all before," he declares.

Devontae points a finger at Dominic, his eyes blazing with anger. "This isn't over, country boy. As long as you're involved with Tiana, you'll always have problems with me," he warns.

Devontae and Shoutel exit the hotel, making their way to the car the valet is retrieving. Dominic follows them outside and waits for them to get inside their vehicle.

Devontae grins and remarks, "You're a bold one, country boy." His words hold a slight warning, "There will come a time when you won't see me coming," he adds with a sly smile.

"Those are the nights that make life worth living. I'm eagerly anticipating our first date," Dominic responds with excitement.

The valet arrives with their car, and as the bags are loaded into the vehicle, Dominic waves goodbye before they drive off from the hotel. He commits the tag to memory and returns to the restaurant to check on Tiana. He sits down next to her, leans over, and kisses her on her cheek.

"No man should ever speak to a woman with disrespect. I apologize for interfering. My mother raised me with good manners."

"I am the one who should apologize to you, Dominic. It seems that my past has caught up with me here in Columbus. I promise to ensure it doesn't happen again, but unfortunately, I have to work with those idiots. That's just how it is."

She reveals, "My ex-boyfriend - who also happens to be Devontae's best friend, and I have a complex relationship because of the business ties I have as their attorney.

"To sum it up, I caught him cheating, and I couldn't handle it, so I left town," she quickly clarifies the situation.

He inquires if their relationship is finished. She responds that, as romantic partners, yes, but as business associates, no.

"It's a common saying that keeping in contact with your ex is never a good idea. Navigating through conflicting emotions can lead to unpredictable outcomes.

"Tiana, I strongly feel for you and think you are amazing. However, I want to take things slow so that no one ends up getting hurt."

"How slow are you going to move?" she asks.

"I'm unsure. The man flashed his gun at me and promised to dance with me later," he says.

She lets out a wail, her words punctuated with fear and shock. "Dominic!" she cries. "I always knew Devontae wanted to be part of that gang life, but I never thought it would go this far."

She wastes no time reaching for her phone, determined to make a call and try to contain the situation.

Dominic places a comforting hand on top of hers. "We're here for breakfast this morning," he reminds her. "Remember what I said earlier: you and your ex are a recipe for disaster. Don't let one slip-up make you want to call him. Forget about him, and let's focus on eliminating this negative energy."

Dominic picks up his menu and scans it for a satisfying meal. "I think I will build my omelet."

"Do you think it's too early to start drinking? This whole unnecessary situation makes me crave a drink," she remarks.

The waitress approaches the table and asks if they are ready to order. He orders an omelet with spinach, tomatoes, cheese, and green peppers. She also wants a drink and adds a blood orange margarita to her order.

He grins at Tiana. "Looks like you weren't kidding about starting your day off with a drink," he comments.

She shrugs, "I need to clear my head, especially since you suddenly want to slow things down. You should have told me that before I was choking on your dick and swallowing your kids," Tiana retorts with a smirk. "Now you're stuck with me."

He chuckles, "You are quite a character. Just be mindful of the promises you make, Tiana. I may not be the best person if you do me wrong."

She shoots back confidently, "Don't you worry. I'll make sure to take care of your heart."

She has no clue about my identity. Does she not realize that if I open up to her and she hurts me, I am capable of snapping her neck? he speaks silently to himself.

Dominic catches the server's attention and gestures for her to come to the table. "Can we dine outside?" he inquires politely.

"Of course, feel free to choose any outdoor seating, and I'll bring your meal out to you," she responds with a smile.

"Thank you, and may I have a glass of ice water with some lemon slices, please?" Dominic requests courteously.

He rises from his seat and extends his hand to Tiana. "Let's watch these people zip across the river," he suggests.

"Has anyone ever fallen into the water while zipping across?" she asks.

"As far as I'm aware, no, but anything is possible."

Spending time with Dominic brings her joy, but she knows she also needs to call Catalina and confess about the unpleasant experience at the hotel. Despite feeling upset, she puts on a happy facade and enjoys their morning outing. However, she plans to return to Charlotte and ensure this situation never occurs again.

"HUMANS USE THEIR TONGUES FOR PLEASURES, PROMISES AND LIES. BUT IF YOU CAUSE ME PAIN, I WILL NOT HESITATE TO RIP OUT YOUR TONGUE, PULL OUT YOUR TEETH WITH PLIERS, AND SLICE OFF YOUR LIPS AS PUNISHMENT."

CHAPTER 15

Devontae swiftly parks the car and rushes into Michael's house, eager to share his experience in Columbus. He's still angry about a country boy provoking him and challenging him to draw his gun.

As he enters, he halts in the foyer and sees two bulky white men acting as security guards for the white woman who is talking with Michael. He shakes his head and steps forward, but one of the guards blocks his path by placing his large hand on Devontae's chest.

"Is this how it is now, Mike? I can't even speak without permission?"

The white woman nods at the security guard, granting Devontae permission to enter the room. Straightening his shirt and giving the guard a menacing stare, Devontae warns, "Don't touch me again, or there will be consequences."

He finally approaches Michael but completely ignores the presence of the white woman. "Man, we need to talk immediately," he insists.

"Devontae, don't be rude to my guest. Gwendolyn, this is my childhood friend. He may be rough around the edges, but he's family."

Gwendolyn extends her hand to greet Devontae, who hesitates before returning the gesture. "Nice to meet you," he says. "Do you mind if I pull Michael away for a moment?"

"Sure, you two can do whatever men do," she says sarcastically. "I'm about to head out and finalize some deals for our upcoming meetings."

Devontae watches as she kisses Michael on the cheek before being escorted out by her security team. As soon as Gwendolyn is out of sight, Michael turns to him sternly. "Don't ever come into my house and disrespect her like that again. She's our golden ticket; whether you like her or not, you will show her the proper respect."

Devontae scoffs, "Whatever, man. I'm not going to pretend to respect some old rich bitch you're fucking. I saw how she looked at you; I know what's going on."

"And what if I am? There's nothing wrong with sleeping with older women who have money," Michael replies confidently. "Maybe you should try it instead of messing around with those hood rats on the streets."

"Speaking of the hood. It appears Tiana has a new neighborhood and a man she's fucking," Devontae says as he watches the arrogant expression on Michael's face droop down into disappointment.

Devontae walks over to the bar and pours himself a drink, glancing at Michael, who hasn't said a word since he mentioned Tiana. Knowing Michael could use one—maybe even two—

Devontae offers to pour him a drink, and Michael nods in agreement. Devontae opens the Black Cognac bottle on the counter and pours their drinks. After taking a sip, Michael places his glass back on the counter and tells Devontae to go ahead and tell him about Tiana.

"You never liked her anyway," Michael adds.

Devontae sips his drinks nonstop. "Ahh, that's some good shit," he expresses. "Tiana is staying in a townhouse overlooking a riverfront. She is hanging out with her friend, Catalina, and dating some country-ass guy.

"When I confronted Tiana at the hotel, he was there with her and dared to pump his chest and run his mouth. I hate Columbus, Georgia, but I'll return to fuck up her boyfriend."

"How do you know he's her boyfriend?" Michael asks.

"It doesn't matter if he's her boyfriend. He stayed the night with her, and that morning, they were coming to the hotel to have breakfast," Devontae says.

Michael sips his drink and chuckles a little. "Bitches forget that they were in the trenches after you place them on a pedestal." He reminds Devontae that she would still be sliding down poles if not for him. But now, he has a lot riding on this project with Gwendolyn, and there can't be any mistakes.

Devontae asks, "What should we do about Tiana?"

Without hesitation, Michael replies, "I'll take care of it."

They exchange nods and finish their drinks. Devontae then suggests they go to the Red Door later that night. Mike agrees, saying he needs to release some energy on some women.

"What's the theme for tonight?" Mike asks.

Devontae pulls out his phone and checks the club's website before answering, "Bunny Tails and High Heels."

Michael grins mischievously and slams his hand down on the counter. "It looks like we're about to get into some wet pussy. Call up some girls and tell them to meet us there too," he suggests.

They leave the house, and as they make their way to the car, Devonta follows Mike's request and contacts the ladies.

Michael starts the car, turns on some music, and drives down I-85 while Devontae tells the ladies their plans.

After forty-five minutes, they pull up to the swinger's club. They park the car and approach the infamous red door that some say is the Devil's Den.

After checking in at the counter, they receive their evening face masks and are guided to the locker room. They change into their outfits and prepare for a night of pleasure.

They emerge wearing identical leather gladiator body harnesses with built-in cock rings. Devontae notices that his harness feels snugger than usual. "Either I've gained weight, or this thing is too tight," he grumbles as it rides uncomfortably up his ass.

Michael chuckles. "Don't worry, man. Once your dick is in a woman's mouth, you won't even remember the tightness anymore."

As they move through the crowded dance floor, Michael notices a tall, black woman with blonde hair moaning as her partner thrusts his fingers into her pussy. She stands around 5'11" with curvy legs and a phat ass that catches his attention.

He halts in front of her and begins to stroke his dick. She locks eyes with him, and a smile spreads across her face.

"Mike, the girls are waiting," Devontae interrupts.

"You always wanted to fuck Ashley. You have my blessing. You can fuck her and Kim tonight," he says without breaking eye contact with the woman.

Devontae smiles and continues to bop through the crowd, excited for his birthday celebration in the VIP suite.

Meanwhile, the mysterious woman dancing in front of Mike stays close to her partner until Mike waves her over. She struts towards him, turns around, and backs her ass onto his crotch. "Do you want this pussy, Daddy?" she asks seductively.

"I have a suite in the back if you want to join me," Mike invites her while kissing her neck.

Michael notes his Lifetime Elite status at the Red Door, a privilege earned by owning most of the shares. He keeps this information to himself and follows all established rules to avoid raising suspicion.

He grabs the wrist of another female passing by. "Entertain her husband while we're away," he instructs. Without hesitation, the mysterious woman winks and kisses his cheek before doing as he requests. Michael leads the woman towards his private suite.

Most women in this club may not know his identity behind the mask, but they certainly remember the intense pleasure his dick gave them.

He effortlessly spins the woman around, her body presses against his, and he asks how many times she wants to cum tonight. She can feel his erection growing against her stomach and reacts by gripping it tightly with her hand, pulling him through the crowded dance floor towards the VIP suite.

The VIP suite has a luxurious bathroom with feminine and masculine shower products, towels, and a vanity mirror. There are also snacks, drinks, a TV, condoms, and a bowl of ecstasy pills.

Without wasting time, he pushes her onto the bed, and she eagerly motions for him to join her. With the press of a button on the wall, the sultry sounds of neo-soul music fills the room, adding to the already heated atmosphere.

He eagerly sucks on her breasts, brushing his tongue over her nipples as she moans in pleasure. "Are you ready for me to eat your pussy?" he calls out.

"Oh god, yes! Please do it," she begs.

He spreads her legs apart and slides in between them, floating over her sensitive clit. Her foot falls loosely over his shoulder as she grips the back of his head and rocks her hips into his face. "Fuck, baby. I love the way you eat this pussy!" she cries out.

His tongue quickens its pace as he laps at her swollen lips and pinches her nipples. She lifts her legs higher in the air, moaning uncontrollably and covering her eyes with one hand.

He slows his tongue's movements and playfully teases her sensitive clit, biting down on the tip. Her moans grow louder as he sucks harder. His neck muscles tense as he moves his face up and down, determined to make her climax. Her body shakes as she bounces up and down on the bed.

"Oh, my God. I'm about to cum!" she screams.

He feels her release wash over his lips but doesn't stop until she pushes him away.

Thinking of Tiana giving his pussy away, he decides to take out his frustrations on this woman. He flips her over onto her hands and knees.

Fitting a condom onto his swollen dick, he skips the extra foreplay and thrusts into her aggressively. Pushing her head into the mattress and slapping both of her ass cheeks, he starts to fuck her hard.

"That's right, take this dick. It's why you came here tonight!" he yells.

Her groans only turn him on more. Climbing onto the bed, he makes her lie flat as he mounts her. He bites her neck and thrusts harder as his pelvis claps against her ass cheeks.

"Oh, my God," she moans.

"Ride me and make me bust," he demands with urgency.

He turns over, and she climbs on top of him, straddling his dick. She moves her hips, grinding against him as he pulls her hair and kisses her roughly.

He tightens his grip on her hair and thrusts harder. She matches his intensity, bouncing up and down on top of him. Their bodies are slick with sweat, and he can feel himself getting closer to cumming.

With a few final thrusts, he pushes her off of him and quickly removes the condom before forcefully pushing his dick into her mouth. He dominates her throat, causing her to gag and spit.

Closing his eyes, he pictures Tiana in his head. "You mean nothing to me!" he screams.

As he reaches his peak and releases himself into her mouth, he demands that she swallow every drop.

They laugh afterward, and he tells her, "I needed that release."

"Me too," she responds with satisfaction.

CHAPTER 16

Sitting outside Gwendolyn's house, Michael watches the security team patrol the lawn like they're guarding a high-profile politician. His insatiable desire to expand his empire has led him down a dark path, where whispers circulate about Gwendolyn ruthlessly disposing of her closest associates, echoing through both high society and the streets. Yet, Michael refuses to back down from a challenge; he knows he needs more money before reinvesting in his real estate ventures in the Caribbean Islands.

He reaches for his briefcase, steps out of the vehicle, and puts on his shades to shield his eyes from the bright sunlight. Confidently, he strides up to the entrance, acknowledging the security team with a nod before continuing up the steps.

He enters the front door and is informed by the guard that Ms. Price is at the pool. After thanking the guard, he navigates through the house, eventually making his way outside for the meeting.

As he approaches the patio, he notices a group of women lying on their stomachs while men apply suntan lotion to their backs and legs. Gwendolyn lounges in the pool, sipping a margarita, and she motions to the server, who hurries over to take her empty glass.

"Why were you in the car for so long, Michael? Are you having doubts about our arrangement?" she asks.

"No, everything is fine. I just needed some time to myself before coming to see you," he responds.

Gwendolyn scoops up some water in her hands and splashes it onto Michael's pants, causing him to force a smile despite his annoyance. *This bitch plays too much. I knew I shouldn't have fucked her*, he thinks while forcing a smile on his face.

"Gwendolyn," he says through gritted teeth, "you're ruining a perfectly good suit. I'm here for business. Let's focus on that first and play later."

She winks at him mischievously before replying, "Always business with you." She sighs, "Fine, let's talk about business. Have you hired Ms. Henley to handle my services yet? My clients are ready to proceed, but I need her to handle some legal matters beforehand."

His response is firm and clear. "No, I have not. I intend to personally bring her back to North Carolina so we can make all the necessary preparations."

She playfully dips her hands in the water, splashing his clothes and repeating the motion until he becomes visibly agitated. "Ms. Price, can you please stop?" he demands, his tone full of frustration.

"Take off your clothes, Michael," she commands, her voice stern and unwavering, while he glances around at the people, pretending not to notice their exchange.

"They know not to make eye contact with me. Undress and enter the pool; I won't ask again," she threatens. "I've already made it clear that 'no' is not an acceptable answer.

"You still haven't fulfilled your duties of bringing Ms. Henley to me, yet you dare to question my instructions? If you don't remove your clothing, my team will hold you under water until you do."

"Gwendolyn, perhaps you've had too much to drink today. It's time to focus on business before things turn sour," he responds calmly.

"Business? Allow me to demonstrate how I handle business." She snaps her fingers sharply. "Face the other way," she commands.

He turns around and finds himself facing three women who are aiming pink flower-engraved pistols at him. One of the women strides forward and presses the gun to his temple.

"Michael Oliver Patterson, this is a business matter. By the end of today, someone will lose their head. It's up to you whether it's yours or not. If I were you, I'd get into this pool and eat my pussy until I cum and forgive you. But if you choose otherwise, she'll shoot you in the head, and then I'll sit on your face while your blood is still warm."

With a sigh, he puts his hands down and slowly sets his briefcase on a nearby lounge chair before undressing.

"You're taking too long," she snaps. "Forget your clothes and get in the pool now."

Despite being on the brink of death, his main concern is ruining his pair of Louboutin shoes. *That bitch is going to pay for this*, he thinks to himself as he slides into the pool next to Gwendolyn.

He looks her in the eyes before submerging himself in the water. As he goes down on her, he struggles to keep from swallowing too much water. Suddenly, he chokes and resurfaces, exclaiming that it's too much to handle. "I can't breathe and eat pussy at the same time!" he yells.

She responds, "You're right, Michael. You can't do both. But that didn't stop you from eating out that woman at the swinger's spot the other night."

"What the fuck?" he says in shock.

"Don't act surprised. You canceled our meeting to go fuck some random bitch. Nothing comes before my business."

She makes it clear that if it weren't for his sexual skills, he would be dead for prioritizing someone else over her. She also instructs him to tell their mutual friend Devontae that his family will suffer if he ever disrespects her again.

"I refuse to be played for a fool. Not by anyone!" she yells, her voice echoing against the pool walls. Michael is still in the water, but she stands above him, using the pool ledge to prop herself up. She pulls him out of the water with a tight grip on his tie and forces him to stand before her.

"My business is fucking you and making money until I say otherwise. I'm not sharing either with other women.

"Michael, get ready to be ridiculed," she says, leading him to the chaise lounge chair. She forcefully pushes him down onto it and then removes her bathing suit, settling herself on his chest. She teases his chest hair with her fingers before pinching his nipples.

"You're going to make up for pissing me off by eating my ass," she demands.

She slithers down from his chest, slowly making her way over to him. He watches intently as she sits on his face in reverse cowgirl position, her hands gripping her ass cheeks and spreading them open for him.

She glides over his face, and he eagerly starts to work, smacking his lips and delving his tongue deep inside her asshole.

She moans and lightly taps her fingers against her clit. "Yes, yes," she moans with pleasure.

He smacks his lips again as she inserts three fingers into her dripping pussy. Michael removes his mouth and inserts two fingers into her ass.

He pulls out his fingers and replaces them with his tongue, causing her sweet juices to drip down her legs onto his chin. "Faster, baby," she moans, urging him on.

Grunting in response, he obeys by pressing his lips firmly against her ass and sliding his tongue in and out at an accelerated pace. The pleasure is intense as their bodies move in perfect rhythm together.

"Michael, you're driving me insane. Don't give anyone else my head and dick!" she cries out.

She moves her fingers in circular motions around her clit, rubbing and slapping at it. She moans louder and pushes four fingers into her moist entrance, causing her to squirt.

"Yes, don't stop!" she yells.

She lifts herself off of Michael's face and continues fingering herself while squirting all over the lounge chair and onto Michael.

He slides away from her and repositions her on all fours, rapidly unbuckling his pants. He tosses off his jacket, removes his tie, and throws it onto the ground.

Pulling his pants down to his ankles, he says, "You tried to kill me, bitch. I'm going to destroy your asshole."

"Please punish me with that thick black cock," she pleads. "Ram it all the way inside of me. Show me how angry you are with me, Daddy."

He thrusts his dick inside of her and moves his hips vigorously while holding onto her ass cheeks. "Talk that shit now, bitch," he taunts. "You love when I fuck you in front of your stupid friends. Admit it, you love this big black dick. I'm going to fuck you so hard that you'll shit on my dick."

He pulls out and watches as her asshole widens. He teases her by inserting just the head before pulling back out again. He repeats this until he's ready to punish her once more.

With a firm grip on her thighs, he pulls her towards him, their bodies connecting with each of his thrusts. She lets out a loud moan, reveling in the pleasure he is giving her. "Oh yes, yes! Fuck me harder, Daddy!" she cries out.

He presses her face into the lounge chair and buries himself deeper inside of her. He starts to pull her hair and spank her ass cheek, intensifying the sensations for both of them.

For a moment, he slows down his movements. "Gwendolyn, can we talk for a minute?" he says. "You were showing off in front of your friends earlier, and now you're about to cry."

"Keep fucking that asshole, Daddy," she moans.

He slaps her ass again. "Who's your daddy, bitch?" he demands.

"Fill me up with that cum, Mike. Fuck me harder!" she screams in ecstasy.

He lifts her from the lounge chair and bends her over, driving himself deeper into her tight hole. They move together, trying to outdo each other with their desire.

"I'm going to cum," Mike grunts.

As they continue to have sex, she snaps her fingers twice. The woman with the gun from earlier walks over. Gwendolyn turns her head to look at Mike. "Unload in her mouth while I watch," she says.

He ravages Gwendolyn's ass for a bit longer before pulling the other woman towards him and onto the ground. He removes his dick from Gwendolyn's hole and forces it into the other woman's mouth.

She eagerly sucks and slurps on his dick as if she had known him her whole life.

"Oh, fuck. You're really going at it," he groans. "I'm about to cum. Open wide, killer."

He pulls out and slaps his dick against her cheek. Smiling, she tilts her head back and opens her mouth wide. He strokes his dick faster and faster until his body starts to tremble, and he releases himself down her throat.

She remains still, continuing to drain his dick, and even sucks on his balls after the last drop.

Gwendolyn smiles with satisfaction but then becomes serious. "Pull your pants up and come upstairs," she commands. "We have work to do, so don't keep me waiting."

She leaves Michael baffled, wondering if this is all just a mind game or if she plans to kill him. Either way, he quickly gathers his clothes and follows after her.

CHAPTER 17

Dominic wrestles with what to wear for his meeting with Tiana's friend, Catalina. He knows he shouldn't feel anxious, but he wants to make a good impression and avoid coming across as the wrong type of person. Fortunately, their meeting is in Atlanta, so he calls his friend Sasha to join him as his wingwoman. As he dials her number, he stares at another outfit while the phone rings.

"Hello?"

"Sasha, I need a big favor."

"Dominic, what's going on?"

"I'm in Atlanta for the weekend, and I was wondering if you and your husband could meet Tiana and her friend?"

Sasha's tone changes with excitement. "What? You're getting serious with this woman? Count me in! But the kids are at a soccer tournament with Robert. So, it'll just be me coming tonight."

"Thanks so much, I owe you."

"Text me the address, place, and time."

"I will. Thanks again."

"Yes, you do owe me big time. And that starts by bringing Tiana to meet the family tomorrow," Sasha suggests.

"Okay, I can do that," Dominic agrees.

"Hurry up and get off my phone so I can get ready. What kind of place are we going to?" she asks.

"It's a Thai restaurant that also offers massages and live music," he replies.

"Okay, I'll see you soon," she responds before hanging up.

"Shit, I should have asked her which outfit I should wear," he mutters to himself.

He returns to his suitcase and imagines Catalina as one of his targets, which helps calm his nerves. While picturing her, he chooses an outfit: a Fedora rim hat, ripped black jeans at the knees, a collared shirt, and ankle-high boots. After trying everything on and admiring himself in the mirror, he nods in approval at his evening attire. He neatly puts everything back in his closet.

With his outfit settled, he grabs one of his burner phones and looks for potential cheating partners to lust over. Ever since meeting Tiana, he has drifted away from his passion for eliminating cheating scumbags from existence.

As he continues browsing through profiles, he feels his dick getting hard in his satin boxers. He reminisces about the thrill of taking out cheating scumbags by snapping their necks or tampering with their cars to cause accidents on the highway.

He lets out a heavy sigh and speaks softly to his inner demons, telling himself to do the right thing. He knows he has something special with Tiana, and maybe she can help him control his urges and become a better person.

His grip on the phone tightens until it breaks in his hand. He pulls out a plastic bag and discards the broken phone, planning to dispose of it later.

He leans back on the bed, stares at the ceiling, and prays all will go well for everyone tonight. He sees Sasha asking a million questions, and he knows Tiana's friend is Puerto Rican, so she will also analyze him as well.

He lies still for what feels like an eternity until his alarm goes off, reminding him to get dressed for his dinner date. He rises from the bed and prepares for the evening, dressing up, brushing his teeth, and spritzing on some cologne.

He rides the elevator down to the lobby and steps outside into the parking lot, a smile spreading across his face as he savors the feeling of being with a woman worthy of his love. Upon arriving at the restaurant and parking his car, he takes a moment to breathe deeply before getting out.

Although he may have never been to Dunwoody, Georgia, he can tell it's a great place to catch cheating partners. The area's stunning ambiance features charming patios, rooftop views, lively bars, inviting restaurants, and various shops lining the streets. As he walks toward the Thai restaurant, he dials Sasha's number. "Do you want me to wait for you before going in?" he asks.

"I'm already here," she responds. "I remembered the photo you showed me and located Tiana quickly. Sorry, but law enforcement is something I enjoy doing."

He shakes his head and retorts, "No, you're just nosy as hell. I'll be joining you in there soon," before hanging up the phone. "She's probably spilling all my business. Hopefully, she won't mention the part about me being committed to a mental ward."

When he reaches the door and enters the restaurant, the live music, oriental paintings, and delicious smells immediately explain why Tiana chose this place for their meetup. He glances around, spots Tiana sitting with her friends Catalina and Sasha, and approaches them with a smile, removing his hat. "Good evening, ladies. Looks like you've already started without me," he jokes.

Sasha says, "Someone had to break the ice and get us in our comfort zone."

"I don't think I need to introduce you all to Sasha," he says, addressing the group.

He then introduces himself to Catalina, who grasps his hand eagerly and pulls him closer. "I have to stand up and hug you. We're practically family now since Tiana talks about you nonstop."

He chuckles and responds, "Well, at least they were good things she was saying."

Catalina's expression changes as she adds, "But I have some concerns."

"I was expecting that. Go ahead, start the interrogation," he invites.

"Please don't take this the wrong way, Dominic, but I'm from Columbus too. When Tiana showed me your picture, I did some digging and discovered that you are the famous Dominic Legend, whose wife and best friend were murdered in your home," Catalina reveals with a severe tone.

His gaze cuts to Sasha, but she quickly interrupts him. "I didn't say anything," she promises.

"Wow, you wasted no time with that one," he chuckles and responds, "Yes, I am him. You must not have dug deep enough because then you would have known you were sitting next to my deceased best friend's wife."

Catalina jumps in shock and blurts out, "What the fuck?"

"It's okay, that was all in the past. I've moved on from it, and you have nothing to worry about, either from me or Dominic," she adds.

He looks over at Tiana, who sips her drink while coyly shifting her eyes towards him. She smiles, rolls her tongue, and winks before returning to her drink.

He senses she's not bothered by his past, making him feel good as things seem to be returning to normal. But then Catalina interrupts again, blurting out, "Tiana used to be a stripper named Mercedes Chanel."

Tiana coughs and splutters as Catalina reveals her secret in front of Dominic and Sasha. She continues coughing as Dominic laughs at Catalina's statement.

"I thought I was going to be the only one up for elimination tonight," he adds with a laugh, appreciating Catalina's quick wit.

"So, Sasha, what do you do?" Catalina asks curiously.

"I'm an FBI agent," Sasha replies confidently.

"Well, this date just keeps getting better and better," Catalina retorts.

"Catalina, is there anything you'd like to share?" Dominic inquires.

"She's a freak hoe," Tiana yells out with a laugh.

"I plead the fifth," Catalina responds playfully.

"Maybe we should call over some masseuses to fully enjoy this fancy restaurant," Dominic suggests.

"I'm ready to eat," Catalina mentions eagerly.

"How about I order the grilled octopus for you?" Dominic jokes, laughing at his own suggestion.

"No, thank you. I'll choose my own meal," Catalina responds firmly.

Suddenly, four women appear behind them, gently massaging their shoulders and necks.

Sasha turns to Tiana and says, "You're all invited to meet my family tomorrow."

"I would love that! I have nothing else planned since Catalina leaves tomorrow morning," Tiana says happily.

"I am happy to have my husband prepare a light meal for us as we continue to get acquainted."

Dominic reaches for his phone and sends a text message to Tiana, asking her to spend the night with him. Upon receiving the text, she smiles and responds enthusiastically, "I thought you would never ask."

They engage in deeper conversations as they enjoy the live band's music. After 10 minutes of relaxation, their masseuses move on to another table. Dominic asks Tiana if she wants to dance, and she eagerly accepts. He leads her to the dance floor and spins her around, pressing her backside against his pelvis.

"Damn, your perfume smells divine," he compliments.

"Just wait until you taste this wet pussy tonight," she says seductively.

"I love it when you talk like that; it's such a turn-on. Do you think I made a good impression on Catalina?" Dominic asks.

"Yes, I'm sure you did. She always looks out for me, and I appreciate that about her."

"I wanted to tell you about my past at the convention center," he mentions.

"It's okay, we all have a past. And yours sounds interesting. Maybe you can take care of yourself," she jokes.

They continue dancing while the band plays, with Dominic occasionally kissing Tiana's neck and expressing his desire for her.

"I want you so bad right now. If you keep grinding your ass on my dick, I'm going to fuck you on this dance floor," he confesses.

"Don't threaten me with a good time," she teases back.

"Let's come up with an excuse to ditch these people and go somewhere else," he suggests playfully.

They scurry off the dance floor and return to their table. Dominic hands Sasha his credit card with a charming smile. "Order whatever you'd like, my treat," he insists.

Sasha and Catalina exchange knowing glances, having seen them dancing closely together. "We know what's going on. You two are going back to the hotel to fuck," Catalina teases.

"Girl, be quiet. You have said enough tonight," Tiana says.

"Whatever. I'll just hang out here with my new friend, Sasha, the FBI agent. You never know when our friendship might come in handy," Catalina jokes.

Dominic thanks Sasha for coming out and says he looks forward to seeing them all again tomorrow.

"No worries," Sasha replies. "Go have fun. Catalina and I will take care of maxing out this card tonight."

Dominic squeezes Tiana's hand and gives her a knowing look before leading her through the crowd and out of the building. He opens the car door for her, and they speed off to their hotel.

Tiana kicks her feet up on the dashboard once they hit the interstate and slyly reveals to Dominic that she's not wearing any underwear under her dress.

She gently runs her hands down her thighs and in between them. She lets out a moan as she urges him to taste how wet she is. Grabbing his arm, she guides his fingers inside of her. "Feel how wet I am, baby?" she asks, still moaning.

"You're so crazy and sexy," he says, trying to focus on driving. "I better pay attention to the road, or we might not make it."

She pulls his hand away from her thighs. "Put your fingers in your mouth. Suck my love," she commands.

He sucks on his fingers while driving and realizes they won't make it to the hotel. Spotting a sign for a dog park, he quickly turns left and parks behind some dumpsters.

Turning off the car, he unbuckles his seatbelt and rushes around to get Tiana out. She's already standing outside waiting for him.

He lifts her onto the car's hood and dives under her dress. She wraps her legs around his neck and guides his movements with her thighs.

He eagerly tastes her as she cries out for more, gently biting on her clit and pulling it out.

"Oh shit, Dominic!" she exclaims. "You have no idea how long I've wanted to fuck your face."

Throwing her head back, she thrusts her hips towards him. He explores the inside of her pussy with his tongue, hitting all the right spots.

"Ooh yes, eat this pussy," she moans. "You are amazing."

"You're going to cum for me, and then you're going to straddle this dick and ride it to sleep. Do you understand?" he grunts.

"Yes, baby. I'll do whatever you want. Just don't stop devouring my pussy," she moans.

He breaks away from her legs, lifting her in the air and slamming her back onto the hood while keeping his face buried between her thighs.

"Oh god, I love a savage like you. That kind of behavior makes me cum even harder. Don't tease me. Show me what that mouth can do."

He eagerly feasts on her, sucking her lips into his mouth like the famous spaghetti scene from *Lady and the Tramp*. She spreads herself open with her fingers, giving him access to pleasure her in any way he chooses. As he trails his tongue from her pussy to her asshole, she rubs her clit faster.

She gasps for air as no one has ever explored the depths of her sunken place before, not even Michael.

She crawls away from him in an attempt to escape the overwhelming pleasure Dominic is giving her. "Damn, oh god. You're going to make me cum," she moans.

He continues eating her ass and fingering her pussy. Her body convulses, and her eyes roll back in ecstasy.

"Yeah, give me that nut, Tiana. Give it to me now," he commands.

"Umm. umm, umm, here it comes."

He sucks on her asshole with more intensity, spreading her cheeks apart as she frantically rubs her clit. She can't resist any longer and has an explosive orgasm from his skilled oral techniques.

He gives her a moment to catch her breath before pulling away and undoing his pants. Although he wants her to ride him, he doesn't want to strip down entirely in the middle of the woods. Instead, he pulls her off the hood of the car and repositions her body against it, bending her over slightly.

He flips her dress up and enters her from behind, giving her the best thrusts of her life as he proclaims that she will soon be married to this dick. She eagerly begs for it, and he penetrates her timidly before pulling her back onto him with each thrust.

She moans about how long she's waited for him to be inside of her as he continues to slide deeper into every inch of creamy wetness.

After a few more minutes of intense pleasure, he bends down again to suck on her clit before standing back up to resume fucking her.

"I had to taste you, and now I'm ready to fuck you."

She pushes back against him, clenching tightly around him as he reaches around to stimulate her clit with his fingers. She leans further across the car, completely lost in bliss, as he relentlessly pounds into her.

He roughly grabs a handful of her hair and pulls her head up from the car hood, letting out a primal yell. She moans in response as his fingers move faster on her clit while his thrusts become more intense.

"Fuck me, Dominic!" she screams, and he obliges by driving harder into her. Her head bounces with each powerful thrust.

In the midst of their passionate encounter, they hear police sirens nearby, but neither of them is willing to stop. They continue to fuck like wild animals, ignoring the approaching sirens.

As the sirens get closer and closer, Dominic looks over at the dumpster and sees the flashing lights heading their way. "Shit," he groans.

"Don't stop," she yells, "fuck the police and fuck me!"

With renewed determination, he thrusts even harder, his breath becoming heavy as he pushes himself toward climax. His ass pops up in the air as he drives his dick into her with all his might.

Closing his eyes and ignoring the approaching authorities, he focuses on reaching orgasm. "Ahh," he grunts, thrusting again and again until finally releasing with a primal roar. The warm sensation floods her body like a tidal wave.

He catches his breath before quickly pulling up his pants. He helps Tiana fix her dress before checking their appearance just as the police enter the dog park.

Tiana whispers urgently, "Stay calm and act normal."

The wailing sirens abruptly cut off as the police cruiser pulls up behind the dumpster. The flashing lights continue to illuminate their hiding spot. They hear the sound of car doors opening and closing as officers approach with flashlights in hand.

"Step out with your hands raised!" one of the officers demands.

Dominic glances at Tiana, who cracks a small smile despite the tense situation.

"Just do as they say," she murmurs.

They emerge from behind the dumpster, slowly raising their hands above their heads as instructed.

"For your safety, we need to ask you some questions first. We couldn't see what was happening behind the dumpster," one officer speaks up. "What were you all doing at this dog park so late at night?"

Once they realize that Tiana and Dominic pose no threat, the officers try to de-escalate the situation. "Listen, this is Dunwoody, where people call the police for every little thing. Whatever it is you were doing here, please stop," one of them says.

The other officers check out the car and yells, "they don't even have a dog."

"I could interrogate you all night, but I can already piece together what happened. I'm just glad I didn't catch you in the act," says the officer with a sigh. "My shift is almost over, and I just want to go home."

Tiana smiles embarrassedly while Dominic laughs, knowing they've been caught red-handed.

"Just remember, next time, get a room or something," advises the officer jokingly.

"Sir, ma'am, can I please see your driver's licenses?"

As instructed, Dominic and Tiana grab their licenses from their car and hand them over to the officer. After verifying their identities and running a check for warrants (which comes back negative), the officer lets them go on their way.

"Alright, you two horny jackrabbits can leave now, but if I catch you here again, you'll both be in trouble," the officer says.

"Thank you," they say together.

"Now get out of here so I can go home to my family," the officer adds.

Tiana and Dominic hop into their car and drive from the dog park towards their hotel room.

"Tiana, your wet pussy almost got us arrested," he says.

"You're the one who couldn't wait and pulled off at that exit," she responds.

"Could you imagine their faces if they saw me throwing this dick?" he laughs. "You were like, fuck the police, just fuck me."

"I say some wild things when the sex is good," she admits.

"I'm starving because we didn't eat before leaving the Thai restaurant," Tiana remembers.

"Let's head to the hotel, shower, and I'll order room service," he suggests.

"Great idea, and maybe I'll suck your dick with the curtains open. Who knows? Maybe someone will see us," she teases.

With the interstate fast approaching, he presses the pedal even harder and speeds back to the hotel. *This woman has me wrapped around her little finger, making me do things I'd never imagine before. But I can't get enough of it,* Dominic thinks while they drive back, enjoying each other's company and sharing laughter and music.

CHAPTER 18

Dominic turns over and gives Tiana a soft kiss on the lips. She opens her eyes and runs her fingers through his wavy hair. He moves down to her nipples, gently sucking on them as she watches him with a playful look in her eyes.

She pulls him back up to her face. "We should probably stop. We need to be at Sasha's house soon," she reminds him.

"Are you sure you don't need a quickie? I'm sure I can pump faster than the speed of light," he teases.

She playfully slaps his butt. "No way, save your energy for tonight. I'll give you a lap dance that will make you lose control," she promises.

"I like the sound of that. Why don't you shower while I start packing?" he suggests.

He rolls off her, allowing her to leave the bed and head towards the shower. As he watches her walk away, he can't help but admire her perfect figure - from her flowing locs to the dimples in her ass and the way her hips sway as she walks.

He feels himself getting hard, but he knows he can wait until tonight. He jumps out of bed and begins packing their belongings, eagerly folding her clothes and even taking a moment to smell a pair of her underwear.

He finds a matching purple lace set and lays it out on the bed with a smile on his face.

As he continues packing, he speaks confidently: "I'm sure she won't mind wearing these for me today."

His phone suddenly rings, and he walks over to answer it. The screen displays Sasha's name.

"Dominic, if you don't mind, pick up some wine before coming here," she says. "And by the way, don't analyze your card transactions too closely. We ordered everything we could at your expense."

"It's okay. I can't be upset about that," he replies. "I can't wait to see you all today."

"Likewise," she responds before hanging up.

Once he finishes packing his clothes, he walks over to the window and takes a moment to breathe in the normalcy of the view outside. He closes his eyes and relaxes until he hears soft tapping on the floor. Knowing Tiana is trying to scare him, he slightly opens his eyes and spins around, shouting, "Boo!"

"Shit!" she screams in surprise and drops the towels she was wearing.

He smiles and admits, "I guess I was looking at the wrong view. I should be exploring your city instead."

She kisses him passionately and interrupts their embrace with a reminder: "Later, you can explore. For now, go shower so we can make it to Sasha's house in time."

She reaches for her phone and settles onto the bed, smoothing lotion over her skin. She dials Catalina's number and sets it on speakerphone. Surprisingly, it goes straight to voicemail; Tiana knows this is unusual since Catalina always answers her calls.

Assuming that she requested a later checkout, Tiana sets her phone down and giggles as she admires the lingerie set that Dominic left out for her to wear.

She loves how he always knows what will make her smile, from opening car doors to remembering her favorite perfume and lipstick shade.

She believes their future together will be incredible, and there's no way she would consider moving back to Charlotte. Her old life is the past, and a fresh start is something she has always dreamed about since she started sliding down poles and lap dancing on men's dicks.

She slides on her clothes and retwists her hair into a cute style, knowing it will drive Dominic crazy once he emerges from the bathroom.

Dominic opens the bathroom door and steps out fully nude, and the shower gel scent was enticing her to say 'fuck her' instead of going to Sasha's.

He catches her staring and rushing up behind Tiana to place a kiss on her ear. "You look stunning," he proclaims. "Promise me you'll never leave me."

Tiana pauses for a moment, teasing him with suspense. Finally, she turns around with a smile and replies, "I'll never leave you. You are my new beginning."

They dress in silence, and once he finishes, he turns on the TV, giving Tiana time to finish getting ready. "Tiana, I'll take some of the suitcases to the car. I'll be back in a minute," he says.

"Okay, I'll be ready when you get back," she responds.

She continues fixing her makeup until her phone buzzes with a text message from Catalina, letting her know she's okay and will call later.

Tiana finishes styling her hair and changes into a casual outfit of shorts, a tank top, and sandals. She remembers Sasha mentioning last night that this was a relaxed family dinner with her husband and kids.

She takes her business phone from her purse and checks for potential new clients while waiting for her man's return. She sees some messages from Michael's team but deletes them without reading them.

Then, she notices one message from Gwendolyn Price that catches her attention. It appears to be a regular business inquiry until she reaches the part where Ms. Price demands that Tiana assist Michael.

Just as she reads those words, the phone rings and Tiana answers with a polite, "Hello."

"Good afternoon, Ms. Henley. This is Gwendolyn Price, and I'm calling to ensure you are-"

Without hesitation, Tiana hangs up and powers off her phone before Ms. Price can finish speaking. "No one threatens me and then has the nerve to call me," she mutters angrily. "Fuck that bitch!"

Tiana suspects that Michael passed her number to Ms. Price, and she plans to confront him about it when they meet. Her anger at his money-hungry ways fuels her determination.

Despite this, she refuses to let this situation ruin her chances of meeting Dominic's side of the family. She has been curious since he doesn't talk much about them, except for mentioning a famous brother in Florida with whom he doesn't get along with.

Tiana knows Sasha won't mind answering some questions, and once they're alone, she plans to get all the inside scoop on Dominic's family.

Dominic returns to gather their belongings before leaving the hotel and driving to Sasha's house. He stops at the store to pick up a bottle of wine. As Tiana watches him go inside, she realizes she is falling hard for him.

She remembers meeting him in the elevator and thinking of how she could use him to squeeze a nut off. Now, they have found each other and are building a future together.

As Dominic comes out of the store with the wine, he hops back into the car and declares that they are ready to continue their drive towards Sasha's house.

They arrive at Sasha's house and park the car. As he turns to face her, he wraps his hands around hers and thanks her for not bringing up his past when Catalina mentioned his deceased wife.

He admits he is never comfortable talking about it, but her understanding made him realize he wants to spend the rest of his life with her. She says she would do anything for him, kissing his knuckles sweetly.

They walk up the driveway hand in hand, laughing together. Dominic prepares to knock on the door, but it swings open to reveal a young woman with hazel eyes.

Dominic recognizes her as Katrina. She was just a child the last time he saw her. She rushes towards him and gives him a tight embrace. "Uncle Dominic, I remember you! You used to tell TJ and me the most amazing bedtime stories."

"Wow, you've grown so much!" he exclaims.

"Come on inside; everyone is in the backyard," she says, leading the way.

As they walk through the house, he introduces his girlfriend, Tiana, to Katrina.

"It's a pleasure to meet you, Ms. Tiana," Katrina says with a smile. "Mom already filled us in on your visit today. She's always in work mode."

They step out into the backyard, where Sasha runs over to hug them and thanks them for coming over.

"Robert, this is Dominic and Tiana," Sasha says, introducing them to her husband.

Robert waves and replies, "I'll be there in a second. Just need to flip this fish real fast."

Sasha gestures towards the patio table and suggests, "Why don't you all have a seat?"

As they reach the table, they hear a young man call out, "Heads up!" as a football sails through the air. Dominic effortlessly catches the ball and soon playfully wrestles with the young man who threw it.

"Wow, TJ, you've gotten so tall!" he exclaims.

"You have to visit more often, especially during football season. Who's your girlfriend? She is gorgeous," TJ says, shaking her hand. "Do you have any young nieces that look as fine as you?"

"TJ, sit your thirsty ass down," Sasha scolds.

Everyone laughs at Sasha's comments while sitting down at the patio table. Robert arrives with a platter of grilled seafood and boasts that it is some of the best in Atlanta. After saying grace, they all start serving themselves from the delicious spread.

Dominic takes a bite of the fish and gives his approval, asking Robert to save some for him to take home.

As they eat and catch up on old times, Dominic's heart is filled with warmth and happiness from being with Tiana. He knows it's love that makes him feel this way.

After spending hours together, Tiana and Dominic prepare to leave, but not before giving everyone hugs and promising to return soon.

"I'll walk them out," Sasha says, heading towards the door.

"Make sure you don't stay gone too long. It's karaoke night," Robert reminds her.

Sasha laughs. "I'd invite you all to stay and sing, but I think the lovebirds have other plans."

Dominic hugs Sasha. "Thank you for everything. We'll be back."

Tiana thanks Sasha for the dinner with a smile.

"Yes, girl. And next time we'll have some alone time, and I'll give you more details about Dominic," she jokes.

As they walk down the driveway, Tiana freezes upon seeing Michael leaning against Dominic's car.

"Do you need something?" Sasha asks, noticing his presence.

"No, ma'am, I'm here for the young lady," Michael replies calmly.

Sasha reaches behind her back and pulls out a gun, cocking it. "Coming to my house was your first mistake."

"Turn on your phone, Tiana," Michael instructs.

Dominic remains silent, his fists clenched tightly and his nostrils flaring in anger, while Tiana's worried voice rebukes Michael for being there. He assures her that he will leave as soon as Tiana checks her messages from Ms. Price.

Tiana apologizes to Dominic and quickly checks her phone.

"Ma'am, can you please stop pointing your gun at me? Like I said before, I'm only here for her," Michael reminds Sasha.

She gasps as she reads the message, covering her mouth in shock. Turning to Dominic, she whispers an apology before attempting to walk away. But just as she takes a few steps, Dominic grabs her hand, pleading with her to stay and work things out together.

"Baby, you don't have to go. We can figure this out," Dominic says.

Despite his pleas, Tiana knows she has to go. She tells him she loves him and that she's sorry before breaking free from his grasp and walking toward Michael. Dominic falls to his knees, crying out for her to stay.

Tiana looks back at him with a heavy heart, wanting to stay but knowing it is beyond her control. As she walks away, she sees Dominic professing his love on the ground, causing her heart to shatter into a million pieces.

Tiana glances at Dominic again before turning her head and striding towards Michael. He greets her with a kiss on the cheek, but she slaps him hard across the face. "I hate you!" she screams as tears stream down her cheeks.

"Tiana, Dominic is right. You know I have connections with powerful people. Please don't get into that car," Sasha advises.

"It will be fine, Sasha. We can go on our girl's night out later, but I have to leave now," Tiana says.

Dominic looks up from the ground and reminds Tiana of her promise not to leave him.

Michael interjects with a playful comment, "This is turning into quite the love story."

Michael then suggests that Tiana enter the car so they can all leave peacefully. Dominic stands up and confronts Michael face-to-face. He stares intently at him before flashing a smile.

"What are you smiling at, country boy?" Michael taunts. "She's coming with me."

Feeling defeated, Dominic steps back. "Tiana," he pleads. "If you leave with him, you're dead to me."

"Please don't say that," Tiana begs.

But Michael opens the passenger door, and Tiana enters without hesitation. He closes the door and walks around to the driver's side.

"Ma'am, country boy. You all enjoy your evening. I got what I came for," Michael smirks.

Filled with fury, Dominic tightens his hand into a fist and thrusts it through the front window, shattering the glass. Tiana instinctively recoils as shards of glass scatter around her from the impact.

Michael only laughs at this display of strength. "Damn, you're one tough country boy," he jokes. "With what I came for in hand, I'll spare your life for breaking my window," Michael declares before getting into his car and driving away.

Sasha quickly holsters her gun and rushes after Dominic, who is already storming toward his car.

Breathless, Sasha catches up with Dominic. "Stop. Let me see your hand," she demands. His hand is bloody and coated in glass particles.

"Dominic, I'm sorry this happened. But let's hear the other side of the story before we jump to conclusions. I have the license plate number and I'll get some information on this guy tonight."

Dominic breaks down crying and laughs while embracing Sasha. "It's okay. I'll be fine. This isn't the first time a woman has left me for someone else," he says with a bittersweet smile.

"Take care of your family. Maybe happy endings only exist for everyone except me," he adds before getting into his car and driving off.

"WHEN A MAN GETS ON HIS KNEES, IT'S TO MAKE A LIFELONG COMMITMENT OR TO SAY A FINAL GOODBYE. DON'T TAKE SOMEONE'S PAIN LIGHTLY; CONSIDER THE CONSEQUENCES BEFORE ACTING."

CHAPTER 19

Tiana's anger intensifies as they drive back to Charlotte. Each time she glances at Michael in the rearview mirror, she unleashes a string of curses and threats. The shattered window from Dominic's outburst only fuels her frustration, and to make matters worse, Michael hasn't bothered to stop for a rental car or even try to cover the broken window, leaving her to endure the biting wind.

After a long and tiring three-and-a-half-hour drive, they finally reach their destination in Charlotte. The driver parks the car in front of a large house surrounded by towering oak trees at Eastover Estates. As they step out, they are greeted by a stylish white woman wearing a pink pantsuit and two well-dressed men.

She slightly nods, and the gentleman hurries to open the car door for Tiana. He helps her out of the back seat and leads her up the steps to stand in front of the woman with authority.

"Welcome, Tiana. How was the journey?" she inquires, glancing at the car and spotting the broken window. She then directs her gaze towards Michael, who quickly protests his innocence regarding the damaged window.

"Tiana, you must be exhausted. Let me show you to your room so you can finally see your friend again," she offers with a kind smile.

Tiana's struggles to break free from the grip of the security guard. Her mind races with one thought: to ensure her friend is safe and unharmed. With determination, she approaches the imposing figure in front of her.

"Ms. Gwendolyn Price, I presume?" Tiana boldly states.

"I have been called many names, but since we are going to be close friends and partners in business, you can call me Gwen," she introduces herself.

"I'm not here to make friends," Tiana states firmly. "Just take me to see Catalina."

Gwendolyn turns her head to the left, watching the guards guide Tiana through the house and up a flight of stairs to a doorway that opens into a spacious room.

The guards shove Tiana into the room, causing her to stumble before she spun around, cursing at them. They slam the door behind her, and she hears the locks click into place from the other side.

"Are you okay? Did they hurt you?" Tiana rushes over to give Catalina a concerned hug.

"You know they can't keep a soldier down," Catalina adds with a hint of pride. "I even managed to slap one of the guards with my shoe before they threw me in their car."

"I'm sorry they brought you here because of me," Catalina apologizes.

Tiana reassures Catalina, "Don't worry. Michael and his accomplices are hatching a major plan, and it seems they need my help to make it happen."

"At least the room is excellent; we have king-sized beds and a pool view, and they will bring room services whenever I request it," Catalina jokes.

"I suppose you're right," Tiana says thoughtfully. "We could have been stuck in some dark basement, chained to a pole with rats scurrying around us."

Catalina then asks if Tiana had the opportunity to contact Dominic.

Tiana shifts her position and admits, "I doubt he'll speak to me for a while after what happened. You should have seen his anger when Michael bragged about taking me with him."

Tiana's voice trembles as she recounts the terrifying moment when he shattered the passenger window while she was already inside.

Catalina's eyes narrow. "I knew it," she seethes. "That bastard killed his wife, and now he's after your ass."

"You watch too much TV," Tiana shook her head. "Dominic may be hurt, but he's not a monster like that. He even stood up to Michael for a brief moment. Dominic doesn't know why I left. I couldn't tell him anything because Gwendolyn threatened to have you killed. I fucked up, and I'll probably never find someone as amazing as Dominic again."

Catalina leans in expectantly. "So, what's the plan for getting us out of here?"

Tiana urges them to devise a plan quickly, but she wasn't sure what they could do. As they hear the bolt on the door unlock, they stop talking and wait to see who will enter.

Tiana frantically searches for something that could be used as a weapon, but they only have a TV remote and some books in the room.

Devontae surprises them by walking into the room carrying a tray of food.

Of all people, why did they have to summon this idiot? Tiana thinks to herself, hating his arrogant attitude. She hates his crazy ass and refuses to eat anything he's carrying.

"Hello, ladies," he greets them with a smirk. "I hope you're enjoying your stay at Gwendolyn's bed and breakfast."

"Fuck you, Devontae," Tiana responds angrily. "Send Michael up here so I can confront him face to face."

"Aren't you tired of acting like you're in charge?" he taunts while playfully snapping grapes at her from their stems.

"Do that again, and I'll claw your eyes out," Tiana threatens, crossing her arms defensively.

"Catalina, don't be like your friend," Devontae says mockingly. "She'll be stuck here for a while, but if you want to make it home tonight, all you have to do is suck my dick," he suggests.

"That tiny Vienna sausage? I might accidentally swallow it and choke," she jokes.

"Fine, have it your way," he says with frustration. "Stay locked up in this place with your friend," he adds as he slams the tray on the table and storms off.

Tiana and Catalina continue laughing about the size of his dick.

Tiana's mind is racing about how to help them both escape this situation. "Catalina, I think we need to strategize and work together for you to return home," Tiana says.

Catalina shakes her head. "No, Tiana. I'm fine being here with you."

"I know, but you're innocent. My hands have been stained with corrupt cases before. This might be karma coming back to me," Tiana confesses.

"Tomorrow, I will start working on gaining their trust, and then I'll devise a plan to take down their entire operation from within," Tiana reveals to Catalina.

"I'm not entirely convinced by that plan. Are you not worried about the potential consequences of concealing evidence? Also, I overheard Devontae saying that the Mayor had stopped by earlier."

"It doesn't come as a surprise to me. The Mayor played a significant role in the success of many of my cases. He and Michael were fraternity brothers, and you know how those Que Dogs operate."

"All this talk of corrupt politicians and criminal activities makes me crave food. If it's alright with you, could you pass me a plate of Mofongo?" Catalina requests.

Tiana seems taken aback. "How can you possibly think about eating at a time like this?" she questions.

"We're both hostages here, but I will not let this food go to waste. The chef is Puerto Rican, and I ordered this dish earlier today."

"What did you order for me?" Tiana asks.

"I didn't even know you were coming tonight," Catalina jokes. "I'll have them make you a hamburger or something."

"No thanks, but I'm glad you mentioned the chef is Puerto Rican. Let's keep him on our side until we can escape this situation," Tiana says.

"By the way, what exactly is Mofongo?"

"It's a traditional Puerto Rican dish with plantains, mashed potatoes, and bacon. Mine also has chicken and shrimp stuffed inside. You know I love my meat," Catalina explains.

"You don't have to tell me. Remember those dick pics you used to send me?" Tiana laughs.

Tiana couldn't help but tease Catalina about her past love interests, and they share a laugh before Catalina digs into her food.

"I'm going to nap on the other bed and think about Dominic," Tiana says.

"Don't think too hard; he might come into your dreams like Freddy Krueger and take revenge for leaving him for Michael," Catalina jokes and takes a bite of her food.

"I keep telling you that my man is not a murderer. Please stop saying that. Why don't you eat your food while I take a nap?"

As she chews and speaks simultaneously, she manages to say, "Don't say I didn't warn you."

"Enjoy your meal and find a way for your Puerto Rican boyfriend to sneak us a phone or something," Tiana suggests.

"His handsome face could slip into this pussy. Handcuff me to the bed, choke me, and smack me around a little. Now that's the kind of kidnapping I would enjoy," Catalina says with a laugh.

Tiana rolls over onto her side, getting comfortable as she sinks into the softness of the bed. "Wow, this bed feels amazing. Gwendolyn, I still plan on kicking your ass, but thanks for this bed. I'll sleep like a baby tonight," she whispers to herself.

"EVEN IN THE MIDST OF A DISASTROUS SITUATION, DON'T LET IT STOP YOU FROM ENJOYING A DELICIOUS MEAL."

CHAPTER 20

Dominic lays on the bed, mindlessly flicking darts towards the ceiling. Some stick, while others fall back onto his face and chest.

For the second time in his life, he has lost someone he deeply cares for, and it's hitting him hard. With his wife, he saw the warning signs and was able to ease his pain by killing her. But with Tiana, she left without explanation, and her ex-boyfriend cruelly took her away from him while laughing in his face.

Tiana promised him she wouldn't leave him earlier that day, and he believed her wholeheartedly. Now, as he replays their last moments together in his head, he can feel his blood racing to his dick.

Sometimes, it feels like he's transforming into a vampire or werewolf, and besides good pussy, the only thing that can calm his urges is watching someone die.

He throws the final dart and watches it fly towards the ceiling before bouncing off and landing on his chest with the needlepoint sticking into his skin. Rather than being disturbed, he laughs before pulling it out and licking the blood off his finger.

His phone has died, which is a relief because Sasha has been calling incessantly to express her concerns. At this moment, Dominic doesn't want to talk to anyone with a pussy; he sees all women as enemies.

He hasn't taken a shower or brushed his teeth, living like a soldier in a warzone. Empty bottles litter the floor, remnants of drinking and urinating.

"Just go down," he pleads with his dick, hoping to distract his demons and move past the drama.

He rises from bed, the stench of not showering for an entire day accompanies him. Raising his arms to sniff his armpits and bringing his hand to his nose after touching himself below, he curses at how unclean he is. "Damn, I smell terrible. I need to shower and wash away this depression and sadness."

He plugs in his phone and turns it on to a flurry of messages. He finally responds to Sasha's check-in by texting her that he's at home and grateful for her concern.

Stripping out of his clothes, he heads towards the shower, led by a hard dick. The inner demons start whispering to him, tempting him with thoughts of killing and watching people cheat. Agreeing to give in to their games, he feels his hardness shrinking back to its average size.

After his shower, he checks the time and travel to Phenix City, Alabama, for a potential opportunity or person to kill. There's an event called Stroke-N-Word tonight, featuring poets and nude models for women to paint.

He can easily slide into this event, hoping his brother isn't aware of it. That's just a typical event for a cheating bastard like him. He deserves to face consequences, too, and their truce may end if he shows up there.

He quickly texts the event information to the hacker and lets him do his thing, leveraging his skills to coerce the host into adding another dancer for the evening.

How hard could it be? Just stand in the middle of the room naked, and let women paint you, he thinks to himself.

To blend in with the theme, he opts for a simple yet comfortable soldier outfit. He pulls on black jump boots, camo pants, a brown shirt, and a camo face mask bandana that covers his head and eyes. The mesh allows him to see out while concealing his face from others.

There are always plenty of thirsty sluts who love military men at these events. It shouldn't be challenging to find someone to satisfy his urge to kill tonight, he thinks to himself.

The event is being held at Webb's Place, a secluded farm located just beyond the city limits. He packs up his disposal bag and clothes and rushes out of the house and into his car.

Driving through backroads and into Phenix City, he turns onto an unmarked path that leads to a beautifully manicured garden filled with fruit trees, lush lawns, and charming farmhouses and cottages; it would make for a perfect wedding venue.

Quickly changing into his costume inside the car, he pulls on the camo pants, slips on his boots, and adjusts his mask. Deciding to forgo the shirt, he steps out and heads inside, confident and ready to charm the ladies.

He sneaks in unnoticed and makes his way to the DJ booth. "What's the lineup?" he asks.

The DJ hands him a basket to pick a number, and he draws number one. The DJ informs him that a poet will perform first, followed by him posing for the crowd. Dominic nods in agreement and surveys the room, eyeing all the women in attendance.

He knows some are loyal fans looking for entertainment, while others may be savages.

The DJ introduces the poet, who performs a piece, and the audience cheers and applauds. When it's his turn, Dominic heads to the center of the stage as *Fuckin' Wit Me* by Tank begins to play.

He kicks off his boots, removes his pants, and stands in green socks and camo briefs before the audience.

"Take it off!" the women scream eagerly.

He puts on a seductive dance, swaying his hips and thrusting his pelvis. Then, with a sly smile, he leans over and takes off his briefs, placing them on the head of a woman sitting at a nearby table.

He returns to his original stance, imagining the death of every woman in the room. His dick grows, stretching and hardening to a nine-inch erection in front of the watching crowd.

He poses while the women sip their drinks and paint, never having done anything like this before. He can see why his brother enjoys the creative arts.

A curvy, light-skinned woman in a green sundress and heels approaches him. "How do you keep it up for so long?" she asks, intrigued.

"As long as I think about killing some pussy, it comes naturally," he responds with a smirk, flipping his dick in the air for her amusement.

The woman giggles and walks away, unaware that she could potentially be his next victim if her life isn't in order.

He stands there for 45 minutes, occasionally stroking his dick, imagining it's a neck he's squeezing the life out of.

The DJ announces an intermission to prepare for the next artist. Dominic picks up his clothes from the floor and heads back to the restroom to change. He has had such a good time tonight that he decides not to kill anyone.

As he pushes open the door to the restroom, he finds a woman bent over the sink being fucked by one of the nude models.

"Are you going to join? If not, get the fuck out of here!" the nude model says.

"I'm good," Dominic mutters through his mask, slipping on his clothes and noticing wedding rings on both participants.

His blood boils, and he knows he needs to act tonight. He takes a moment to calm down before leaving the bathroom and returning to his car. With a quick text to his hacker, he obtains information on the nude model he desires and discovers that he is indeed married.

Dominic opens his trunk and searches for something to make a statement tonight. Satisfied with his choice, he gazes at the stars and whispers, "Tiana, you're the reason I'm here."

He patiently waits in the car, listening to music and fantasizing about everything he wants to do to the male model and the woman. He asks his hacker to intercept their messages so he can read what they are saying to each other.

The nude model asks the woman to meet him behind one of the cottages in five minutes so he can fuck her throat. The greedy bitch eagerly responds with a tongue-out smiley face and says she'll be right there.

Dominic steps out of his car and gives them a head start before following them stealthily. After ten minutes, he creeps up behind the cottages, pulling out his X-2 dart pistol.

As he approaches, he drops his bags and finds the woman on her knees, deepthroating the model's penis. He positions himself beside them and clears his throat loudly. "Ahem," he announces, "I would like to join in on this fun now."

The man turns his head, causing the woman to stop performing oral sex on him. Without hesitation, Dominic takes out the pistol from behind his back and shoots a tranquilizer dart into the model's neck and the woman's arm.

As the man rushes towards him, Dominic quickly sidesteps and hits him in the face with the butt of his pistol. The man collapses to the ground, and Dominic finishes him off by stomping on his head until he is unconscious.

Dominic then turns to the woman crawling on her knees, attempting to escape. He towers over her, blocking her path. "Come here, you filthy slut," he taunts. "You're married, yet you're here having sex with random men in a bathroom. You didn't even use a condom, and now you want to bring those nasty fluids home to your husband?"

He pulls out a 550 cord from his pocket and wraps it tightly around her neck, pressing his knee between her shoulder blades to make breathing harder for her. Despite her attempts to fight back, she eventually succumbs to death after two minutes of being strangled.

Dominic then retrieves his disposal bag and considers what to do with the model. He wasn't trying to cause too much damage to the man but wants to send a message to all the cheaters out there.

After scratching his head momentarily, he decides he needs more time to be creative. However, this is not the time for that.

Instead, he takes out his knife and approaches the model lying on the ground. Tilting his head back, he swiftly slices his throat from ear to ear before making any further decisions on what to do with him.

After dragging the lifeless bodies through the grass, he props them up against a nearby tree and secures them with rope. He carefully carves the words "RELATIONSHIP KILLER" into the bark above their heads, a fitting tribute to his handiwork.

Content with his accomplishments for the night, he carefully tidies up any traces and hides his inner struggles deep inside himself.

Excited to leave this scene behind, he eagerly awaits returning home to shower before indulging in some delicious waffles at Waffle House.

CHAPTER 21

Gwendolyn is kind enough to return Tiana and Catalina's possessions; she even took them on a shopping trip yesterday. However, she clarifies that she will not hesitate to harm Dominic if they make any mistakes.

Tiana feels guilty about breaking his heart and is determined to protect the only person she truly cares for. She tried to persuade Catalina to return home, but her friend refused to leave without her.

The day begins with breakfast downstairs, surrounded by Gwendolyn's team. Tiana knows that Michael will be at the table, and this will be the first time she sees him since he took her away from Dominic. As they reach the bottom of the stairs, the mouth-watering smell of sizzling bacon and freshly baked biscuits greets them, along with the aroma of warm butter and maple syrup.

Gwendolyn was already seated and beckons over. "Come on over and meet the family," she announces.

Tiana and Catalina join her at the table as the staff rushes over to take their drink orders. Tiana requests a Mimosa for herself and Catalina as she braces herself for whatever nonsense they would be discussing at this meeting.

Gwendolyn asks everyone to bow their heads as she blesses the food and expresses gratitude to God for their new family. The table choruses, "Amen," and the plates start moving from left to right as everyone chooses what they want for breakfast.

Tiana glares at Michael, but he does his best to ignore her. She's not having it this morning. She scoots her chair away from the table. "Gwen, since we're family, I need to speak with Michael privately for a moment," she says firmly.

Gwen nods understandingly, and Tiana quickly exits to Gwendolyn's library for a heated conversation with Michael. He follows behind her and attempts to charm her with a smile that she once loved.

"Get the fuck away from me," she snaps. "Don't make me embarrass you in front of your new friends."

He smirks and winks at her. "Calm down, Tiana," he says arrogantly. "You know you're curious about how much money we can make with Gwendolyn. You should be thanking me for setting you back on the right path."

She reminds him that even if she is curious, she has the right to decide her future and shouldn't be forced into anything.

"I have no idea who you are anymore. Definitely not the man I met many years ago," she mentions.

"No, I haven't changed," he retorts. "You're just letting your successful career blind you from seeing that you're just as manipulative as everyone else at that table.

"Please cooperate with Gwendolyn and remember that she doesn't handle rejection well. She was the one who came up with the plan to abduct Catalina and ruin your perfect romance with that country boy," Michael admits.

"His name is Dominic, and he's a real man, despite what you might think. He'd never let me catch him getting his dick sucked at a party," she reminds him before storming off.

He hastily grabs her arm to stop her from leaving. "Listen, bitch. Your attitude has been shitty lately. You need to remember who the fuck I am and what I'm capable of. I'm only cutting you some slack because I still have feelings for your ass. Now come on, let's go eat some pancakes, and talk business," he says.

He releases her arm, and she reluctantly returns to the table and sits beside Catalina. Catalina senses something is wrong and asks if everything is okay.

Tiana whispers, "I'll be fine. Let's just get through breakfast, and I'll fill you in on my plan later."

Gwendolyn looks concernedly at Tiana. "Are you two alright now?" she asks.

"We're fine," Tiana responds, focusing on sliding eggs onto her plate.

As everyone continues to enjoy their breakfast, Gwendolyn introduces each person at the table and emphasizes that they are all like family to her.

Gwendolyn toys with her pearl necklace as she carefully observes the men at the table. After giving them a moment to settle, she stands up from her seat. With a snap of her fingers, a man enters the room wheeling in an old-fashioned chalkboard.

She walks to the board, grabs the chalk, and writes, *Why are we here?*

She then turns to face Michael and asks him directly, "Mr. Patterson, do you understand the purpose of today's meeting?"

Michael confidently responds, "We are here to make each other rich," and waits for her response.

Gwendolyn repeats this question to all the board members, who agree with Michael's answer. However, when she turns to Tiana and asks for her opinion, Tiana hesitates. She swallows her food and quickly sips her orange juice before responding, "Honestly, the solution to your problem is not about money. We all know that will come eventually. We are all here because you need to trust us."

Gwendolyn nods thoughtfully and turns to the chalkboard to place a checkmark next to this point. "Thank you, Tiana. Your critical thinking skills make you such an integral part of this family. You always consider different perspectives and variables before finding a solution."

Gwendolyn snaps her fingers, and one of her employees enters the room with a wooden box, setting it on the table. The initials G.P. are engraved in gold letters on the lid.

"Yesterday, there was an issue at one of my secretly owned companies in New York," Gwendolyn shares.

She then turns to Michael and asks him, "What were the two things I told you not to do on your first day working for me?"

Michael pauses before answering, "Never tell you no, and don't fuck you over."

"Correct," Gwendolyn nods, flipping open the box to reveal a gun. Before anyone can react, she shoots and kills the man sitting in the chair on the side of her. His face lands on his plate of eggs, causing some people at the table to cringe.

"Tiana, thank you for mentioning trust. It's another one of my pet peeves," Gwendolyn comments as she calmly wipes her hands with a napkin.

Gwendolyn reveals that the dead employee had been with her for ten years but, for the past six months, had been involved in insider trading—stealing from her and funneling the money to his friends and family.

With a snap of her fingers, two men are instructs to take the body away and bury it where it will never be found.

After wiping her hands with a napkin, she calmly cleans the gun and places it back in the box. Then, without missing a beat, she returns to her seat and slices into her pancakes, acting as if nothing unusual had just occurred.

Tiana's jaw drops in disbelief as she whispers, "What the fuck?" to Michael.

He slyly pulls out his phone from between his legs and types a message, *I'll make sure you and Catalina are safe. I'm sorry for dragging you into this.*

Tiana reads the text but doesn't respond. Instead, she grasps Catalina's hand under the table, forcing a smile, though her mind is racing, trying to formulate a plan.

After considering all that has happened, Tiana understands the urgency of her next move. She repeats to herself, *I need to get Catalina away from here,* while nibbling on a piece of crispy bacon.

CHAPTER 22

Sasha swivels in her desk chair, staring at the ceiling and dreading the upcoming briefing with her team about the Forbidden Tree case in Phenix City. The recent incident where Dominic punched a car window while Tiana was inside has raised concerns about his potential for violence.

"Strangely, the bodies were only discovered a week after Tiana broke up with him… It can't be him," Sasha sighs to herself. "I've seen how much he loves Tiana and how happy she makes him. I'll have to visit him this week to check on him."

Gathering her things, Sasha heads to the briefing room where her specialized team of agents is waiting. Local authorities often call her team for cases requiring their expertise.

"Pull up the photo," she commands as she enters the room.

The tech expert follows her instructions and displays the photo on the large screen. Sasha looks at the gruesome scene - she's seen worse during her time on the front lines.

Using the remote with a pointer and laser, she focuses on the words "RELATIONSHIP KILLER" carved above the victim's head. "What do you make of our unsub leaving this signature?" she asks her team.

One of the youngest agents raises his hand, mustering up the courage to ask a question that has been on the minds of Sasha's team for years. "Agent Thomas, please forgive me for being so forward. But do you believe the perpetrator is responsible for what happened to your family many years ago?" The room falls silent as everyone waits for Sasha's response.

Sasha takes a moment to look around at her team, seeing the anticipation written on their faces. She turns off the screen before setting the remote down on the table. "I'm not sure if this unsub has any connection to my late husband, but since the murder took place so close to my previous duty station, it has definitely piqued my interest," she says thoughtfully.

"Why are we discussing personal matters? Let's focus on the case so we can better understand our suspect," she redirects the conversation.

"And just so we're all clear, everything discussed in this room stays in this room. Is everyone comfortable with that?" she asks, ensuring her team feels safe and supported.

As she sits back in her seat and takes a sip of water, Sasha prepares herself to delve into her agents' personal lives. She never allows someone onto her team without thoroughly knowing their past and present situations. Before she begins, she makes it clear that no one will be embarrassed or singled out during this discussion, but she knows some secrets may lurk at the table.

"Cheating is breaking a promise to someone special in your life. Instead of leaving that person, cheaters are selfish and enjoy having their cake and eating it too. They would rather harm others with their twisted narcissistic ways than end their relationships honestly.

"The act of infidelity has spawned a dangerous entity known as the Relationship Killer. He sees himself as a vigilante, punishing those who stray from their committed partners."

She grabs the remote and turns on the screen without looking in that direction. "Look at what you all have created," she says, passing the remote to one of her agents. "Zoom in on the photo, please."

"The bruising around the victim's neck implies that he wanted her dead quickly, perhaps as retribution for her infidelity. She was petite and weighed 130 pounds. As we approached the male victim, his throat was sliced, indicating he didn't have time to make an example out of him. Instead, he left his calling card as a warning that he would come for all cheaters."

Taking a sip of water, she stands up and paces around the room. "For those of you who are cheaters in this room, this could be your fate," she warns. "Phenix City is just down the street from Atlanta, so don't think you're safe. As my team members, I'm asking you to stop betraying your relationships. Despite my warning, I know some people will still cheat. But that's fine with me. People like you will turn the Relationship Killer into a notorious killer like Ted Bundy, Jeffrey Dahmer, or Gary Ridgeway."

She asks if they did a background check on the significant others to see how much life insurance they had for their partners.

One of the agents raises their hand. "It has been revealed that the policy was valued at over a million and was established two years ago."

Sasha turns off the photo and pulls up information about the deceased spouses. She orders two teams to visit Phenix City this week to speak with the spouses, and report back before the weekend.

"Before it's too late, get your affairs in order. Cherish your loved ones at home. As I've said before, no one cares until it happens to them," Sasha reminds them as she gathers her notes.

As she leaves, Sasha can't help but smile, knowing that no one on her team is cheating. She doesn't want to project her feelings onto the question about her deceased husband. She never likes discussing that day and always ignores Dominic when he brings it up. The discovery of her best friend sleeping with her husband completely changed her life.

She secretly went through therapy and probably would have grieved longer if she hadn't met Robert. He helped her heal, accepted children who weren't his own, and showed her that there are men who are faithful to their vows.

As she thinks about Robert and his promises, she remembers that she still owes Dominic a favor. She enters her office and contacts one of her private investigators. When he answers, she asks if he has any updates on the license plate and the person of interest at her house.

The PI informs her that the individual in question is Michael Oliver Patterson, a property owner with multiple estates throughout Charlotte, North Carolina. He also mentions that Tiana Henley is his ex-girlfriend and defense attorney.

She asks, "Do you have any other information on Mr. Patterson that could be useful for my investigation?"

"Agent Thomas, this is not within your jurisdiction," the PI responds. "Are you sure you won't do anything that could lead back to me?"

"Michael came to my house uninvited, so I'm just returning the favor," Sasha says determinedly.

"I understand," the PI replies. "I also found out that Michael is working with Gwendolyn Price, a well-known real estate and hotel mogul in North Carolina."

"Yeah, I've heard of her and her connections to social elites syndicates. Her family has been involved in illegal activities for decades without getting caught," Sasha remarks.

"Please meet me tomorrow with all the documents, and I'll start my investigation from there," she instructs.

It dawns on Sasha that Tiana may have been coerced into defending some of Michael's cases. Under normal circumstances, she wouldn't care about Tiana's ex, but they broke Dominic's heart, which means they will have to face the consequences.

She reaches into her desk drawer and pulls out a photo of her, Jennifer, Dominic, and Tyrese at the military ball. In the picture, they look young and deeply in love. It's a memory she keeps hidden from her husband and kids. But as she gazes at it now, she knows it's time to let it go and move on from the past. She walks over to the shredder and feeds the photo into the slit, watching it disappear.

It's family night again at home, and she can't help but feel the weight of bringing work home with her. She takes a moment to close her eyes and focus on her breathing, chanting that work should not control her life and that family truly matters.

With a deep inhale and exhale, she opens her eyes and prepares to leave for the evening. She knows that one day, she will retire from the agency and leave behind the daily grind of being Agent Thomas.

When that day comes, she plans to relocate to a private island far away from the constant news and social media barrage. But until then, she will continue to be Agent Thomas at work and Mom/Wife at home for her beloved family.

CHAPTER 23

For the past week, Tiana has been working closely with Gwendolyn's defense team on strategies to dismiss a money laundering case involving one of her hotel managers.

As she sifts through paperwork, her mind wanders, and she reflects on why Gwendolyn is drawn to Michael's properties instead of her wealthier business connections. She takes screenshots of a company called Fadu LLC, which appears multiple times in various businesses.

Tiana has performed her role so well that Gwendolyn trusts her enough to give her freedom around the house. She even has the opportunity to go shopping with Catalina at times, but the only rule she must follow is to return to Gwendolyn's home every night.

After completing her final notes for the case, Tiana stands up and informs the team that she believes she has all the necessary information. They gather their papers, thank her for her help, and prepare to leave for the evening.

Watching them from the library window as they drive away, Tiana can't help but envy their freedom to go home after a hard day's work.

Dominic's kisses and tender embraces are what Tiana misses most about Columbus. She silently prays that she can finish her business and escape from Michael and Gwendolyn.

Tiana slips off her stilettos and rubs her aching feet, longing for a soak in a luxurious bubble bath. Just as she starts to fantasize about it, Gwendolyn appears in the doorway and suggests that Tiana take some time to rejuvenate herself.

"If you agree, then you won't mind if Catalina and I go out for some pleasure," Tiana challenges Gwendolyn.

Gwendolyn says there is a certain beauty in experiencing and witnessing pleasure. "If you ever need cream between the Oreos, don't hesitate to invite me along," Gwendolyn says playfully while flashing a flirtatious smile.

"During my pole dancing days, I would give lap dances to and even have my pussy eaten by a woman or two. But as I grew older and became the person I am today. I only take requests from the man you took me away from," Tiana reminds Gwendolyn.

Undeterred, Gwendolyn snaps her fingers and summons a man to take Tiana and Catalina to a place called Down and Dirty. Despite the shocking name, Tiana is grateful for the opportunity to escape the house and ignores any previous offers of threesomes from Gwendolyn.

In an attempt to manipulate Tiana, Gwendolyn sweetly insists that other options are available for them all to explore together.

Despite inwardly dismissing Gwendolyn's words as empty promises, Tiana masks her true feelings with a fake smile and displays false gratitude towards Gwendolyn's gestures.

"I'll head upstairs to get Catalina, and then we can hit the road. And before I leave, I have to say, I think I've done a great job on this case. Would it be possible for Catalina to go home while I stick around and help out as much as needed?" Tiana asks respectfully.

"You have truly exceeded my expectations and outshined my entire team. Your abilities are unparalleled." Gwendolyn expresses her thoughts, "I don't see any issue with Catalina leaving."

Tiana nods gracefully in response, sliding past Gwendolyn, who stands in the doorway, unwilling to move and purposely brushing against Tiana's butt.

Tiana desperately wants to slap the piss out of Gwendolyn. Instead, she bites her tongue and continues upstairs to get Catalina.

"Come on, hurry up!" Tiana shouts as she bursts into the bedroom.

"I'm not even dressed yet," Catalina responds nonchalantly, still eating and watching *Boy Meets World*.

"That shit will still be on later. Let's go before Gwendolyn changes her mind," Tiana urges, pulling Catalina up by the arm.

The two women walk downstairs and are greeted by a chauffeur who opens the car door. They thank him and settle into the car for their trip to the spa.

As they ride to the spa, Tiana uses this opportunity to vent about the job and Gwendolyn's behavior towards her.

"Catalina, can you believe Gwendolyn asked for the Mercedes Experience?" Tiana tells her friend, shaking her head in disbelief.

"No way!" Catalina exclaims.

"I'm dead serious. She said she wanted to taste my pussy," Tiana replies with a mix of shock and disgust.

Catalina bursts out laughing and continues until Tiana reveals that Gwendolyn also wanted her as part of the deal.

"You've got to be kidding me. I think it's time for me to go home; I'm not about to lick any Botox pussy," Catalina jokes.

"You're crazy. And speaking of going home, your ass is leaving soon because I can't risk you getting killed by Gwendolyn," Tiana says with a hint of concern.

"I've been taking sick leave from work already and still have bills to pay. Gwendolyn might not murder me, but my bills definitely will," Catalina jokes.

The driver pulls into the spa parking lot, and Tiana and Catalina continue to chat and laugh. As they enter the spa, they are greeted by a friendly staff of women welcoming them to Down and Dirty.

The staff explains the mud bath process and directs them to a changing room, where Tiana and Catalina quickly change into towels, disposable slides, and rush back to the staff. They are then led into a room with an open pit that resembles an empty kiddie pool filled with dark brown mud.

"What the hell is that?" Catalina asks the staff.

The staff explains that it's a mixture of mineral water and therapeutic mud, known for its various health benefits, such as improving skin conditions, reducing inflammation, and providing deep hydration.

"Ha, wouldn't it be great if this mud bath also gave us an orgasm?" Catalina jokes as they drop their towels and enter the mud.

The staff informs them that they have thirty minutes until their facial appointment, followed by a mineral bath in the hot springs and a massage.

Tiana raises her hand and asks for some wine before she's ready to unwind fully. As the staff leaves, Tiana starts making plans for when Catalina returns to Columbus and updates Sasha.

Catalina asks if she'll be okay while she's gone.

"I'm untouchable within her organization, as long as I keep up my good work," Tiana explains.

The staff brings over a tray of glasses and a bottle of Pinot Noir, which Tiana graciously pours for herself and Catalina. They clink their glasses and toast themselves before sinking deeper into the mud until it reaches their necks.

"I might put my head under the mud," Catalina jokes.

"You know what? You only live once," Tiana responds with a smile. "After I finish this glass, I'll join you."

"What are we going to do with Michael? Do you want me to inform Dominic that you're safe?" Catalina asks.

Tiana falls silent, sipping her wine before responding. "Forget about Michael. I'll deal with his ass. And as for Dominic, I think he needs some time to process everything that's happened. We can let Sasha tell him."

"Yeah, that's probably best, considering he might try to kill you like he did his wife," Catalina reminds Tiana.

"I don't need your reminders. It's time for you to go back to Columbus because you keep insisting my man is a murderer," Tiana retorts.

"Well, someone is killing people down there. I saw on Facebook this morning that a couple was found murdered at the wedding venue in Phenix City. That's close to us," Catalina informs Tiana.

"It could be anything," Tiana dismisses with a shrug before finishing her wine. "Let's sink our heads in this mud. Are you ready?"

"I'm going down," Catalina sings playfully as she sinks into the mud.

Tiana laughs at her eccentric friend and makes a mental note to read about the murders when she has time.

CHAPTER 24

With a sinister grin, Dominic lounges in his seat, relishing the sight of Truth and Lacey tied to the X frames. He has been subjecting them to various forms of torture for the last four hours, deriving satisfaction from their agony.

His current method involves drenching them in sticky maple syrup and watching as fire ants crawl up their bodies, causing excruciating pain with each bite. In his eyes, this is the just punishment for their betrayal of their vows, and he remains unmoving, savoring every moment of their torment.

Ants crawl up Lacey's legs and scurry between her thighs, finding a sticky haven that will soon become their feast. She screams as they swarm over her clitoris.

He is intrigued by this scene, so he grabs another jar of ants and syrup and sneaks over to Truth. He crouches down, spreads open his ass cheeks and pours syrup between them. He then sprinkles an entire jar of ants over his exposed anus, watching with satisfaction as they invade like soldiers on D-Day.

Stepping back to his seat, Dominic enjoys that their screams will go unheard in this abandoned basement. He has all night to do whatever he wants with these unfaithful muthafuckers.

Truth and Lacey are married to each other but they refuse to get a divorce. They preach about separation publicly but have been invading other people's homes and hearts for three years now.

Innocent people suffer because of their lies - they promise their current lovers they will leave their spouses and remarry but never follow through. Tonight, Dominic will ensure they fulfill their vows until death does them part.

"Why do you two insist on toying with people's emotions? You seek out individuals to fuck, but as soon as they start developing feelings or questioning your fidelity, your go-to response is always, 'I told you I was married when we started this.' It's all just a game for both of you. You continue living with the people you are cheating with but refuse to fully commit to them, afraid that it might hurt you financially in a future divorce. But tonight, there's no need for either of you to sign any papers," he says.

He reaches into his toolbox and pulls out a pair of heavy-duty industrial scissors. He moves towards Lacey, gripping her jaw tightly and locking eyes with her. With a chilling smile, he takes her hand and spreads her pinky finger away from her palm, placing it between the blades of the scissors.

"No, please don't do this. I won't tell anyone I saw your face. Just let us go," Lacey pleads.

"Do you think I care if you've seen my face?" he scoffs. "You'll both be dead before the sun rises. Now, why did you refuse to get a divorce from Truth?" he calmly asks.

She stutters, struggling to find the right words as her lips and thoughts tremble. Suddenly, Dominic grabs onto the handle and ruthlessly slices off her pinky finger, causing it to drop to the floor.

"You're too slow, bitch," he taunts.

He moves the scissors to her other fingers and slices through them one by one, leaving only her thumb untouched. Lacey's screams and pleas fill the air as tears stream down her face.

"Release her!" Truth screams. "Take me instead."

Dominic glares at Truth. "You were supposed to be the man in this marriage, leading by example and taking charge. But you're nothing but a pathetic excuse for a husband."

Grabbing Lacey's hand, he unties her wrist and shoves her thumb into her mouth. "Suck on that like you suck on those dicks."

Lacey spits out her thumb. "Fuck you!" she yells.

"Fucking is what got you in this situation," Dominic retorts.

"Untie me, and let's see how tough you are then!" Truth shouts.

Dominic nods, amused by Truth's boldness despite ants crawling out of his ass. "Do you enjoy having things shoved up there? Don't worry, I have something special for you. Those blue pills I made you take earlier are starting to work their magic."

As if on cue, Truth's penis grows and hardens to its maximum size.

Dominic leaps into the air with excitement before landing on the ground. "It's time to test out my latest invention," he says to Truth slyly.

Dominic retrieves a catheter with a bag of hot sauce and water from his kill box. He mentions that he usually uses lubricant, but since Truth likes fucking bitches raw, this shouldn't be a problem.

He holds Truth's penis tightly and carefully inserts the catheter, causing Truth to scream in agony. Despite not being a doctor and having doubts about the effectiveness, Dominic finds it exhilarating to watch.

Before taping the bag to Truth's leg, he checks to see if the hot sauce flows appropriately. Satisfied with his work, he instructs Truth to stay still while he goes back to retrieve some pliers from his kill box.

He returns to Lacey's breasts, which are round and firm. Their shape is accentuate by the tight grip of the pliers attached to her nipples, which stretch and turn red from the pressure. He looks up at her face, watching as her expression twists in pain.

He squeezes her titties, clamps the pliers tighter on her nipples, and slowly pulls the pliers. Watching her nipples stretch from the areole, he smiles, stares into her eyes, and yanks her nipples off.

Lacey's screams echo through the warehouse, and he bounces up and down with excitement. "Yes!" he exclaims. "This is exactly what I'm talking about."

He delights in the art he has created, finally having time to fully dedicate himself to it.

"Truth, is the hot sauce flowing through your urethra?" he asks.

Truth grits his teeth in agony and shouts, "You're a psychotic son of a bitch!"

"I'm not psychotic," Dominic replies calmly. "You and others like you, drove me to this."

He dashes across the warehouse and grabs a rolling table, positioning it in front of Truth. With a push of a pedal, the table rises to waist height.

He searches his arsenal for the perfect weapon, laughing maniacally as he approaches Truth with a meat tenderizer.

He grabs hold of Truth's dick, placing it on the table. "I'm going to beat all that hardness out of your dick," he declares.

With each strike, the catheter attached to the bag comes loose, causing Truth even more pain. "Damn it, there goes my hot sauce," Dominic chuckles before resuming his brutal assault on Truth's dick.

After a few minutes, he stops and takes a seat. "I'm tired of looking at your sorry ass," he sneers. "You should have signed those papers when you had the chance. Now it's time for the grand finale."

He walks over to the wall and presses a button, triggering a pulley chain system that hoists the wooden X-frames into the air. The frames tilt and lower Lacey and Truth a couple of feet above the floor. He hits another button, causing the floor to split open and reveal two bathtubs filled with hydrofluoric acid.

"This evening will be the honeymoon you've always dreamed of. I promise that you and your Lacey will spend eternity together in the next life." Dominic pushes another button on the wall, causing the ropes to unravel, releasing Truth and Lacey into their own individual tubs, both shrieking in terror.

He moves swiftly across the room, grabbing a broom and begins to sweep all the evidence up. As he does, the once beautiful and perfect bodies of Truth and Lacey begin to melt away, their skin bubbling and peeling off to reveal the raw, exposed flesh and bones underneath.

He silently hopes to witness the effects of the acid on someone's eyes, but he realizes it may not come to pass. With a touch of disappointment, he finishes cleaning up the evidence and gets ready to give his statement before leaving.

Yesterday, he blackmailed a graffiti artist to create a massive mural of the words "RELATIONSHIP KILLER" in vibrant colors and bold letters on the clean white wall. The paint is still fresh, and some parts are dripping. The graffiti style has a hint of retro flair, almost like something you would see on an 80's hip-hop album cover. Overall, the mural is impossible to ignore and immediately captures attention.

When the morning comes, he will ensure that the bodies are found, and their discovery will spread fear throughout the town that The Relationship Killer is on the hunt and no one is safe anymore.

CHAPTER 25

Dominic stands outside Marco's Pizza, observing the constant flow of patrons entering and exiting Snap Fitness. He has been staking out this location for a week now, keeping a close eye on a certain fitness trainer who seems to be sleeping with every woman he trains or meets at the gym.

Dressed in head-to-toe black workout gear, complete with a weighted vest and breathing mask, Dominic is determined to kill this new-age Instagram influencer who preys on vulnerable women in the name of fitness.

Dominic is anxious to kill Marcus Devon Graham, who borrowed that name from the 90's movie *Boomerang* starring Eddie Murphy.

For the first time in his life, he feels that the world deserves to witness someone's death live on video. Every time he takes a life, he is reminded of Tiana. He eagerly awaits the day when he can strip her skin off her body.

His watch beeps, signaling that it's time to act on his demonic urges. He puts Tiana on the back burner for now and walks across the street. He scans his phone against the entry pad and enters Snap Fitness.

Dominic knows that Marcus is the only one who works out during this time. As he moves towards the weight room, the doors automatically lock behind him. He steps inside and sees Marcus dominating the leg press machine with six hundred pounds of weights, trying to impress his followers. Like most fitness influencers, he's shirtless and grunts louder with each rep of the weight he presses into the air.

Dominic ignores Marcus' outburst and starts his biceps workout at the dumbbell rack. He looks at himself in the mirror and imagines how satisfying it would be to punch Marcus in the face with a dumbbell.

"That's how you do it!" Marcus yells into his phone, trying to motivate his followers to get active.

After a few minutes, Marcus calms down and answers an incoming call through his Bluetooth earbuds. He rolls out of the leg press machine and stops his live stream. Based on Marcus' demeanor, Dominic can tell that a woman is on the other end of the line.

Dominic continues to listen as Marcus discuss meeting the woman tonight.

"Melissa, I've told you multiple times that I'm going to fuck other bitches. You knew what this was when we started talking. Why do you keep pressuring me about being your man?" Marcus says into the phone.

Marcus continues talking as he walks over to the flat bench and adds more weights. "Melissa, I'm not leaving Monica for you. It's less stressful at home. Monica never questions who I'm with or who I'm fucking. After my last set, I'll come over and give you some dick," he exclaims before ending the call.

Marcus complains to Dominic, "Women can be so damn annoying sometimes. They should stick to sucking dick and leave it at that."

Dominic chuckles in agreement, replying, "You've got to be careful who you give good dick to. A good fuck can turn even the most amazing woman into a nagging nightmare."

"Tell me about it," Marcus agrees. "Can you spot me so I can impress my viewers by lifting this weight?"

"No problem," Dominic says, setting down his dumbbells and moving behind the bench to spot Marcus. With three forty-fives on each side of the bar, Marcus didn't need help on the first set.

Dominic's phone chimes, so he pauses to check his messages before spotting Marcus again. The screen reads: *It's on. Are you ready?*

A smile spreads across Dominic's face as he knows he has the green light to do something wild with this fitness freak.

His heart begins to race, and adrenaline surges through his veins.

Just then, Marcus' phone rings, and he answers it. "Hey, baby. I'll be home later tonight. Right now, I'm working out with a client… I'm not lying," Marcus insists. "The client is here, helping me with a set."

Marcus explains to Monica on the phone that he's not cheating and, for once, his workout partner is a man instead of a woman.

"I refuse to let you meet my client. You're always accusing me of things, and it's affecting my motivation."

Dominic gives Marcus a reassuring tap on the shoulder. "I got your back, man. FaceTime her," he says.

"Give me a second. Add two more plates," Marcus replies.

While Dominic adds the extra weight, Marcus retrieves his phone and sets it up on the tripod before sitting back on the bench.

As Marcus talks to Monica on the phone with his back turned, Dominic discreetly secures the plates with bar clips. He then steps out from behind the bar and waves at the camera, greeting and confirming that Marcus is telling the truth for once.

Monica dares Marcus to lift an even heavier weight for her. Dominic knows that Monica is stroking Marcus' ego, and he's ready to take advantage of his prideful nature. Marcus confidently boasts that he can easily lift the weight, comparing it to how effortlessly he throws Monica's legs up.

Marcus allows Monica to watch him bench-press the weight. He reclines on the bench and inquires about Dominic's unusual mask, comparing it to the villain Bane from *Batman*. With a sly grin, Dominic explains that it's just a cool accessory, but secretly, it helps with his asthma.

Marcus shifts his wrists, adjusts his hips, and shouts in determination. He knows this set is for Monica. With a burst of energy, he pumps out the first three reps effortlessly and continues strong through the seventh rep.

"You got this, Marcus! You can do thirteen more," Dominic encourages, dangling a tempting bet of a thousand dollars before him. With determination, Marcus continues lifting the weights, and his arms tremble at sixteen reps. But Dominic assists him, pushing him to reach his goal.

Marcus fights the pain and pushes out the nineteen reps before struggling with the last one. With Dominic's help, he completes the final rep, and they both cheer in triumph as the bar is lowered back to his chest for the last rep.

Marcus' face contorts in intense exertion as he struggles to complete the final repetition of his weightlifting set. His mouth hangs open in a plea for assistance. Dominic reaches out his arm, almost reaching the bar before ultimately letting go and causing the weight to slam down onto Marcus' chest.

Dominic emerges from behind the bar, leaving Marcus to struggle under the bar's weight on his chest. He grabs a thirty-pound kettlebell and heads towards the camera, waving at Monica, who eagerly waves back, knowing what will happen next.

Dominic hoists the kettlebell above Marcus' head, his anger boiling over. "Cheaters deserve death!" he screams before bringing the weight crashing down onto Marcus' face. The impact of the kettlebell breaks his nose, and blood spurts out in all directions.

With a fierce expression, Dominic slams the kettlebell down and then up in a continuous motion. Monica's voice echoes through the phone as she screams delightfully, "I love it! Keep going! Fuck him up!"

Marcus sobs and pleads for help, but his efforts are pointless as Dominic mercilessly continues to pummel his face until there is no more fight left in him.

Dominic lets out a hearty laugh and pounds his chest in excitement. This is the kind of thrill he lives for. He looks at the screen of Marcus' phone and sees Monica's arousal, sparked by her dead husband.

"Can you come over and wear the mask while we fuck?" Monica asks, adding a new addiction to Dominic's twisted pleasures.

"That's a new request. Let me clean up here, and I'll come to your place. I could definitely use some good pussy."

CHAPTER 26

He chuckles upon seeing his reflection in the rearview mirror, imagining how the gym-goers and managers will discover Marcus' mutilated body in the morning. Dominic left him butchered on a weight bench, his abdomen sliced open, and his intestines ripped out. In a twisted display of satisfaction, he used Marcus' blood to scribble "RELATIONSHIP KILLER" on the gym mirror.

The thought of fucking Monica, who had watched him commit this gruesome act for the first time, sends a surge of excitement through his dick.

He knows he has a purpose, and it involves satisfying his sick desires with her. He loves that she wants to be fucked with a mask on, indulging in their twisted game where he is the Joker and she is his Harley Quinn.

He drives to Lake Oliver Estates, a peaceful suburban neighborhood where he once murdered a corrupt doctor who fucked female patients for illegal medication. The doctor's wife was thrilled by his death and used her inheritance money to relocate to Paris with her children.

As he navigates through the subdivision, he spots Monica's house and pulls into her driveway. He steps out of the car and walks up to her front door, which she opens for him without hesitation or question.

She stands in the doorway, her silhouette framed by the dim light of the room behind her. The mulberry drape fringe chemise hugs her curves, cascading down her body in a soft, sheer fabric. The G-string lingerie set complements and accentuates her figure, while the matching six-inch heels elongates her legs.

Monica catches a glimpse of the delight in Dominic's eyes, and her anticipation grows for what she knows is to come with the monster standing before her.

Dominic steps into the room, and Monica quickly shuts the door behind him. This was not his usual approach, but he hadn't fucked anyone since Tiana left him. If anything goes wrong, he won't hesitate to choke the life out of Monica.

"Would you like something to drink, or do you want to get straight to it?" Monica asks, breaking the silence.

He shakes his head, declining the offer, and stands before her in all black. She steps closer and takes in his scent, enjoying the mix of blood and her husband's lingering aroma on Dominic's body.

She takes his hand and guides it to her mouth, sensually sucking on two of his fingers as she moans in pleasure. "I love what you did tonight," she whispers before pressing her lips to the mouthpiece of the mask.

She pulls him upstairs to their bedroom. She wants to be used and dominated in the very bed she once shared with her husband.

Looking at his watch, Dominic realizes he only has an hour left before sunrise and needs to return home. He follows her up the stairs and watches her as she seductively crawls onto the bed.

She runs her fingers over her wet pussy and motions for him to join her. He moves closer to her as she pulls down his compression pants and exposes his dick. She takes his hand and guides it to the back of her head, then opens her mouth and slowly takes in his rod.

He grabs onto her hair tightly and thrusts into her mouth. He lets out a muffled moan through his mask, rejoicing in the pleasure. "This is heaven!" he exclaims.

She continues to pleasure him, her mouth drooling and her hands gripping his balls while she bobs back and forth. Pausing momentarily, she looks up at his face and praises his features. She compliments his distinct and sexy eyes, saying they would be unforgettable if someone survived to tell the tale.

He moans softly in response, explaining that he wants his victims to see beauty before their inevitable death. Pushing her head back down, he watches as she spits on his dick before taking it into her mouth and using her hands to stroke his shaft.

Dominic's eyes were drawn to the large mirror that covered one wall of her bedroom. He couldn't resist pulling his dick out of her mouth to take a closer look. With his pants removed, he stands naked, leaving only his vest and mask on.

He gently lifts her from the bed, and she wraps her legs around his waist as he carries her to the mirror. She licks her hand and uses the moisture to lubricate herself.

"Fuck me, Killer," she gasps and moans eagerly.

Without hesitation, he enters her without any protection, eager to experience the raw sensation that had been lacking in her sexual encounters due to her husband's infidelity.

As soon as he is inside of her, she excitedly mounts him, clenching his dick deeper into her. He unleashes all his pent-up anger with every thrust, making her feel his wrath.

His hands grip her ass tightly as they charge towards a full-length mirror at full speed. With one final powerful slam, her back collides with the glass and shatters it.

Blood runs down Monica's back, and she screams, "Yes, Killer! I love it! Fuck this pussy!"

He tightens his grip on her throat and pounds into her relentlessly. His intense gaze pierces her soul as he watches her scream in ecstasy.

"Harder, Killer!" she yells. Wrapping her thighs tighter around his waist, she clenches her walls around his dick.

As he ravages through her pussy, he lets out a muffled noise through his mask and tightens his grip around her throat, showing no mercy.

The heat from his breath intensifies as he ravages through her pussy. A dark thought crosses his mind - *What would happen if I squeezed the life out of her and then fucked a corpse? How long would the warmth of her pussy last?* His inner demon contemplates this as he continues to dominate Monica's body.

His arousal intensifies as he imagines having sex with a dead woman, causing his dick to become even more rigid. He takes out his dark thoughts on her lifeless body, thinking of his first wife, Tiana, and all the unfaithful people he knows.

With each thrust of his hips, he tightens his grip around her neck and screams at the top of his lungs. Suddenly, everything goes black, and all that matters to him is busting his nut.

His hands, once clenched tightly around her neck, release her as he lifts her and flings her onto the bed, her limbs splayed out in every direction. The sheets crumple and ruffle beneath her as she lands.

In this moment, he savors the feeling as he strokes himself and watches Monica struggle to catch her breath. He cracks his neck and strides over to her, ordering her to kneel. Spreading her butt cheeks wide, he enters her forcefully.

At first, she is tight, but with each thrust, she relaxes, and he can slide deeper inside of her. She finds her voice again and screams as she climaxes from the thought of being dominated in the bedroom.

She gushes over the sheets, trembling as she looks back at Dominic, who continues to penetrate her with force.

He leans in closer, his voice a low growl as he pushes deeper. Through the mask, he yells, "I'm cumming, bitch!"

She responds eagerly, "Yes, cum for me, Killer! Make me shit your babies out of my asshole!"

He relaxes and shudders slightly as his body releases the last drops of cum. Gathering his clothes, he slides off the bed and starts getting dressed. Monica sleeps soundly on her stomach, snoring loudly, as he quietly slips back into his shoes and leaves the bedroom.

Making his way to the front door, he pauses to admire how glad he is that he came over tonight. Entering Marcus' birthday into the keypad, he exits the house and waits for the doors to lock behind him. Dominic always plans ahead; initially, he had planned to kill Marcus at home, but the gym was a more exciting location.

Sitting in the driver's seat of his car, he starts the engine and heads towards home, riding in silence with the windows down. The wind carries the scents of Marcus and Monica into his face, and he knows she will never confess to what happened tonight. She may be attractive, but she's not his type of woman.

He plans to stay in touch with her since she's a plastic surgeon, knowing that someday he might want her to perform a sex change on a man for entertainment purposes—utilizing various gadgets and toys before ultimately killing him.

Pulling up to his gate, he enters his code and drives to his garage, only to find a car blocking him. With a heavy heart, he thinks to himself, *I despise having to end this woman's life.*

CHAPTER 27

Sasha made an impromptu visit to Dominic's house, determined to find out if he is involved in the recent killings in the area. Several clues point to him as a potential suspect. She knew he wouldn't have changed the locks, and she still has a spare key. She had forgotten about it until she encounters it while sorting through her old military boxes.

With the key in hand, she let herself in and began searching the house. As she walks down the hallway, looking at pictures and books, she sees a copy of James Patterson's *Kiss the Girls* and remembers how Jennifer used to compare her to the main character, Alex Cross.

Unable to resist her curiosity, she pulls open the bookcase door and takes out the book. As she did so, the bookcase shifts to the left, exposing a hidden room behind it that leads down to a basement.

She hesitates for a moment before descending the stairs. She is surprised to find no spiderwebs blocking her path - indicating that this space is frequently used.

Ignoring any sense of danger, she continues snooping around, and as soon as she steps off the last step, motion sensors activate and illuminate the entire room.

The room is the size of two standard bedrooms and is filled with an array of spy gadgets and deadly weapons. Pictures of

Jennifer and Tiana hang on the wall, used as targets for an improvised ax-throwing range.

Sasha's curiosity leads her to a cabinet stocked with laptops, passports, and disposable phones. She couldn't help but wonder what Dominic is planning as she continues to explore the room.

On another wall are blueprints of various workplaces, homes, and federal buildings in Columbus and Phenix City. But what truly unsettles Sasha is the shelf lined with various latex face masks.

Suddenly, she hears creaking from the door leading to the basement, followed by footsteps descending the stairs. Sasha's hand moves quickly and determinedly toward her gun, grasping it tightly as her gaze sweeps across the room, searching for any signs of movement while she holds her weapon at the ready.

Dominic's voice calls out, breaking the silence in the room. "Sasha, why are you here without my permission?" she hears him ask.

"I'm armed, Dominic. Please don't make me use my gun to protect myself," Sasha responds.

"What the fuck? You broke into my house," he accuses her.

"I've had a key for years, and I came because I'm worried about the murders happening in Columbus," she explains.

"Well, I'm not armed, so you can come out, and we can talk this out like real friends," he suggests.

Peeking out from behind the counter, Sasha sees Dominic standing there dressed in all black. "Where have you been?" she asks.

"I have been doing God's work. People at church call it ministry," he proclaims proudly.

Stepping away from the cabinet with her pistol still aimed at his head, Sasha demands, "What is all of this stuff, Dominic?"

"Sasha, you were never supposed to see this side of me. But trust me when I say you won't shoot me. Put the gun down. And if I wanted to kill you, you would already be dead," he reassures her calmly. "We need to talk. You need to be honest."

She responds, "Okay, what's on your mind?"

"Put the gun down," he instructs her as he removes his weighted vest and drops it to the ground.

Sasha responds, "I'm not putting anything down because I don't trust you."

"Fine. Answer me this. How did you feel the night Jennifer and Tyrese were killed?" he asks.

"It was like losing both the love of my life and my best friend all at once. It still hurts to think about," she confesses.

"Stop with the lies and tell me the truth," he demands. "You were angry because they were having an affair. They've been cheating behind our backs for years, and deep down, you're upset that you didn't get to kill them yourself."

"Dominic, that case was never solved. The killer was never caught, but I've moved on from it. I've built a better life for myself and my family."

"Well, I don't have a family anymore. Tyrese made sure of that. Your husband and my wife were shitbags. Tell me the truth, Sasha. How did you really feel?"

She hangs her head and lets out a heavy sigh. "You know what, Dominic? I found out they were having an affair a year before they were murdered. But I didn't want to put my kids through a nasty divorce either. So, yes, I wanted them dead. Are you satisfied now?" she asks.

"Ecstatic. And that's why I took care of our problem. I remember pulling the trigger and watching the bullet fly through the air, splattering their brains all over the sheets."

"Now you're confessing, Dominic? And let me guess - you're responsible for these new murders, too. You're not a hero, just pure evil," she accuses.

"Every city needs someone like the Relationship Killer to stop cheaters," he retorts.

"But you're killing innocent people," she argues.

"Innocent? All cheaters deserved to die. But don't worry, after I kill Tiana, I'll turn myself in or maybe even have a shootout with the police. Either way, I won't ever have to suffer heartbreak again," he admits.

"Dominic, I have to take you into custody. You can't continue hurting innocent people."

"Do whatever you need to do, but my mission is not complete until I've killed Tiana, her ex-boyfriend, and the loudmouth guy from the hotel," he responds. "Lights off," he commands, triggering the room's blackout feature. Sasha braces herself in a corner, ready to defend herself against Dominic's attack.

"Dominic, turn the lights back on. I swear, if you come any closer, I'll shoot you," she threatens.

He hears her voice but stays silent, watching her through his night vision goggles. He pulls out a knife and moves closer to her.

Suddenly, he grabs a book and tosses it to one side of her. She instinctively turns and fires her gun in that direction.

In that moment of distraction, Dominic rushes forward, knocking the gun out of her hand and holding his knife to her throat.

"Sasha, calm down. I won't kill you, but I can't go to jail either," he says. "Lights on," he commands.

He leans in close to her face and whispers, "Go home, Sasha. Your family needs you. I'll turn myself in after I finish this mission."

He releases her from his grasp and returns her gun to her before guiding her out of the basement. She's frustrated that he caught her off guard but grateful that he spares her life.

"Dominic, I'll go home tonight, but I can't guarantee what I'll do tomorrow," she tells him.

"Fair enough," he responds.

They exit the basement and ascend the stairs to find a young teenage girl sitting in the living room, enjoying a bowl of ice cream while watching an episode of *House of Dragon*.

Sasha turns to Dominic with a look of disbelief. "Are you kidnapping children now too? You're a monster, and someone needs to stop you," she accuses.

He shakes his head and takes a deep breath. "I'm not in the business of harming children, but there's something even worse than me after that girl. Let's hope he hasn't made it to town yet," he warns.

CHAPTER 28

Tiana embraces Catalina tightly, whispering in her ear to find Sasha and update her on everything. Catalina nods and promises to take care of it. She gazes into Tiana's eyes and squeezes her hands even tighter.

"Lord, please protect my friend while I am away. Keep her safe, and may these wicked people face your wrath," Catalina prays before kissing Tiana on the cheek.

"I don't think you're supposed to ask God to strike people down," Tiana comments.

"Why not? He has the power to do whatever He wants," Catalina responds confidently.

"Well, I guess this is goodbye for now. I'll call you once I get to Atlanta," Catalina says.

They exchange one last hug before Tiana watches her friend enter the car Gwendolyn provided for her journey home. Tiana stands patiently on the porch as Catalina starts the car and drives away from the estate. With Catalina gone, Tiana can finally move forward with the second phase of her plan.

Tiana's eyes take in the vibrant pinks, oranges, and purples painting the sky as the sun sets, creating a breathtaking view. She ponders about Dominic and wonders if he longs for her and if there's a possibility of reigniting their romance.

Tiana knows the only way to get back to Dominic is by working on these cases and hoping that Sasha's connections can help her escape this predicament.

"It seems that Gwendolyn has freed Catalina. That's a good thing," Michael comments as he approaches Tiana from behind.

Tiana's nostrils flare with anger, her eyes narrow into slits as she shoots daggers at Michael's smirking face. "I hate your bitch ass for pulling me into your wicked schemes.

"You think you have everything under control, but you don't," she continues, anger evident in her voice. "Gwendolyn calls all the shots, and once she's done with you, do you believe she'll let you walk away unscathed? I lost a great man because of you, and I'll never forgive you for that shit."

"Are you still crying over that country-ass hillbilly?" Michael retorts. "All the things I did for you, and this is how you talk to me? Spitting in my face like I didn't elevate your life from the stripper pole to the courtroom."

Tiana scoffs at him. "And that's the only thing you did; I'm sure your investment was repaid three times over since I worked my ass off for your business while you cheated on me repeatedly. Now, if you'll excuse me, I have better things to do," she says, bumping her shoulder against his and walking inside.

She ignores Gwendolyn's security team and heads straight for the pavilion, imagining the pool as the crystal blue waters of Jamaica, where she first met Dominic. Her heart beats faster when she thinks of him, especially now that Catalina can no longer distract her with friendly conversations.

She notices Michael leaving the house and heading towards her. She stands up from her chair and meets him halfway. "I'm not finished talking to you, Tiana," he says firmly. "You are my woman, and we need to work on our relationship."

"Okay, please tell me how we can fix it," she responds.

Michael was taken aback by her response and found himself at a loss for words. She notices he is standing too close to the pool and gives him a quick shove in the chest. He stumbles and falls into the water, sinking below the surface.

He resurfaces and punches the water in frustration. "Fuck you, Tiana. Your ass is going to pay for this shit," he warns.

Ignoring Michael's threats, Tiana storms back to the house in search of Gwendolyn. She demands that something be done about Michael's behavior. Gwendolyn was summoned from the library by Tiana's loud cries.

"Why are you screaming like a madwoman in my home, Ms. Henley?" Gwendolyn asks calmly. "How can I assist you?"

"I'm sick and tired of dealing with Michael's bullshit," Tiana fumes. "He needs to stop harassing me and let me enjoy my day peacefully."

With a snap of her fingers, Gwendolyn comes to a realization. "You're right," she says firmly. "Bring Michael in immediately,' she commands.

The two men hurry out of the room, their expressions resolute as they bring in a dripping and furious Michael. Gwendolyn snaps her fingers and calls for the chef to bring her a knife from the nearby kitchen. The chef returns with a sleek, lengthy blade and presents it to Gwendolyn.

Gwendolyn approaches Michael and uses her fingers to push his head back. She reaches into his mouth and extracts his tongue forcefully.

"It's a real shame. You could be putting that tongue to good use, licking my sweet pussy. Instead, you're messing around with my business." She holds the blade up to his tongue, ready to cut it off.

Tiana's scream of shock echoes as she desperately begs Gwendolyn not to go through with it.

"Tiana, my dear. Only address me if you actually want a solution to the issue. It appears that you're still dealing with Michael's nonsense. I suggest you both figure things out before I have to intervene and take drastic measures," Gwendolyn says sternly, her tone leaving no room for argument.

"Next week, we have a hearing to try and drop the charges against my hotel manager. Tiana, it would be helpful if you concentrated on that. And Michael, get out of my damn house and do something productive before I change my mind about letting you live," Gwendolyn sternly advises.

Tiana can hardly process everything unfolding on the same day Catalina departs from the property. She knows she needs to handle these cases and figure out how to escape earlier than planned.

"I'll be prepared for the hearing, and I'm sorry for causing a scene in the house," Tiana states.

She walks away from Gwendolyn and Michael, heads upstairs, and seeks solace between her legs. She plops onto the bed and slips out of her shorts and panties, letting them fall to her ankles.

She reaches for her trusty multi-speed wand massager, turning it on and marveling at its familiar hum. Closing her eyes, she thinks of Dominic, letting her mind wander to their last encounter.

She hovers the toy over her most sensitive spot, letting out a moan as she gently moves it along her outer lips and over her clit. The fantasy of Dominic's skilled tongue on all of her erogenous zones plays in her mind.

She lifts the wand away, spreading open her lips and running it up and down with increasing speed for a more intense pleasure. "I need this," she moans. "It feels so good."

Kicking off her panties and shorts, she stands against the wall, lifting her leg and placing her hand behind it for support. With the wand inside her wet slit, she tightens her grip and feels the sensation of her juices.

She stretches out her leg, bouncing back onto the bed before lying down on her back. The buzzing of the toy and her moans create a melody as she pushes it in deeper.

"Oh fuck," she gasps.

Turning over onto all fours, she slips the wand between her thighs and stimulates herself from behind. The vibrations tickle her sensitive clit as she lowers herself onto the wand and allows it to penetrate her. She cries out in ecstasy, panting heavily, before tossing the toy aside.

Rolling over onto her back, she slides her fingers inside, making circular motions around her swollen clit. Spreading her legs wider, she smacks her wet folds and delves deeper inside.

She needs to cum and can't wait to release the pent-up frustrations from the day. Raising her hips off the bed and into the air, she revels in the pleasure of filling herself with her fingers. Her body trembles, and she moans and breathes even heavier.

She plunges her fingers in deeper, reaching for the center of her arousal. Her pace quickens as she stimulates herself. Her breasts are quivering as she approaches an orgasm.

With a scream, she releases all her pent-up frustration towards Michael and her longing for Dominic. As the pleasurable sensations subside, she gently withdraws her fingers and fans her legs back and forth, allowing her mind and body to relax.

The nut has temporarily relieved her from the impending war and thoughts of revenge against Michael. She is grateful for it; thankful to be able to find solace in something so simple as cumming on her sheets.

CHAPTER 29

Dominic shakes his head at the teenager sitting on his couch and lets out a heavy sigh, still reeling from his earlier confrontation with Sasha. "Graciana Lanaé Valdez. Why are you in my damn house?" he yells at her.

Graciana takes off her headphones and turns to face Dominic and Sasha. "Uncle Dominic, there's no need for all that yelling," she responds calmly. "I am sitting right here."

She sets her bowl on the table and rushes to hug Dominic, confusing Sasha. Graciana pulls away from the embrace and says, "Uncle Dominic, we're out of Cookies and Cream ice cream. We have to go to the store as soon as you finish talking with your lady friend."

Dominic clears his throat. "Sorry for being rude. Sasha, this is my niece, Graciana. Graciana, this is my battle buddy from my Army days. She's practically family, and we're just friends," he clarifies.

"Too bad. She's beautiful. You could use a good woman in your life," Graciana adds.

"Sasha, we can finish our conversation later. I have to deal with my niece right now," Dominic says.

"I don't see why she has to leave, Uncle Dominic. You two already interrupted my TV show with a gunshot and arguing about whether or not you're a killer," Graciana remarks.

"I broke into your house earlier and have been here since Mrs. Sasha arrived. I was hiding when you came in, attempting to imitate John Wick. But now that I've overheard everything tonight, I can't wait to tell Mami all about it," Graciana says excitedly.

"Let's keep this between us. Asperilla doesn't need to know about my life," says Dominic.

He guides Sasha to a recliner on the other side of the room and stands before Graciana. "Now, how did you manage to make it here from Tampa?" he asks.

"It's a long story but an exciting one. Yesterday, Mami caught me hanging out with my boyfriend."

"Boyfriend? You're too young for that shit!" he exclaims.

"Relax, Uncle Dominic. We weren't having sex. We planned to teach a bully at school a lesson by stealing his car. But, as I was pulling out of the parking lot, Mami caught me, took away the keys, and beat up my boyfriend without even asking. The school called my boyfriend's Mom, and she got into a fight with Mami. The police showed up, and Mami got arrested," she explains.

"Okay, okay, enough details. Just tell me how you got here already," interrupts Dominic.

"After Mom got arrested, Papi went to bail her out. I saw an opportunity and stole the car again to drive from Tampa to Columbus. I made sure to pay for everything in cash along the way. They treat me like a kid, and you never come down to visit," she says with a hint of longing in her voice.

Sasha smiles at Graciana's obvious admiration for Dominic. "Wow, Dominic. I wish I could have met her sooner. She's a sweetheart."

"She's a fucking Annabelle doll with wicked intentions like her crazy-ass Mama. Don't fall asleep while she's in the house. She will steal everything you have and slit your throat," Dominic says.

Dominic checks his watch and calculates the hours from Tampa, Malakai bailing out Asperilla, and the amount of time Graciana claims to have been in the house.

"Shit! That means your Dad is probably already snooping around or would have rung the doorbell by now. I need to finish my mission before he shows up and ruins my whole plan. Graciana, I'm calling your mom. It's time for you to go home," Dominic says, trying to get her out of the house before her father arrives.

However, Graciana pleads to stay as she finds it fascinating that her Uncle is a ruthless killer. She puts on her headphones and continues watching TV while eating ice cream.

Meanwhile, Sasha and Dominic leave the living room to go outside. Dominic turns around before they open the front door and walks back to Graciana. "Grace, what did you do with the car?"

"I parked it at the police station in a handicap spot. They can figure out how it got there. Then I took an Uber to the convenience store on the main road and walked back here," Graciana responds nonchalantly.

Dominic shakes his head and gestures for Sasha to follow him outside. They step onto the porch, and Sasha immediately starts bombarding him with questions.

Throwing her hands in the air, she exclaims, "Wow, what the hell was that?" after hearing about Dominic's family and his estranged niece.

"Now you understand why I don't talk about my family," he replies.

Sasha reminds him of his past actions by saying, "Says the person who carves RELATIONSHIP KILLER above his victims."

"I promise not to kill anyone new, but I will seek revenge on those mentioned downstairs," Dominic reassures her. "I have a soft spot for my niece, and her birth helped me control my inner darkness."

He then explains how Graciana's mother had once hired him to kill her boyfriend, who was known as The Poetic Whore. But before he could carry out the hit, the target revealed himself as Dominic's long-lost half-brother, sharing the same father but a different mother.

"The reason I despise my brother is that I've never met anyone more dangerous than myself. I still harbor anger over being caught off guard and almost killed by him years ago."

Sasha sighs heavily, exhausted from the events of the morning. She's not sure if she can handle hearing another story.

"Dominic," she says with concern, "you need to be careful. I shouldn't even be helping you; this could ruin my career and damage my family's reputation."

She promises to do her best to throw off anyone searching for him on behalf of the agency or local authorities.

"Sasha, I don't want to burden you. I promise to turn myself in after completing my final mission. You can return to Atlanta and not get involved in my affairs."

She slaps Dominic on the chest and reminds him, "Never leave a fallen comrade."

He winces at the impact. "Your hand is hard as a rock," he says, rubbing his chest.

"You can go back in there and comfort your niece. I'll take your advice and head home."

After saying goodbye to Dominic, Sasha walks to her car, her mind spinning with everything he's revealed to her. She knows she can't just let Dominic take his own life or spend the rest of his days behind bars.

As she starts her car and her Bluetooth connects, she receives a call from Catalina. Her friend's voice is frantic and rushed as she asks where Sasha has been.

"Calm down, Catalina," Sasha responds. "Where are you and what's going on?"

"It's a long story, but I'm almost in Atlanta," Catalina explains.

"Well, come home. I'm currently in Columbus, and we can talk over breakfast," Sasha suggests.

"Okay. I'll call you when I'm home," Catalina says before ending the call.

CHAPTER 30

Sasha waits outside Bodega1205, a restaurant that prides itself on its Italian American cuisine and appreciation for family, culture, and community. Catalina had recommended this place for their delicious food, privacy, and her connection to the owner.

Sasha checks her watch and realizes Catalina is running late for their breakfast plans. She texts Catalina to find out her estimated arrival time, and Catalina responds that she will be there in less than two minutes after finding a parking spot.

Sasha locks her car and walks towards the restaurant to wait for Catalina. After leaving Dominic earlier that morning, she feels like there is nothing Catalina can say that could be more shocking than what she just went through with Dominic's family.

When she sees Catalina approaching with a purposeful stride, Sasha stands up and greets her friend. Without hesitation, Catalina grabs Sasha's hand and leads her inside the restaurant. "Come on, girl, I have so much to tell you. But first, let's order some food because I'm starving," she says.

They find a table in the corner, and a waitress comes to give them menus. But Catalina confidently places their order before they can even look at them. "No need for menus," she declares. "Just bring us two glasses of orange juice, water with lemon, and two Breakfast of Champion specials."

She then specifies her meal preferences: "I'd like my steak cooked well-done, scrambled eggs with cheese, and please add a pancake as well."

Sasha glances at the waitress and then back at Catalina. "Damn, you didn't even ask me if I like steak."

Catalina shrugs. "Girl, fuck all that. Everyone likes meat. Whatever you don't eat, I'll take home with me."

The waitress walks away, and Sasha can't believe how much food Catalina has ordered. Catalina takes a deep breath and tells Sasha that her mission is to see her first. She shifts in her seat and explains, "After our drinking marathon at the restaurant, I put my suitcases in the truck when a black van suddenly pulled up. Two men jumped out, grabbed me, and forced me inside. They placed a bag over my head, tied me up, and threatened to kill me if I tried anything funny."

"Oh, my God! Catalina, I'm so glad you're okay. How did you escape?" Sasha asks.

"This is the part you're not ready for," Catalina adds. "I was taken to a huge house where I was treated decently well," she continues. "Good food, nice place to sleep, and shopping sprees."

"Catalina, you didn't bring me all the way here for another one of your wild sexcapades, right?" Sasha says with an exasperated tone. "I could have been in Atlanta by now."

The conversation is interrupted when the waitress brings their drinks. Catalina quickly grabs her glass of orange juice and takes a large gulp, setting it back on the table. She then gets to the point, sensing that Sasha isn't interested in hearing the whole story.

"I was kidnapped by a woman named Gwendolyn Price, who is working with Tiana's ex-boyfriend. Tiana is being held against her will at this place. They forced her to leave Dominic because they threatened to kill me if she didn't come to North Carolina."

Sasha buries her head in her hands and shakes her head in frustration. She mutters under her breath that she can't handle all this shit today.

Catalina pleads for Sasha's help to save Tiana before it's too late, suggesting they call the FBI and storm into Gwendolyn's home.

"Catalina, it doesn't work like the TV series you watch. There's a protocol I have to follow. I assure you that I will do everything possible to get Tiana to safety," Sasha informs her.

As their food arrives, Sasha feels relieved to have something else to focus on. They bless their food before eating silently until Catalina suddenly drops her fork onto her plate.

"I have a possible solution since you're in charge of enforcing the law. What if we approach Dominic and accuse him of killing his wife? Maybe he'll feel the need to kill again to save Tiana."

Sasha chokes on her steak as Catalina shares her thoughts. She gulps down some orange juice to clear her throat before responding.

"You're being foolish, Catalina," Sasha says. "Dominic is a good guy, and he loves Tiana. You saw them at the restaurant."

"I'm just going off of what I read in articles online and what Tiana told me about how Dominic begged her to stay," Catalina counters. "I may not be a killer, but I wouldn't hesitate to take revenge on someone who left me crawling on my knees for their ex."

"Your theory is entertaining," Sasha chuckles, trying to change the subject as she digs into her food.

"You never told me how you got out," Sasha asks.

"Oh, I guess I didn't," Catalina responds in between bites of eggs. "It wasn't an escape. Tiana agreed to keep working for them so that I could leave. Once she gained Gwendolyn's trust, I made a quick exit. They never wanted me anyway. I was just a pawn in their money laundering scheme.

"Shit! I almost forgot. Gwendolyn killed a man right in front of us without batting an eye. That was the only time I was terrified," Catalina confesses.

"Why didn't you mention that before?" Sasha asks incredulously. "That should have been the first thing you told me.

"Catalina, thanks for meeting me here, but I need to make some calls," Sasha says, feeling overwhelmed by everything she's learned about the situation.

Catalina interrupts Sasha, "Wait a minute. You're not expecting me to pay for this, are you? I'm already traumatized, and now you want me to spend my hard-earned money?"

Sasha responds with a smirk, "There's nothing wrong with your ass. And no, I won't make you pay." She pulls a one-hundred-dollar bill from her purse and sets it on the table.

"Thanks," Catalina says, relieved.

"Don't tell anyone else about this," Sasha warns Catalina as she leaves the restaurant. "I'll call you tomorrow with updates. We can't afford to make any mistakes."

"I understand," Catalina nods and runs her fingers across her lips to show she'll keep quiet. Sasha hurries out of the restaurant, leaving Catalina behind to finish her breakfast.

She continues eating and thinks she doesn't need anyone to remind her to stay silent. She reaches over and takes some of Sasha's food, scraping it onto her plate.

"This is my lucky morning," she tells herself. "I get all this delicious food for free and can sleep in my own bed tonight."

Out of nowhere, a stranger appears before her, causing her to startle in her seat. He stands tall before her, with a dark complexion and a perfectly trimmed beard. His gray sweatpants hug his well-defined legs, showing off his muscular build. She can't help but notice the dick print in his joggers, and she feels a warm flush spread across her cheeks.

The man's scent is a mix of musk and cologne, intermingled with the smells of the bustling restaurant. A hint of sweat and spice is in the air, making Catalina's heart skip.

He chuckles and says, "A beautiful woman like you deserves all the good things in life. And judging by all this food, you'll definitely need a comfortable bed to rest in afterwards."

She blushes at his compliment and takes in his handsome features and confident smile.

"I don't want to intrude, but I had to come over and introduce myself. I'm only in town for some business, and you happen to be on my agenda."

"Mira papacito, no vas a robarme de mis pantaletas," Catalina says in Spanish.

"Uno no puede robar lo que no se pone," the gentleman responds in Spanish.

Catalina laughs and agrees with the gentleman. She signals for the waitress to bring a to-go box and turns her attention back to the man, inviting him to sit.

He sits down, smiles, and gazes into her eyes. "Catalina, right? I have something I need from you."

She jumps at the sound of her name, especially since she never told him what it was. And she can't help but wonder how a black man with a slightly country accent is speaking fluent Spanish.

Sasha, why did you leave so suddenly earlier? she wonders calmly, feigning nonchalance as she tries to decipher the situation.

His voice is smooth and alluring, captivating Catalina's attention. She feels a pull towards him and the task he mentions, intrigued and wanting more information. His words have a playful tone, with a touch of mystery that piques her curiosity.

He can sense her nervousness and teases her, asking if it's her pulsating clit that caused her to jump from her seat. "Let me introduce myself. My name is Malakai, and my purpose is to protect our loved ones."

CHAPTER 31

Dominic takes a swig from his Corona bottle, enjoying the sound of the fizz and Graciana's shovel hitting the ground in a steady rhythm under the blazing sun. It feels like fitting retribution for her breaking into his home. He notices something unusual as he watches her closely - she isn't sweating or complaining about the intense heat. Intrigued, he steps out from under a shade to observe her work with a smile on her face. Seeing her so content while performing such a grim task is unsettling.

Graciana never questioned why a tombstone was marked with Jennifer's name in his backyard. Dominic knows that Jennifer's body is actually buried in their family plot back in her hometown, but seeing her name always brings him a twisted sense of pleasure.

Today, he can relax as Graciana digs the perfect spot for Tiana's final resting place. He hasn't decided yet if he'll bury her alive or without a head, but just thinking about displaying her head above his fireplace makes him grin wickedly.

Returning to reality, he checks on his niece and offers her a break from digging for an hour straight. He even offers her some water to drink.

Graciana keeps digging, focusing solely on the task at hand. She declines his offer without even glancing in his direction. "I learned survival skills from my mother in elementary school," she yells. "Digging a grave is nothing compared to the time she tied me up and threw me in a pool. I almost drowned. But I managed to escape and was rewarded with ice cream during a trip to the city."

"Your parents are some of the sickest people on Earth. You deserve so much better." He tells her to finish digging and come inside when she's done.

"Uncle Dominic!" Graciana calls out, stopping him from leaving.

He turns around and asks, "What do you need?"

"I want to go on a recon mission with you, if that's okay."

"Absolutely not. Put down the shovel and go home," he says, pulling out his phone to Facetime Asperilla.

He holds up the phone to his face and wastes no time expressing his frustrations. "Come get your daughter. Out of all the places she could have run away to, she chose my house. And now she wants to go on a reconnaissance mission with me? And what is this about you almost drowning her as a lesson?" he scolds Asperilla.

"Dominic, I'm getting a pedicure right now. But keep that badass carbona over there with you. It's peaceful here without her and Malakai for once. And as for almost drowning Graciana, she was laughing the whole time. Give her the phone," Asperilla replies.

Dominic approaches Graciana with the phone, interrupting her from her digging. "Grace, your mom's on the line," he taunts. "Looks like you're in trouble now."

Graciana looks up and greets her mother over the phone. She explains that Uncle Dominic has her helping him dig a grave, eagerly awaiting the day they will put a body in it. Asperilla laughs at their exchange and comments on how much trouble Graciana can be. She jokingly adds that Malakai can bring her back home.

"When did you get out of jail?" Dominic asks.

"Jail? I haven't been there for a year. Is that what she told you?" Asperilla scoffs at the idea as she reveals that Graciana ran away because she mutilated the pit bull next door. Apparently, the dog was barking too loud while Graciana was trying to sleep, so she took matters into her own hands by slicing off its ears and feet, removing its insides, and leaving each body part in a circle drawn with chalk on the main street.

Dominic glances at Graciana and accuses Asperilla of creating this demon seed along with Malakai. He is ready to end the conversation before Asperilla shares one final piece of information.

"Graciana will be okay. She's not an issue at the moment. You should probably check on your brother. He tends to try and rescue hoes in distress, so he'll likely find Tiana before you do," she points out.

"How the hell y'all know her name already? I can't even have a pleasurable moment without everyone else getting involved. Fuck y'all!" he shouts into the phone before angrily hanging up.

"Graciana, I have a job to do. There's enough food in the house for you to stay put. Don't even think about touching my wine bar or you will regret it."

She shrugs with a smile. "No problem. I don't drink alcohol anyway. You always have to be alert."

He rushes into the house, changes his clothes, and gathers all the necessary items before heading out on his latest mission. He opens his trunk and is shocked to find Graciana already inside. "How did you get in there so quickly?" he demands.

"I stole your spare key the other night," she confesses.

"Get the hell out of there," he growls as he grabs her arm and pulls her out of the trunk.

He drags her around the car and tosses her into the passenger seat before slamming the door shut. "I need to keep a closer eye on you."

He drives away from home and into the city, stopping at a costume shop to find an outfit for Graciana. As they enter the store, he greets the owner with a handshake - someone he served with in his platoon. Inside, he searches for the perfect disguise and grins when he finds a Girl Scout uniform complete with boxes of cookies. He hands it to Graciana. "Try this on in there," he orders.

Gracy shrugs her shoulder, steps into the dressing room, and emerges wearing her chosen outfit. "Ta-da!" she announces with pride, twirling around to show off her new look.

Dominic can't help but laugh at Graciana's vibrant personality and can easily understand why he and her parents have a soft spot for her theatrical ways.

"Alright, grab the rest of your clothes. Let's head out to see an old friend who just can't seem to stop cheating," he says.

They leave the store, get into the car, and drive towards the Midland Fall apartment complex. Graciana connects her Bluetooth speaker during the ride, and *U My Everything* by Sexyy Redd plays.

Dominic turns down the volume before Graciana sings to the annoying chorus. "Not today, Satan. Let's ride and talk for a bit."

"Sure, what do you want to talk about?" Graciana asks.

"Life is full of choices, especially at your age. You have the potential to become anything you want. But be careful not to succumb to the darkness that surrounds us. During my time in the military, I was forced to kill foreign enemies and even children who were suicide bombers. It was something I never enjoyed, but it was necessary for survival.

"Then, one day, my whole world shattered when I discovered my wife was cheating with my best friend. It changed me forever and awakened a dark side that I now embrace. Sometimes, I question if I'm sick in the head or if this world deserves the justice I deliver.

"But true love can save you from this fate. I'm telling you this because I don't want you to end up like me or your fucked up parents. Despite their love for you and desire for your well-being, their past mistakes will always come back to haunt them. As for me, I know karma will catch up to me one day, but I hope to be gone before it does."

He pauses, lost in thought, before continuing, "You still have a chance to break this cycle. Don't let the sins of others dictate your future."

Graciana takes in everything he says without showing any signs of fear or remorse. She places her hand on Dominic's. "It's okay, Uncle Dominic. Death is coming to us all one day.

"I have a story too. My father told me how he was ready to leave his dangerous life behind when trouble found him. He recounted the tale of a powerful man who kidnapped me as an infant and manipulated my parents into trying to kill each other in exchange for my safety. Thankfully, my father never gave up because if it were up to Mami, none of us would have survived.

"Uncle Dominic, please forgive my language. I understand our family is fucked up, but we're still family. If my father is in town, he's not trying to interfere with your plans; he's trying to save you like he saved me," she explains.

"Only time will tell, Graciana. Only time will tell," he responds.

He continues to drive until he reaches the gates of the apartment complex. He enters the code and watches as the gate opens for him. Looking over at Graciana, he says that he never imagined going on a reconnaissance mission with his niece. She meets his gaze and responds that she will be honored to accompany him as his plus one for the day.

He informs her that he will retrieve his belongings from the trunk while she heads up to apartment 365 to try and sell some Girl Scout cookies to a woman named Yasmina Jones.

She confesses that she has never sold cookies before in her life. He reassures her, telling her to use her charm and pretend she is the movie's lead actress. He advises her to walk normally, not too quickly, and wait at least five minutes before knocking on the door. She snaps her fingers excitedly and says that she can definitely do that.

As they drive through the complex, he pulls into a parking spot and turns off the car engine. Graciana grabs the cookie boxes and heads toward apartment 365.

Quietly, he walks behind the complex disguised as a maintenance worker, having meticulously planned this reconnaissance mission for months. He never actually executed it until now.

The maintenance room was located behind the complex. He rushes inside, grabs a ladder, and continues on his way. After setting up the ladder, he climbs to the top and glances around to ensure no one is watching before jumping up and reaching for the balcony railing on the second floor. His body sways back and forth as he pulls himself up.

Once outside Yasmina's patio window, he can hear the sound of masculine moans coming from inside the house. As he suspected, her cheating ass is in there giving someone her best demon throat.

The window provides a small, secretive view of the scene inside. He sees Yasmina on her knees, her mouth moving back and forth on his throbbing dick as he thrusts his hips forward. Her hands are gripping his shaft, her fingers moving up and down in a quick motion.

Dominic hears a knock on the front door and watches as the man begs Yasmina not to stop because he is close to cumming. Yasmina tells him she will finish when she returns but must answer the door first. She quickly throws on a long T-shirt and slides on her slippers before leaving the room.

Dominic watches from outside on the patio as Yasmina checks who is at the door. Another round of knocks sound against the door, causing the man to throw a pillow at the wall in frustration, get up from the bed, and stand in the doorway.

Taking this opportunity, Dominic retrieves his gun and quietly opens the door. He enters with his gun pointed at the back of the man's head and smiles, knowing he could quickly end his life with just one pull of the trigger.

"Psst," he hisses, catching the man off guard and causing him to flinch.

"Take a seat if you want to keep your ass intact," Dominic says calmly, pointing towards the bed.

CHAPTER 32

As the sun set over the riverfront, Malakai was hypnotized by Catalina's words as she explains the details of her kidnapping. Her lips move like a symphony, each word a note dancing across her tongue and releasing into the warm air. Her Puerto Rican accent adds an exotic touch to the already magnetic scene.

But despite being enraptured by her, Malakai knows he will forever be a whore in rehab, and if it wasn't for Asperilla, he would fuck the shit out of Catalina.

He redirects his focus and starts to think about Dominic. He understands that he must push the thought of pussy deep in the back of his mind and create a strategy for ensuring the safety of everyone.

He turns to Catalina and asks if he can ask her a question.

She couldn't help but think how fine he is and replies, "Sure, go ahead."

He tells her he has all the necessary details but wants to know if Tiana truly loves his brother. He knows he can research people, but understanding their true intentions requires deeper observation, and time is not on their side. As Tiana's best friend, he hopes Catalina can shed some light on the matter.

Catalina shares that Tiana would have never left Dominic willingly, and during their time in North Carolina, her main concern was always his heart.

"Every day, she aches for him and wants to reach out, but Gwendolyn's threat to kill Dominic stops her every time. That's why my first stop was to find Sasha and confide in her, revealing all the details I have shared with you. By the way, I asked Sasha to join us at our gathering," she mentions.

"I was expecting you to contact her," Malakai replies. "It's important for all of us to be on the same page. When do you anticipate her arrival?"

Catalina hesitates before responding, "I don't have a definite time yet."

He nods, his head bobbing up and down in agreement. "It's cool," he says. "By the way, I did some digging into Tiana's ex-boyfriend's business. Turns out Michael has been quite successful in real estate." He leans in closer. "I think I know how to get close enough to Michael.

"I need you to go back to Charlotte for me," he continues. "Things could get dangerous, but I promise to protect your cute ass," he adds with a smirk.

"Aww, you think I'm cute, Papi?" she teases.

"You're all right," he replies, smiling as they watch kids rollerblading and people walking their dogs.

She notices the ring on his finger. "I'm not one to break up a happy home, but your fine ass can definitely have this pussy," she admits boldly.

He bursts into laughter and playfully slaps her thick, tattooed thigh. "Catalina, you should stay as pure as your name suggests," Malakai says.

"I'll slut you out for my pleasure, penetrating this dick in your throat and gut. Have you ever experienced someone reciting poetry while fucking you in the ass? I'm wild and unrelenting in the bedroom, willing to do whatever it takes to please you. Your pussy will never have a moment of rest; I'll even eat you on your period. Giving head until you think you are dead. Pure ecstasy is second nature to me. Blood doesn't bother me; I'll consume it just like a vampire."

Catalina squeezes her legs tightly together, her hands balled into fists at her sides. Her flushed face and wide-eyed expression reveal her disbelief. The sensation between her legs is like someone has placed a heating pad inside her pussy walls, causing them to heat up intensely.

Sasha walks up and introduces herself, saving Catalina from her thoughts about Malakai's capabilities. "It's nice to meet you, Sasha," Malakai says with a smile.

"Thank you for coming," Sasha responds with a flirtatious giggle and wink towards Catalina. "Your brother didn't mention how handsome you were," she says.

"Dominic said you're like a category five hurricane when you visit," Sasha continues as she admires his pearly white teeth. Looking at the riverwalk, she adds, "I can almost see rainbows and unicorns appearing at this beautiful spot. Let me stop flirting. My married ass isn't going to do anything for real," Sasha says.

"Yes, get off my dick," Catalina blurts out.

As they all share a laugh, the awkward joke fades away, and a friendly atmosphere takes over. Malakai reveals to Sasha that he used to love being the calm before the storm, but lately, he's been feeling more like a tornado: fucking shit up and leaving within minutes.

"Speaking of causing trouble, I ran into your lovely daughter the other day," Sasha says, taking a deep breath and shaking her head.

"Graciana takes after her mother, but she has her father's strategic mindset. She's currently in training, and once I retire, she'll be a frightening force to be reckoned with.

"As for Graciana, she's here in town to keep Dominic at bay and away from Tiana. But we can't rely on her presence for long. Our plan needs to be executed swiftly and with precision. I've arranged to meet with Michael once I arrive in Charlotte.

"Sasha, I'll need you and a few of your trusted team members ready to take down Gwendolyn Price at a moment's notice. My sources say her entire empire is built on illegal drugs, and now she's using a secret basement under her hotel to manufacture synthetic opioids. It's quite the operation; guests check in, use their room for illicit activities and then check out with whatever product they can afford.

"Sasha, if you successfully bust this drug operation, your FBI career will skyrocket to the level of Elliot Ness. You'll become a legend in the South. My brother will also be in Charlotte soon. He's after Devontae, Michael's business partner," Malakai confirms.

Sasha's eyes widen in amazement as she asks, "How do you know all of this?"

Malakai replies, "That's always my first move. Find the middleman with the most information and convince them to talk.

"I can handle Michael and getting access to the hotel," Malakai continues, "but Dominic is the wild card. My brother and I aren't exactly on friendly terms right now. It's crucial for Tiana's well-being that you all make him see how much she truly loves him."

Catalina chimed in, "But what if he refuses to listen?"

"Catalina, that's why I'm counting on you. You're the only one who can get close enough to Tiana without raising suspicion. Act like everything is normal and convince her to leave the house."

"There are too many variables and potential dangers involved. Do you honestly think we can make it out of this without anyone getting hurt?" Sasha asks.

"I don't know, but what other choice do we have? We can't guarantee Tiana's safety with three people after her," Malakai replies.

"Three?!" Catalina exclaims, clapping her hands together. "I knew it! I told Tiana that Dominic was a cold-blooded killer. He must be coming for her now."

Malakai warns, "Once he discovers you took Tiana out of the house, he might also come after you."

"What the fuck?" Catalina says.

Malakai suggests meeting in Charlotte the following night to take care of business and ensure the safety of their family. He bids them farewell with a hug and watches as they walk away from the Riverwalk.

He sighs and watches the sunset in solitude. A grin spreads across his face as he remembers the words he told Catalina. He could have easily seduced her with some poetry, but he's relieved that he is not the whore he once was. Though, sometimes, the desire to feel some new pussy resurfaces. However, the fear of Asperilla catching him in the act always ends his wandering thoughts swiftly.

He takes out his phone and commands it to call Jaz. After a brief pause, the phone connects.

"Hey boo," she answers.

"Can you fly to Charlotte tonight?" he requests.

"Sure thing. See you soon," she replies and hangs up.

CHAPTER 33

Dominic hears his niece's voice at the front door and feels a sense of pride seeing her successfully influence Yasmina to buy Girl Scout cookies. He knows it's not the cookie-selling season, but Yasmina is too focused on pleasing her lover to think clearly.

"Put some clothes on, now!" Dominic urges in a harsh whisper. "If my niece walks in here and sees you naked, I'll shoot two rounds through your asshole and wait to see where the bullets come out."

The man scrambles to grab his scattered clothes and hastily dresses himself, trembling with fear. His eyes beg for mercy as he looks up at Dominic. "Please, sir, just let me go. I won't tell anyone about this," he pleads.

"You should be telling your wife why you're cheating and lying about working late," Dominic retorts. "But it's okay. She'll find out soon enough.

"Do you remember that night a few months ago when you and Yasmina were at that Italian restaurant downtown?" Dominic asks with a sinister smile. "I watched as you dragged her out of the bathroom with "STOP CHEATING" written on her forehead. Looks like you didn't learn from that mistake, and now I'll make sure you both pay for it."

"Sir, please don't harm us. I am pleading with you for another chance. I swear I will gather my belongings, be a faithful man, and never cheat again. My name is Andrew Lewis, and I am the owner of a construction company. I can transfer any amount of money to you right now if you just let us go."

"I don't want your damn money. Just call Yasmina and get her funky ass in here so we can get this over with," he demands.

As he calls for Yasmina, his eyes fill with fear and shame as he stares at the ground, where a small puddle of urine forms at his feet.

Dominic looks at the ground and laughs. "You better not shit yourself, or else I'll make you eat it. In fact, I hope you do shit; then I'll make both of you whores eat it."

Dominic hears Yasmina's footsteps approaching the door as she sweetly says, "I'm coming. I had to get rid of the little girl at the door."

Yasmina's gaze widens with terror as she takes in the sight of Dominic standing in the corner, his firearm aimed straight at her. Paralyzed with fear, she drops to her knees and clasps her hands together in a desperate plea. "Please," she cries out, "don't hurt us."

"Today is your lucky day," Dominic says calmly. "Do you want to die slowly and painfully or quickly and painlessly?"

Dominic turns to the couple, waiting for their response, but before they can answer, he hears someone approaching. The door slides open, and Graciana walks in, happily eating a bowl of ice cream.

"What did I miss?" she asks innocently. "This lady didn't close her front door all the way, so I came inside to check out her fridge. Turns out she likes Cookies and Cream ice cream just like me," she announces with a grin.

"Your ass was supposed to go to the car," Dominic scolds. "You're one hardheaded little girl."

Yasmina pleads with Dominic, promising to do anything if he lets them go. Before he can respond, she crawls towards him on her knees. But instead of accepting her offer, Dominic lifts his leg and kicks her in the face. She falls backwards and accidentally bumps into Graciana, causing her ice cream bowl to drop and spill onto the floor.

Dominic watches in shock as Graciana moves with fluid grace and precision. He notices the glint of metal as she reaches inside her hair and pulls out two hatpins. His focus was drawn to the tip of the first blade as it pierces through Yasmina's shoulder, followed by the second hatpin aimed at her eye.

In a moment of desperation, Dominic fires a bullet through the mattress, causing Andrew to jump off the bed and Graciana to stop her attack. She kicks Yasmina in the face while she is still lying on the ground and yanks out the hatpin. "Maldita Perra," she curses in Spanish, "that's for my ice cream!"

"You better watch your mouth," Dominic warns her. "Go get in the car right now."

"But Uncle Dominic," Graciana whines, stomping her feet in frustration. "It wasn't my fault!" She storms out of the room, slamming the front door behind her, and once she's gone, Dominic turns his attention back to Andrew and Yasmina.

Dominic chuckles to himself, trying to shake off the day's events. He knows it can't get any worse. "Let's just get this over with," he says, proposing a twisted game.

"I know all about your successful construction company, and it's refreshing to see a black man doing well in our community."

Dominic looks at Yasmina and continues talking to Andrew. "Of all the women you could have fucked in this city, you had to choose your wife's sister."

Yasmina looks away guiltily. "It wasn't intentional," she mumbles.

"And the most disrespectful part? Your sister is at home taking care of your kids while you're swallowing Andrew's kids," Dominic says, revealing that he knows about the prenuptial agreement and the loophole that would require them to split everything equally in the event of infidelity in the marriage.

His sadistic sense of humor takes over as he announces his game. "Okay, I'm ready for my game now," he says eagerly.

"Andrew, I need you to muster up your strength and fuck Yasmina for 120 seconds in her favorite position. And if you don't cum within that time frame, I'll shoot you in the head and toss her off the balcony with a rope around her neck.

"Yasmina, what is your preferred position for fucking? Choose carefully, as the price of pleasure may be death," he warns with a sinister smirk.

Yasmina rises from the floor, not willing to risk her life on Andrew's stroke game. "Andrew, strip and lay on the bed," she commands.

As Andrew complies, his dick shrivels from the fear of his impending demise. Yasmina asks for a few moments to get him hard before they fuck.

"I understand the pressure you're under. You have one minute," Dominic says with a hint of amusement. "But first, give me your phone so I can capture this for your sister."

With a flick of her wrist, Yasmina tosses her phone to Dominic, lifts her shirt over her head, and crawls onto the bed. She grabs Andrew's shaft firmly in one hand, her long fingers enveloping it tightly. With her mouth open and ready, she eagerly takes him in, sucking tightly around his head.

Saliva drips from her lips onto his dick as she takes it into her mouth. She picks up the pace, straining the muscles in her neck as she sucks with more force. With one hand, she massages his balls while using the other to stroke his shaft. "Get hard, Drew," she urges, determined not to die today.

She licks and sucks on his balls while continuing to thrust her fists up and down his length. "That's it, baby," he moans in pleasure. Feeling him reach full hardness, she releases him and climbs onto the bed. Positioning herself over his dick, she lowers herself onto it and begins to ride with enthusiasm.

Dominic couldn't help but notice the tattoo of a Capricorn on Yasmina's left ass cheek as she bounces and jiggles on Andrew's dick. Mentally, he gives them an extra thirty seconds for his visual enjoyment.

"Nut for me, muthafucker. You better throw this dick into this pussy!" Yasmina shouts while riding him with ferocity and slamming her ass onto his thighs.

As she continues to ride him harder and harder, the bed creaks against the wall, and she catches Dominic's eye, flashing him a mischievous smile before winking at him. Her movements become even more chaotic as she rises onto her toes and presses her hands down on Andrew's chest. "Cum for me," she pleads as he wraps his arms around her, thrusting upwards to match her rhythm.

Andrew's moans grew louder and more urgent. He begs her not to stop, saying, "I'm almost there. Fuck me, baby."

Dominic can see that squatting is Yasmina's favorite workout at the gym, judging by the way her butt slams onto Andrew and bounces back up into the air. She raises her hand and smacks Andrew in the face. "Come in this pussy, bitch!" she screams.

She puffs heavily, her arms wrapped around Andrew's neck as she rides him intensely. His dick slips out, but she expertly sucks it back in without using her hands.

Yasmina moans, and Andrew yells, "I'm cumming!"

Dominic watches as Yasmina continues to ride on top of Andrew, her pussy overflowing with his release. She refuses to stop, but Dominic interrupts by yelling, "Time's up!"

Yasmine dismounts and rolls off the bed, squatting in the middle of the room. She squeezes her vaginal walls, releasing Andrew's seed onto the hardwood floor.

After catching her breath, she stands up. Dominic congratulates her on a job well done, admiring her skills. He then instructs her to sit on the bed and wait for his next command.

Dominic walks across the room with a cold, calculated stride. He lifts his gun, holding it by the handle, and without hesitation, brings it down with a forceful swing onto Andrew's head. His eyes narrow in satisfaction as Andrew slumps unconscious.

"My reputation is built on keeping my promises, Yasmina. I won't take your life, but I will make sure this video gets to your sister. She deserves the money from Andrew. You'll have to find a way to regain your sister's trust and forgiveness. But don't think about cheating again. If I hear about it, my sister-in-law will come after you. She has a fondness for women who can't control their desire, and she'll use her connections to lock you away and let men pay pennies to abuse your body."

She nods in affirmation, and he tells her he loves how she winked at him while riding Andrew. He says that moment saved their lives.

"When people ask what happened here today, you can tell them that The Relationship Killer spared both of you because of your dick-riding skills. Keep my identity hidden, and the two of you will have a chance at a long life together. Andrew may not have much money to spoil you, but at least you'll be alive and breathing."

He picks up the bowl of ice cream and the spoon, then exits the bedroom and the apartment. He finds Graciana waiting by the car, complaining about the heat and ready to leave.

With a flick of his wrist, he tosses the bowl towards her, and she catches it effortlessly. "You have much to learn," he remarks, remembering the DNA and fingerprints she left all over the apartment.

"Did you take care of them?" she asks with curiosity.

"I didn't miss a damn thing," he replies coolly. "Everyone is still alive."

He gestures for her to get into the car and reminds her not to touch his radio before getting in himself.

CHAPTER 34

Sasha and Catalina sit patiently in the car outside Dominic's house, hoping to convince him not to go after Tiana. They are uncertain if he will listen, but they promised Malakai they would make one last effort.

Sasha notices Catalina staring out the window and asks why she seems lost in thought. Catalina responds that she can't believe the man Tiana has fallen for is also responsible for the recent string of murders in the city.

Sasha sighs, admitting that the truth is hard to accept. She has known Dominic for the longest time, and his dark side scares her.

Catalina asks, "What are your emotions towards your late husband? Did you feel remorse or guilt or relieved he was gone? If I had discovered that my husband was unfaithful and had died alongside my best friend, there's no way I could have brought myself to attend their funeral."

"I don't want to be reminded of that day. Thankfully, my children were too young to comprehend what was happening entirely. Let's not dwell on that moment, if you don't mind. Instead, let's focus on convincing Dominic to change his mind before we have to attend another funeral."

Catalina glances at her watch, anxiously awaiting his arrival. She expresses her concerns about potentially saying the wrong thing and getting a negative reaction from Dominic.

"I'll do all the talking," Sasha assures her. "And with Graciana by his side, he won't hurt us. Have you figured out where to bring Tiana once you successfully get her out of the house?"

"Definitely," Catalina replies confidently. "We're going to Men in Motion, a male revue. It's secure and unexpected, plus we can enjoy some eye candy while we're there. You should join us."

Sasha declines, explaining that she needs to be ready to take down Gwendolyn and her associates when Malakai gives the signal.

Catalina's tongue slips out from between her lips as she brings up the all-male revue, twirling it playfully in the air with a mischievous sparkle in her eyes. "More eye candy for us," she says with a smirk.

Sasha gestures towards the car approaching the gate. "Here comes the moment of truth," she says, her voice filled with anticipation.

As the garage door opens, Dominic navigates the car into the space. Sasha and Catalina sit calmly as if it were a routine occurrence.

Dominic takes his time turning off the car, believing that he has made his intentions clear to Sasha. He instructs Graciana to gather her belongings and assures her he will join her after talking with Sasha. He waits for Graciana to enter the house, steps out of the car, goes over, and knocks on Sasha's window.

Sasha lowers the car window at Dominic's request, and he informs them of his plans to leave soon. He advises Sasha to stay out of his business as he doesn't need her help and warns her that she could end up on his list.

Catalina interrupts with a question, "What happened to the charming Dominic I first met?"

"Hello, Catalina. Let's not waste any time. Contact Tiana and inform her that I plan to dismember fifty body parts from her and bury them in fifty different cities across all fifty states."

Catalina's eyes widen in horror at this side of Dominic, which she had never seen before. She slinks back into her seat, hoping and praying that Sasha will quickly drive away.

Sasha tells Dominic that they have gone through battles together, and she tries to clarify that this was all a miscommunication and that Tiana never intended to abandon or harm him.

Dominic chuckles and leans closer to the car. "That bitch had me begging and crawling on my knees for our love. Her fuck-nigga came to your home to ruin our family gathering. They humiliated me, leaving my heart shattered and unable to beat. They trampled on it, picked up the pieces, and tossed them in the trash. Love is no longer welcome here. I will not forgive her, and I respectfully request that you all leave my property and stay out of my life."

He turns and heads towards the garage, causing Sasha to cry out for him to stop. She begs him to send Graciana with them so they can drop her off with her father. Dominic runs back to the car with a furious expression on his face. His muscles tense as he raises his leg and forcefully kicks the side of the car, denting the door. The car visibly shakes from the impact, causing Catalina and Sasha to jump in surprise.

"You are talking to Malakai? You're turning your back on me, too? After everything we've been through? I'm the Godfather of your children, and this is how you repay me?" his voice rises to a scream. "Get off my property and make sure to inform my brother, if he wants his daughter, he can come get her himself once we reach Charlotte."

With a swift movement, he draws his gun from its holster and fires it into the air. The sound of the gunshot echoes through the air, but it's unclear where the bullet will land. "Get off my property!" he yells, aiming the gun at them. "If you don't leave now, the next two bullets will be your heads."

Sasha interjects, trying to protect her friend and plead her case. "I'm saving you from going to jail," she says passionately.

"1, 2, 3," he counts slowly and deliberately, while his finger twitching slightly on the trigger.

Sasha's hands tightened around the steering wheel, her manicured nails digging into the leather as she diligently held on. She leans forward in her seat, her jaw set in anger as she blares her horn. "I can't stand your arrogant ass!" she shouts before starting up her car and driving off, following the instructions given to her.

"Now, what do we do? That muthafucker is crazy, and we left a little girl alone with him," Catalina voices her concern.

Sasha reassures her, "I'm sure she'll be alright. She's just as unstable as her Uncle. I heard her Mother is even worse. We might be safer going to Charlotte without her. Who knows? She would probably try to strangle me with a shoestring while I'm driving.

"One thing is certain. I will no longer take Malakai or his brother's advice for my life. I am bringing my team in and taking matters into my own hands to put an end to Dominic, also known as The Relationship Killer. He has threatened my life twice now, and it will be the last time."

As Sasha vents her frustrations, tears well up in her eyes. Seeing Sasha upset, Catalina can feel the anger and frustration bubbling inside her.

"Sasha, I understand how you feel, but perhaps it would be best to stick to Malakai's plan rather than trying to call your own shots," Catalina advises. "Right now, we need to focus on Tiana. This feud between you and Dominic can wait."

"As a highly skilled FBI agent, I take my duties seriously. My emotions are running high, but that doesn't change the fact that everyone must abide by the law - including Dominic and his brother, Malakai. I have a duty to protect people, and unfortunately, innocent lives have been lost under my watch," Sasha states passionately.

"Strictly speaking, those people were not blameless. At least, not in Dominic's eyes. I am no expert on criminal behavior. Nevertheless, what if the situation was reversed and you caught your husband fucking your best friend? Can you honestly say you would not have reacted similarly?

"Let's take a moment to calm down and carefully consider our options before making a decision that could put our lives at risk," Catalina suggests.

"We can drive to Charlotte, make it through the weekend, and hope for a safe return to our normal lives."

Sasha is aware that Catalina has spoken some harsh truths. She acknowledges that she could have killed Tyrese and Jennifer, possibly worse than Dominic. But in her line of work, the devil is Dominic, and he must be stopped.

As they drive up the interstate, Sasha looks at Catalina and admits, "You're right about everything. I need to calm down, breathe, and clear my mind."

She turns up the music to drown out the negative thoughts. Deep down, she wishes things could return to how they used to be with Dominic. But after this weekend, there is no going back. If Dominic puts her in a problematic situation, Malakai will find out what it's like to lose a brother.

CHAPTER 35

Mayor Oliver Rittenhouse was wrapping up his speech when he notices a woman entering the room from the back. He couldn't see her face clearly, but he could admire her figure - her dress perfectly cinched at the waist to accentuate her curves and create an hourglass shape. The sleeveless design shows off her toned arms, while the strappy back adds a playful touch to the elegant ballgown. The flowy fabric sways with her movements as she walks, emphasizing her rounded hips. And with each step, the thigh-high slit reveals a glimpse of her thick yellow tone leg.

As he finishes his speech and greets his supporters, Mayor Rittenhouse makes a mental note to meet the woman in the wine-colored dress at the back of the room.

Arrogant and entitled, he believes his position gives him unlimited access to pussy. He sees no issue with fucking any woman who attends his charity events.

With his charming smile still on display, he goes over to chat with his wife and her best friend, Josephine - whom he has been fucking since his time as a city councilman.

He informs his wife that he has some business to attend to with potential investors before returning home later that night. While technically not a lie, he plans on sealing the deal with Gwendolyn Price first before indulging in some "yellow pound cake" - a term he uses for attractive women of color like the one he had spotted earlier.

As he says goodbye to his wife, he wraps his arms around her and slips his fingers behind her, gently caressing Josephine's hand. Josephine smiles and tells him she loves him in a whisper.

Walking away, he heads towards his campaign manager, who is conversing deeply with the gorgeous woman who captivated him during his speech. With extended arms, the woman greets him with enthusiasm. "Hello, Mayor Rittenhouse. I am a fan and supporter of your vision for Charlotte."

He reciprocates her smile and asks for her name. "I never gave it," she responds as she shakes his hand.

Tilting his head up slightly, he signals to his campaign manager that he can leave as he turns his attention to this beautiful woman with alluring green eyes.

"I detect a slight accent," his eyes drawn to the rose tattoo with five delicate petals adorning her chest.

"I'm a little Creole Queen from New Orleans, but Houston is my home," she reveals. "By the way, my name is Jazmine, but everyone calls me Jaz."

He takes her hand, bringing it to his lips for a gentle kiss. "Would you like to discuss my vision somewhere else?" he suggests.

"Sure, let's see if your mouth is as good as the promises you made during your speech," she teases back with a smirk.

His lips curve up into a grin. A woman with a good sense of humor always catches his attention. He decides to have one of his security team members escort her to where he will be in a matter of minutes. As he walks away, he takes out his phone and sends a text message: *Bring that bitch to the private bathroom upstairs in five minutes.*

He leisurely walks through the crowd, eventually taking the elevator to the second floor. He waits for the woman to be delivered to him so he can devour her like all the others before her.

He enters the bathroom and sits on the stool in front of the sink. He calls Gwendolyn and informs her that he will see her after the banquet. She reminds him that time is money and he better not be late. He chuckles into the phone and assures her he will be there shortly.

There are three knocks on the door, and he yells, "Come in."

Jaz slides the door open seductively and struts towards him with one stiletto heel placed carefully in front of the other. He looks up and sees her twirling her fingers through her soft curls.

She stops in front of him, lifts her foot, and presses the tip of her heel against his chest. "I want you to bend me over this sink and fill me with your vision," she demands.

"But first, you're going to eat this pussy," she adds with a sultry smirk.

"I've never been afraid of Creole food," he boasts as he loosens his tie, unbuttons his shirt, and tosses it carelessly onto the floor.

She slowly slides her lacey black panties down and stuffs them into his mouth. "Suck on these," she instructs.

She moves around behind him, circling him like a predator stalking its prey. Her lips brush against his ear as she leans in and kisses it softly. Her hands glide down his chest, fingertips tracing every curve and dip of his body until they reach his pants. Confidently, she unzips them and pulls out his dick through the opening.

Her fingers wrap around him, stroking and teasing him as he moans and muffles sounds against her panties. "You love how I touch you, don't you, Mayor?" she whispers huskily into his ear. "Just wait until after you eat my pussy and bend me over. I want to feel your vision explode down my throat," she teases.

His dick twitches in her hand, and she lightly tugs on his earlobe with her teeth. "Are you ready, Mayor?" she asks.

He nods eagerly, unable to resist the dominance that radiates from Jaz. Among all the women he's slept with, none have controlled him like she does. It turns him on as he closes his eyes and waits for the first taste and scent of her pussy on his tongue.

With a swift movement, she grabs the panties from his mouth and twists them tightly around his throat. As he falls to the floor, she presses her knee into his back, immobilizing him. The Mayor never had a chance to regain control. With both knees planted firmly between his shoulder blades, she pulls on the panties with all her strength, attempting to cut off his air supply.

Gasping for air, he frantically tries to break free from her hold. But she clings on with determination, as if riding a mechanical bull. With one final tug, she yanks his neck back and slips her panties from around his neck, pulling him into a rear choke hold. She applies more pressure as his body convulses, and he falls unconscious.

Shifting him onto his back, she notices his limp dick and can see why he's known for fucking the women in the city. "It's quite attractive," she muses.

She reaches into his pocket and pulls out his phone. She quickly tucks her panties back into her dress before walking out the door. The two security men who escorted her upstairs were waiting for her outside. She flashes them a flirty smile and a wink. "So, who's going to escort me downstairs? Or am I supposed to make my own way?"

They exchange a look before replying, "Ma'am, you can go ahead, but we'll need to wait for the Mayor to leave first."

She chuckles, "Looks like it might be a while. My skills have him on the floor."

Jaz quickly heads towards the exit of the building while the security guards barge into the bathroom, paying no attention to her. She hears their voices and footsteps receding as she rushes away.

The guards immediately notice the Mayor laying on his back with his pants unzipped and his private area exposed. They carefully lift him off the floor, trying their best to avoid touching him. One guard refuse to go near his dick, while the other reluctantly fixes the Mayor's pants. He notices his colleague looking away in discomfort and announces, "All done," when he's finished.

The team member's head snaps towards the Mayor in a sharp movement. The man who was previously kneeling on the floor jumps up and delivers a punch, striking the other guard's chin with incredible speed. The guard stumbles backwards, his face contorted in pain as he slams into the wall nearby. Fueled by a surge of adrenaline and armed with expert fighting techniques, the man charges at the guard, unleashing a flurry of elbows and kicks until his opponent collapses to the floor.

He stands at the sink, his knuckles coated in deep red blood. A satisfied grin stretches across his face as he washes away the evidence of his vicious act. The water turns a sickly shade of crimson, mixing with the soap suds to create an unsettling sight. "Damn, that woman made my job easy," he muses to himself while admiring his reflection in the mirror.

Turning back to Mayor Rittenhouse, he taunts, "Look who we have here. You should really learn to stay away from these kinds of women."

With a swift slap to the face, he continues, "Get up, you cheating muthafucker."

As he drags the trembling Mayor towards the toilet, he sneers, "The funny thing about cheaters is, they never know when to stop. Your wife may be dumb as fuck, but that Josephine... she's one sick and twisted lady. And she's the reason I'm about to kill your sorry ass."

He chuckles darkly before adding, "Sometimes, things don't end well when you piss off your side chick."

Disguised as a security guard, Dominic easily infiltrated the Mayor's event. He knew the Mayor would be upstairs fucking a woman, but he didn't anticipate the woman's own hidden intentions. As the Mayor gasps for air in his final breaths, Dominic smirks with satisfaction before discreetly disposing of any evidence and leaving the Mayor's head floating in the toilet. Using a sharpie, he scribbles "HERE LIES THE CHEATER OF CHARLOTTE" and signs it "RELATIONSHIP KILLER."

This is only the first kill of the night in Charlotte, and Dominic can hardly contain his excitement for his next target.

"MEN WITH INSATIABLE GREED PLAY A
DANGEROUS GAME WITH MULTIPLE WOMEN WHO
KNOW AND UNDERSTAND THEIR SITUATION. THEY
WILL CONTINUE TO PLAY THEIR ROLES. AS LONG AS
THEY FEEL LIKE THEY ARE THE MOST IMPORTANT
PERSON IN YOUR LIFE. BUT IF YOU STOP MAKING
THEM FEEL THAT WAY, THEY WON'T HESITATE TO
HIRE SOMEONE LIKE ME TO ELIMINATE YOU. IN
THEIR MINDS, IF THEY CAN'T HAVE YOU, NO ONE
ELSE WILL EITHER."

CHAPTER 36

Dominic waits in his car, knowing the chaos that will soon erupt at the Mayor's event. Before leaving his disposable phone inside the building, he made sure to call the police and inform them that the Mayor's head was floating in a toilet. He also mentioned that The Relationship Killer was in town, and there may be more murders tonight.

As the approaching sirens reach his ears, Dominic glances in his rearview mirror and watches the police and EMS vehicles speed towards the building. The officers rush out of their cars while the EMS team unloads a stretcher and hurriedly follows them inside.

It always baffles Dominic why medical services would take a dead body to a medical examiner when he had already informed them of how the Mayor died. To add insult to injury tonight, he called Thompson Funeral Home and paid them to come pick up the body from the scene. Of course, the police won't release it until they have completed their investigation, given the Mayor's political status.

Dominic puts on his telescope glasses and adjusts the focus. He sees Josephine comforting the Mayor's wife. She is notorious for being a cold-hearted mistress but fiercely loyal to her friends. Before the Mayor's death, she never asked for any financial favors and assured Dominic that all his assets would go to his wife and children.

Dominic watches as the paramedics bring the limp body out of the building and load it onto the ambulance. The corrupt city will likely spin a story about the Mayor suffering a sudden and severe heart attack.

As he turns on the car radio, a familiar song starts playing - *Love and Happiness* by Al Green. Dominic can't help but yell in excitement and beat his steering wheel to the rhythm of the music.

He believes that if he's not killing, he's not truly happy; it's what the universe is telling him. He starts driving towards his next target, debating whether or not to make it a slow and painful death or take him instantly. The more he thinks about it, the more aroused he becomes, feeling his dick pressing against his pants.

While driving, he uses Bluetooth to call Graciana. She answers, scolding him for not taking her along for tonight's mission. He laughs and tells her she is like a ray of sunshine in his dark world.

"Go ahead and call your dad. Tell him where you are," Dominic says.

"Do I have to?" Graciana responds over the phone.

"Yes, you do," he insists, "unless you want me to call your mom."

Graciana quickly agrees to call her dad instead, not wanting her Mami to come looking for her. "I had a great time visiting you," she adds.

"I'll make sure to come and see you more often," Dominic promises. "And when I do, we'll rent a yacht and swim with dolphins or something."

Graciana can hardly contain her excitement at the idea of a luxurious outing with her Uncle. It's something she has never experienced before. "Uncle Dominic, please be careful tonight. I love you."

"Love you too, Grace," he responds before ending the call.

It's the first time that he has smiled since Tiana left him. Now, he's having doubts about getting into a firefight with the police.

He continues driving down I-85 until he reaches Belmont and pulls into the project's parking lot. He takes a moment to survey his surroundings and notices a few children who should be home by now since it's after midnight. Other than that, most of the guys from the neighborhood are at the club trying to get some pussy.

According to his sources, Devontae always stops by to see his child's mother every other Friday. She may not care about his cheating ways but is resentful that he forces her to stay in the hood while he lives it up with other women in a fancy condo downtown.

When Devontae confronted him at the Columbus hotel with Tiana, Dominic put his plan into motion. It was an easy set-up, and Devontae's baby mama wouldn't have to pay a penny. She had the foresight to always insure Devontae with a policy worth over 2 million dollars.

Dominic pulls two sets of army green brass knuckles from his kill bag and slides them onto his hands. He slings his bag over his shoulder and walks towards the apartment complex door.

In the midst of everything else happening, Devontae's baby mama had initiated a heated argument fifteen minutes ago, and it was still raging. She was shouting for him to leave while Dominic could hear Devontae yelling back at her, "Fine, I'll go. Why do I even waste my time with you and your trashy ass?"

Dominic drops the bag onto the ground, standing still as he waits for Devonte. The front door swings open, but Devonte, preoccupied with his ex-girlfriend, barely notices. Finally, he turns around to leave, and that's when Dominic strikes, hitting him in the mouth with brass knuckles and landing another punch to his eye.

The phrase "country boy" enters Dominic's thoughts, and he despises being labeled as such. He quickly raises his arms and delivers a series of blows to Devontae's face with the brass knuckles on his hands. Blood gushes out, and a few teeth fly onto the floor.

Dominic's fists continue to pummel Devontae's face as he yells at Veronica, "Lock yourself in the bathroom!" He hears her footsteps retreating up the stairs but doesn't glance up.

He has one goal: to damage Devontae's eye sockets and jaw. When he's content with the bloody masterpiece he has created on Devontae's face, he rises from his seat, retrieves his bag from outside, and forcefully shuts the front door behind him.

Dominic hears Devontae's cries of pain as he rummages through the bag, searching for his sharpest knife. Upon finding it, he turns back to Devontae and reaches inside his mouth, gripping his tongue tightly as he pulls it out. Despite Devontae's screams and pleas, Dominic ruthlessly slices through his tongue with the sharp blade.

Dominic's sinister laugh echoes through the room. "You dumb fuck, you weren't even supposed to be on my list of targets. But lucky for me, you're a cheater."

He stands up and rummages through his bag again, removing his brass knuckles and retrieving a rope. He effortlessly ties the rope into a noose around Devontae's neck and drags him up the stairs, his limp body bouncing along like a lifeless puppet. Upon reaching the bedroom, Dominic starts to search for a sturdy object from which to hang the rope.

He angrily tosses the mattress aside and yells, "You're a cheap bastard! Your baby's mother is sleeping on these metal rails? This bed frame probably cost less than two hundred dollars."

He ties the rope tightly around the other end of the frame, then picks Devontae up from the floor. Dominic glances at Devontae one last time; he couldn't see or speak after the vicious attack. With a smirk on his face, Dominic blows a kiss into the air. "Kiss your ass goodbye," he scoffs. "Who's the country boy now?"

Devontae is thrown out of the window, his body colliding with the unforgiving red bricks of the building. He crashes into the window frame with a resounding thud, causing it to shake slightly. The bed rails tremble but remain sturdy in their place.

Dominic exits the room and pauses by the bathroom. "Veronica, make sure your children are taken care of," he instructs her. "Follow our prepared script when speaking with the police, and enjoy your new life," he adds as he gathers his belongings and leaves the apartment.

He steps out the front door, glad the children have vacated the area. Everyone in the complex dislikes Devontae, so no one will report what happened tonight.

With his voice changer on, Dominic calls 911, "What's your emergency?" the operator asks on the other end of the line.

"As promised," he says with a grim satisfaction, "there has been another killing. The body is hanging out of the window at the Belmont Housing Project." Without waiting for a response, he hangs up and tosses the phone out the car window as he drives away.

After a successful kill, he can't wait to get some eggs and hashbrowns from his favorite spot. "The fucking Waffle House, here I come," he mutters to himself with a dark grin.

CHAPTER 37

After receiving a call from Graciana, Malakai arrives at the cottage and knocks on the door. Graciana greets him with a hug and offers him breakfast. He admires the cozy interior with wood panel walls and a stone fireplace, and particularly enjoys the scent of his favorite meal: an omelet, grits, and T-bone steak.

"If your mom were here, she would love this place. I can't believe your Uncle didn't make you stay at Motel 6 just to fuck with me," he jokes.

"It's becoming clear to me that you and Uncle Dominic have more similarities than you realize. He said the same thing to me." She laughs softly and plops down in a chair next to him.

She presses the power button on the remote and switches to the local news channel. "There hasn't been much coverage on the Mayor, but I feel he's no longer alive. While scrolling through Facebook, I've seen countless conspiracy theories claiming The Relationship Killer was involved in his death," she shares with her dad.

As the news reporter on TV begins covering the story of a body found hanging outside a project window, Graciana cheers and claps excitedly. Convinced it's Uncle Dominic's doing, she beams with satisfaction, celebrating his revenge being complete.

Malakai cuts through his steak with a grunt, paying no attention to Graciana's admiration for her Uncle. She laughs when she notices the look on her Papi's face.

"Don't worry, Papi. Mami told me how amazing you were back in your day. But now you're just a retired man who loves poetry," she reassures him.

"Retirement and caution are two different things," he responds defensively. "And I don't want to draw too much attention to my organization."

"Ahh, but I can't wait to see 'Malakai the Great' in action again!" she exclaims.

"Speaking of greatness," he interjects, "you did an incredible job keeping your Uncle out of trouble while you were in Georgia."

"Oh, that was easy," Graciana says nonchalantly. "I even got to stab a woman in the shoulder during one of our adventures."

After breakfast, her father reminds her that they have a meeting in the suburbs, and she eagerly agrees to ride with him.

"I'm so glad you're excited about Uncle Dominic. If he keeps getting into trouble, you can use your college fund to buy him cigarettes for the next fifty years," he jokes.

"Uncle Dominic is too slick for prison. I've seen him in action; he's like the Equalizer, tearing apart his enemies," Graciana adds confidently.

Malaki tries to silence Graciana's praise for her Uncle, insisting that the eggs are flawless. He's not envious, but he believes his daughter should only idolize him.

He casually drops his fork onto the plate and confidently declares that the Equalizer doesn't stand a chance against John Wick. With a swift motion, he pushes his chair back and jumps to his feet. "Let's ride," he says with a smirk. "I'll show you who's the most feared man in this family."

Graciana can't help but giggle as she covers her mouth with her hands. Her mother always said that a daughter's love could stroke a man's ego and drive him to do anything for her. Today, she will see if the stories about her Papi are true.

They make their way outside and get into the car. "Since you're so curious about your Uncle and his reckless ways, I'll show you how things should be done," he says, clearly annoyed by his brother's actions. "I should have just left you at home with your mother."

Graciana shrugs, unfazed by his complaints. "Everyone always says that. But how will I learn about our family business and protect myself when necessary if I stay home?" she retorts confidently.

As he starts the car and drives towards their destination, he can't help but think aloud, "I wish you could have stayed a baby forever because this world is too overwhelming for someone as anxious as you."

Graciana keeps talking throughout the drive to the River Runs Golf Community. Malakai parks his car behind another one in the driveway next to a brick house adorned with a "for sale" sign on the front lawn. The neighborhood reminds Graciana of those extravagant homes featured on one of those *Real Housewives* shows on Bravo.

She couldn't help but wonder if anyone would come to their house and cause problems. "Do you ever worry about people causing trouble at our home?" she asks.

"I had only experienced that once in my life, and someone on the inside did it," he explains as he reaches under his seat to retrieve two silenced Glock 34s. "These are the same ones used by John Wick in the movies," he adds with a smile.

"You have a .22 caliber gun under your seat just in case someone comes out of the back. Let's put all the training I've given you to the test."

He checks his watch and sets a five-minute timer before walking towards the house. As the doors open, Graciana watches as her father swiftly takes down a man with one blow to the head and rushes inside.

Gunshots ring out throughout the house, and Graciana can barely contain her excitement as she sees another man trying to make a run for it from behind the house.

Following orders, she reaches under the seat and retrieves her 22. With the gun in hand, she exits the car and aims it at the man. "Don't move, or I'll shoot," she warns.

"Get out of my way, little girl," he sneers as he charges at her.

Without hesitation, she pulls the trigger twice, hitting both of his kneecaps with precision. The man collapses to the ground, howling in pain. "You little bitch!" he screams.

Her laughter echoes as she playfully scolds, "I told you to stay put!" She leans against the car, waiting for her Papi to emerge from the house.

Malakai storms out of the front door, pushing some unfamiliar guy along with him. Malakai kicks the man in the butt, and the guy stumbles down the steps. With a rough hand, he pulls him back up and slaps him on the head with his gun. "Hurry up," he grumbles. "It's all your fault I'm stuck in this town.

"Get the zip ties, Graciana," Malakai orders as he drags the man towards the car.

Graciana quickly binds the man's hands with the ties while Malakai opens the trunk. "Get in there," he barks at the man, shoving him towards the open trunk.

The man yells out, "You might as well just kill me now. I'm not going anywhere with you all!"

"Michael Oliver Patterson, you've probably seen the news by now. Your childhood friend Devontae is dead. Don't end up like him," Malakai warns.

Malakai gives a strict order to Grace: "If this man makes any sudden movements, shoot him in the head."

Malakai's hand moves with lightning speed as he sheathes his gun and grabs Michael's head in a tight grip. He forcefully slams Michael's head against the car trunk multiple times, causing his body to convulse until he loses consciousness. "I hate having to say things twice," Malakai mutters through gritted teeth. "You have me fucking you up in front of my daughter."

Graciana's face lights up at the sight of her Papi's ruthless side. But along with that excitement comes a hint of fear; she has only ever known him as someone who smiles and laughs.

With a forceful shove, Malakai pushes Michael into the car's trunk and slams it shut. "Alright, let's hit the road," he says to Graciana as they drive off with Michael in tow.

"You know, Papi, I take back my comment about retirement. You definitely still have some tricks up your sleeve," Graciana remarks in awe.

CHAPTER 38

Catalina cautiously approaches Gwendolyn's heavily guarded home, feeling a tremor run through her body as she exits her car and waits for an escort inside. Once she's in, she sees people frantically shuffling boxes, shredding documents, and IT experts hunched over laptops in the library.

She lets out a sigh of relief and says a silent prayer that they can get Tiana out without any issues. After navigating past the chaos downstairs, Catalina makes her way upstairs to find Tiana packing a bag for their evening plans. She greets her with a hug and whispers about the commotion downstairs.

Tiana pleads, "Please tell me you've spoken with Sasha, and she has a plan to get me out of this predicament."

Catalina responds, "Yes, there is a plan, though I'm not sure how great it is. Let's discuss everything once we're at the rooftop. The loud music will ensure that the guards won't overhear us."

Tiana mentions that she's been cooped up in the house since Catalina left, and while Michael usually drops by to annoy her, he hasn't shown up today.

"Then consider yourself lucky," Catalina urges as she hurries Tiana. "Let's get out of here before Gwendolyn tries something shady."

They quickly exit the room and hop into Gwendolyn's SUV, accompanied by two bodyguards in the front seats. Catalina gives the driver their hotel address, and he inputs it into the GPS before starting the vehicle and driving towards their destination. As they ride, Tiana asks Catalina if she's seen Dominic.

Catalina pauses, stares out the window for about thirty seconds, then responds. "Yes, I have, but we can talk more about it at the club. Right now, let's focus on relaxing and seeing some dicks."

"You're wild, girl, and I love you for it," Tiana laughs. "Thanks for convincing me to get out of the house this weekend. I needed this adventure."

After driving for forty-five minutes, the SUV stops at a hotel with a rooftop bar called Sky's the Limit. The bodyguard in the passenger seat exits the car and tells the driver to park before joining them upstairs on the rooftop.

He then helps Tiana and Catalina out of the car. "Have fun tonight, ladies, but please behave. I don't get paid enough to babysit," he warns.

Catalina playfully shoves her hand in his face. "Moverse estúpid," she says in Spanish as they walk past him.

"Don't forget to tell your partner to take our luggage to the Presidential Suite," Tiana reminds him.

Once inside the hotel, they rush to the elevator and press the button for the 22nd floor, where the rooftop bar is located.

As the elevator doors slide open, a lively scene unfolds before them. Strings of colorful lights dangle from the high ceiling, casting a warm and welcoming glow over the space. People of all ages and backgrounds mingle. Their vibrant attire and expressive faces add to the festive atmosphere.

The reserved section offers an unobstructed view of the starry night sky, twinkling with thousands of stars. Behind a sleek counter, a skilled bartender mixes drinks while taking orders. The open-air setting allows a refreshing breeze to flow through, gently rustling their hair and clothes.

Catalina glances at the guard standing nearby. "Can you back up a little bit?" she asks, then shakes her head. "Never mind, just stay where you are." She smirks knowingly. "I have a surprise for you later on. I bet you'll move then."

"Leave that man alone, Catalina," Tiana chides playfully. "Let's focus on enjoying the show." She peruses the drink menu and selects their first round before sinking back into the plush cushions of her lounge chair.

Music fills the air as they wait for the evening's entertainment to start. When the host finally appears on stage, he electrifies the crowd with his infectious energy and gets everyone pumped for what's to come.

Catalina purposely chose this spot because of the diverse range of dancers, both men and women, who will perform tonight. And even though there is a mix of genders in the audience, no one here will be offended by any suggestive movements or displays of dicks and titties during the show. It's all part of the fun and freedom of being at this particular venue.

"The moment you have all been anticipating has arrived. Ladies and gentlemen, are you prepared for the one and only Mr. Wetness?"

The crowd gathered on the rooftop is a mass of anticipation, eagerly awaiting the arrival of the main event. As booming music blasts from the speakers, their faces light up excitedly. And then, he appears - a tall, muscular black man oozing confidence, with 10-inch dick appeal. He struts confidently, his bare chest glistening under the lights as he approaches center stage. Adorned only in calf-length boots and a brimmed hat, his body is a masterpiece.

"Ladies, don't be shy - who's ready to get soaked?" the host yells into the microphone.

In the center of the room stands a chair directly under a metal pole with a shower head attached. Mr. Wetness sits in the chair. The fluorescent lights make the water shimmer and sparkle as it sprays and flows over his toned muscles, each droplet clinging to his skin like a precious gem. He moves gracefully to the music, a mesmerizing sight to behold.

The hosts call out, "Mercedes Chanel, are you in the audience? You have been chosen to be the first one to ride Mr. Wetness. Get up and slide on his dick!"

Tiana looks over at Catalina, clearly hesitant. "Come on, girl! Just do it," Catalina urges.

But Tiana responds, "I can't just jump on some random guy's dick. I'm trying to fix my relationship."

During a moment of carelessness, Catalina lets slip, "You need to hop on that man's dick before Dominic shows up and kills you anyway."

Catalina gasps and immediately covers her mouth, holding onto Tiana's hand. "I didn't mean to say that, Tiana. I wasn't thinking before I spoke."

Confusion and anger wash over Tiana's face. "What the fuck are you talking about? Is Dominic trying to kill me?" She demands the truth about what happened when Catalina returned to Columbus and warns her not to lie. Tiana's tone is stern and severe.

As Catalina remains silent, the host calls out, "Ladies, unfortunately, Mercedes is not present. Moving on to our next contestant, Diana."

Tiana doesn't bother to find out who Diana is or why her friend kept it a secret before she storms off the rooftop with Catalina and their bodyguard following close behind.

They enter the elevator and select the 18th floor. Tiana can't believe what has happened. Her mind is racing, and she can feel her breathing becoming shallow and erratic.

"This can't be true. Dominic would never want to hurt me," she says to Catalina in disbelief. "Tell me you're lying and just playing a prank on me."

"I'm sorry, Tiana. I didn't mean to scare you," Catalina apologizes, placing a comforting hand on her friend's shoulder.

"We'll be safe though. We have Gwendolyn's bodyguards with us." Catalina gives one of the guards a sidelong glance, clearly doubting their abilities. "I hope they know how to fight instead of just talking shit," she mutters under her breath.

"I'm afraid the night has become too dangerous," he states, pressing the button for the lobby. "I must call Gwendolyn and ensure everyone's safety before returning to the house. We will skip the room and head straight downstairs."

Catalina reluctantly nods in agreement as he instructs the other guard to retrieve their car and meet them outside the hotel.

They rush out of the building and eagerly wait for their SUV to arrive. The loud roar of the engine temporarily drowns out their racing thoughts as the vehicle screeches to a stop in front of the hotel.

The guard swiftly opens the back door, ushering them inside, and closes it behind them.

As the guard opens the passenger door, he catches sight of a flash of bright yellow before being struck with a sudden blur of movement. He stumbles backward and falls onto the pavement, clutching his chest in pain.

Meanwhile, the guard on the driver's side removes his sunglasses and calmly speaks over the chaos. "Welcome home, my love," he says before closing the passenger door and accelerating away from the scene.

Dominic's finger hovers over a sleek panel; with each press of a button, the doors and windows lock in place. The glass window separates him from Tiana and Catalina, his gaze fixed on them as he activates the speaker box. He stares hungrily at Tiana, taking in her beauty and anticipating how he wants to slice her clitoris off.

Catalina pounds on the glass with her fist, screaming for Dominic to release them and pleading that he didn't have to kill the guard because he did nothing wrong. But Dominic ignores them, fully focused on his "prize" for the night.

"Relax, Catalina," he snaps impatiently, "the guard only took a beanbag to the chest. He'll recover. Now, sit down before I tie you to the back of the SUV and drag your body down the interstate."

Catalina's body slumps in defeat as she sinks back into her seat, her shoulders drooping and her head hanging low. She reaches out to touch Tiana's leg, trying to comfort her and reassure her that everything will be okay and she won't be left alone with Dominic.

Tiana gazes through the window while Dominic checks her reflection in the rearview mirror, flashing her a smile. He pushes the speaker button and taunts Catalina, asking her if she told Tiana about his plans to dismember her body. But he quickly reassures Catalina that he won't kill her unless she admits to being a cheater like the bitch sitting next to her.

"Catalina, take a moment to observe your friend," he states calmly. "Sitting there in silence, she knows she's guilty. But I'm sure she wasn't so quiet when she was giving my pussy to her ex-boyfriend. I can picture it now - her moaning his name, riding his dick, and letting him fuck her throat." He honks the horn in frustration. "You're such a filthy slut!" he yells angrily.

"I'm going to teach you a thing about respect and commitment. Your pretty ass will learn what it means to be faithful. You'll be the last woman I give my heart to…"

He pauses, waiting for her response.

"Say something, you nasty bitch. You thought you could leave me begging for your love? Yeah, I got your ass now, and you are going to pay for breaking my heart."

Tiana sits in shock, realizing she never knew the monster that lives inside Dominic. She wishes she had stayed with Gwendolyn instead of going out with Catalina.

"Catalina," he says, "once I reach my destination, you can take the car and find my brother. Let him know I've won another round on the chessboard. Checkmate."

CHAPTER 39

Malakai remains quiet and attentive as Sasha briefs her task force on the plan to take down Gwendolyn and her associates. He doubts the plan's effectiveness and is uncertain if it will even work. His phone suddenly rings, and he answers it during the meeting, interrupting the briefing.

After listening for a moment, he tells the caller that he will walk outside in a few minutes before ending the call. As he starts to leave, he overhears one of the agents questioning why he's even there since he's not a part of law enforcement.

Taking a deep breath, Malakai considers walking away, but his sense of pride won't allow him to let anyone disrespect him in this way. He turns around and confidently walks to the front of the room. "Sasha, I'm sorry, but I have to say something. I'm here to ensure that no innocent people get hurt while you are trying to storm the hotel. My information led you here, and you are here only as my backup."

The agents grumble and express their disapproval at being put in their place by a civilian. But Malakai stands firm and scans the room before pointing out their amateur mistakes. He then walks outside into the parking lot, determined to fulfill his role as protector and leader for his family.

As he walks towards the SUV, Catalina runs from the driver's side, screaming, "He has Tiana! Your crazy ass brother is going to kill her!"

Watching her charge towards him, he can't help but think that all Latino women are crazy. He wishes he could slap the shit out of her and tell her to calm down. But instead, he calmly asks her to repeat what she said.

Catalina bends over, resting her hands on her knees as she struggles to catch her breath. She raises her finger in the air, signaling to Malakai that she needs a moment.

"I couldn't tell you everything over the phone," she gasps. "Dominic kidnapped us as we were leaving the hotel. He told me to take the truck and tell you 'checkmate' when I see you. I fear for Tiana's life. You must do something before it's too late."

"Things are really heating up tonight. Dominic won't harm her until he has all the necessary pieces for his plan. Go inside and let Sasha know I'm heading to the hotel, and she can meet me there. Are the keys to the SUV still in the truck?"

"Yes, they are."

"Perfect. Take some time for yourself and relax. I promise you and Tiana can have breakfast tomorrow morning," he guarantees.

Catalina's arms cling tightly around Malakai's neck, her head nestled against his shoulder. She breathes in deeply, savoring his scent - a blend of traditional and bold, fresh and mild, strong and sensual - that lingers on his shirt.

"I have to admit, Catalina, you are my type. But I have a feeling there may be another Hispanic woman keeping an eye on me right now."

He chuckles, pulling away from her embrace and giving her a playful slap on the ass. The sudden impact sends a shiver through her body. She grins, shaking her head in amusement before walking into the building.

He slides into the driver's seat of the SUV, presses the ignition button, and pulls out of the parking lot. He senses that Sasha is a kind person, but he doesn't fully trust her because she works in law enforcement. He promises to provide her with a big drug bust that will boost her career, but he fails to mention that Gwendolyn may not actually be at the hotel.

After Jaz successfully seduced the Mayor and stole his phone, Malakai was able to uncover valuable information that he chose not to share with Sasha and her team.

He drives towards the Sanctuary, a luxurious neighborhood with golf courses, sports facilities, and a private boat.

He dials Jaz's number and asks her to ensure Graciana doesn't go near Michael. "She's been reading a book on different ways to torture people, and I'm afraid she might have some wicked plans in mind."

Jaz assures him that everything will be alright because she is Graciana's beloved Auntie.

He hears Michael yelling in the background while talking on the phone with Jaz. "Sorry, I have to go," she says abruptly before ending the call.

After a forty-minute drive, Malakai arrives at the gates of the sanctuary. He pulls in, and a guard aggressively questions him about who he is visiting. At that moment, he wishes he would have brought Catalina with him to make it seem like Tiana was also in the car, but his top concern was keeping her safe because situations can escalate quickly.

"I'm here to see Gwendolyn Price," Malakai states.

Rather than consulting the log to confirm if Gwendolyn has visitors arriving, the guard decides to assert his power and commands Malakai to exit the SUV.

As Malakai steps out of the vehicle, he notices another guard lounging and scrolling through his phone. He follows instructions and turns to face the SUV while the guard conducts a thorough pat-down, searching for any weapons.

Malakai suddenly pivots and strikes out with his elbow, hitting the guard on the side of his head and causing him to fall to the ground. In one swift motion, he grabs the guard's gun and presses it against his temple, then helps him up to his feet.

Malakai knocks on the door with the gun. The sound echoes through the room, the sharp rap of the metal against the wood filling the air. The young guard's phone drops to the ground with a clatter as he looks up and sees his coworker held at gunpoint.

"Put your weapon on the desk, and we won't have any issues tonight," Malakai says sternly, clarifying that he means business.

The younger guard obeys Malakai's demand. Malakai shoves the guard towards the other one. He quickly grabs the second guard's gun, makes the guards handcuff each other, and then forces them into the nearby bathroom.

"These guards are incompetent and useless. They could never work for me. The level of protection has significantly decreased," he remarks before climbing back into the SUV and driving towards the pier where Gwendolyn's private boat is anchored.

He drives through the exclusive neighborhood, taking a right turn and continuing down the two-mile road. The only light source comes from the dimly lit streetlamps, casting a faint glow over the houses and trees.

The darkness lingers, creating an unsettling feeling. But as he nears the end of the road, the bright lights of the parking lot shine brightly, dispelling the darkness that had enveloped everything before it.

He pulls the car into a parking spot, takes a moment to inspect the firearms he acquired from the guards, and makes his way toward the dock. Memories flood his mind of the last time he was on a pier and how his enemies ambushed him.

His neck whips abruptly from one side to the other. The air resonates with the thudding of his rapid footsteps as he races towards Gwendolyn's boat, his aim swift and precise as he takes down the first guard at the bottom of the ramp without hesitation.

He pivots smoothly and fires at the second guard on the top of the ramp with the same determination and speed.

His heart quickens like a hummingbird's erratic flight as he dashes onto the boat, his feet pounding like drums on the wooden planks. He dives behind a nearby table, seeking refuge from the onslaught of bullets that whistle past his head like a deadly symphony. He realizes with a sinking feeling that this situation will require every ounce of his bravery and skill, and perhaps even more than he thought he had.

With his stomach pressed against the ground, he slowly inches towards the corner of the table. As soon as he has a clear shot, he pulls the trigger and hits the guard's knee before firing a fatal shot to his head. The other guard hears the commotion and rushes in. Malakai carefully listens to each bullet being fired from the guard's gun, counting them in his head as he waits for the perfect moment to strike.

"You should have saved your ammo, you trigger-happy muthafucker."

He springs up from his position and fires two shots into the guard's chest before he can reload. Without hesitation, he rushes towards the stateroom and cautiously peeks around the corner. To his dismay, two more guards stand in front of Gwendolyn's door, ready to defend it at all costs.

"I'm only here for Gwendolyn. If you surrender, I'll let you all live!" Malakai yells.

One of the guards yells, "Fuck you!" and pulls the trigger, sending a bullet flying towards Malakai.

Malakai shakes his head and sighs. "I gave you a warning," he says sternly. "Now, you can die with your friends upstairs."

He dashes up the stairs, taking the steps two at a time. His eyes dart around the deck, searching for the propane tank he had spotted earlier. Finally, he spots it near the bar and makes a beeline towards it. He swiftly grabs the propane tank and rushes back down the stairs to the staterooms.

"Okay, are ya'll ready to die?" Malakai asks.

More bullets fly through the air in response, leaving behind a trail of smoke and sparks. Malakai's grip tightens on the propane tank as he expertly hurls it around the corner. Like a predator swooping in for its prey, he launches himself forward with precision and agility, finger firmly on the trigger. With deadly accuracy, he fires a single bullet that strikes the propane tank and triggers a massive explosion, filling the air with smoke and sparks.

As Malakai lands on the ground with a thud, his body still vibrating from the intense moment, he watches flames engulf the guards' clothing in a blazing inferno—the water from the sprinkler glimmers against the dark backdrop of the stateroom. Smoke billows out, creating an eerie haze.

The guards burst through the stateroom and leap out the window to extinguish the flames engulfing them. But Malakai knows Gwendolyn isn't inside; she must have escaped up top while he was engaged in his first shootout.

He ascends the staircase, frustration evident in his voice. "Gwendolyn, please stop running. Let's have a civilized conversation."

"Who's running?" she yells back in response.

"You need better security," Malakai shouts after her. "Listen, if you give up now, I promise you'll live and won't serve any time. But you only have a few seconds to decide your future."

Gwendolyn is skeptical. "Why should I trust you?" she asks, waiting for a reply. When she doesn't receive one, she shouts at him, "Answer me, dammit!"

"Gwendolyn, I have more than just your life to worry about tonight. You can either listen to me or not; it's up to you. I'm well aware that the second I turn this corner, your firearm will be aiming at me.

"The FBI is currently raiding the hotel your drugs are in. I know you've taken precautions to cover your tracks, but there's an agent on her way who intends to bring your ass down. I can stop that from happening if you put down your weapon and hear my plan. You have two seconds to decide before I take action," Malakai warns.

Gwendolyn scans the boat, her gaze resting on the lifeless body of her guard. The stateroom below is engulfed in flames, and she realizes she is stuck on a boat with a dangerous lunatic. With no other options, she gambles and accepts Malaki's offer.

She hurls her gun away from her. "Fine, I'll take your deal," she concedes. "I'd rather live another night than die."

Malakia appears around the corner, his gun at the ready. "I can't believe you actually bought into all the shit I was saying. I lied to you. Your ass is going to jail for everything, and you'll never get out, my friend."

Malakia flashes a mischievous grin and leans in to plant a playful kiss on Gwendolyn's cheek. His eyes shimmer with amusement as he chuckles at her startled reaction. "I'm just fucking with you, Gwen Gwen," he says with a laugh. "My word is as good as gold."

Her eyes are locked onto his—dark and intense—mirroring her determination and fury like pools of obsidian. She can't help but say, "Why must all my foes be sexy and black?"

"I cannot vouch for your adversaries. I am a one-of-a-kind individual with a strategic mindset. You've just been fucking with the wrong family. Let's disembark from this boat, and I will fulfill my promise to you."

He leads her back to the SUV, and she comments, "This looks like my vehicle."

"It is," he responds. "I'm borrowing it for now."

He takes out his cell phone and calls Sasha, anxiously waiting for her to answer. When she does, she immediately starts barking about how Gwendolyn was not at the hotel.

He quickly explains that he has Gwendolyn with him and that he didn't trust her team. He tells Sasha to come alone to a location where he will send her a text.

After ending the call, he dials Jaz's number. "Our hideout is about to have some more visitors. Once I arrive, you can leave, and I'll take care of everything with Michael."

Jaz confirms and hangs up the phone. Malakai glances over at Gwendolyn as he drives. "I'm getting too old for this John Wick style work," he comments. "And Gwen, it's time for you to retire from your business and live a legal life."

CHAPTER 40

Tiana sits huddled in a dark, locked room with her knees pulled up to her chest. She has tried to reason with Dominic countless times, but it seems futile. This is not the man she fell in love with, the one she wanted to spend the rest of her life with. Despite her anger, some may consider her foolish, but she can't help how she feels for him and blames herself for his transformation into a cruel version of himself.

As she reflects on their relationship, the sound of bolts unlocking breaks through the silence, and a sliver of light from the central warehouse seeps into the room. She looks up to see Dominic standing there, gesturing for her to come out.

In the warehouse, he has set up a romantic dinner with candles. Two Waffle House bags sit on the table. The bags contain delicious breakfast items: eggs with melted cheese, scattered and smothered hash browns, grilled chicken and pork sausage patties. She hasn't had anything to eat since yesterday morning, so she eagerly digs through the bags and sets her plate on the table. With a swift motion, she flips open the lid and grabs a fork to begin her meal.

Dominic catches Tiana just as she was about to take a bite of her scrambled eggs and cheese.

Dominic glances at her with disapproval. "Where are your manners, Tiana?" he scolds. "We always say grace before eating."

He continues, "You've been gone too long and seem to have forgotten some of the qualities I loved about you."

Dominic extends his arms and invites Tiana into his sacred space. He prays to the Heavenly Father, asking for the removal of any impurities in the food and to give strength to their meal. He thanks God for creating life and for allowing Tiana to return home to share this final meal with him. He finishes with an, "Amen."

"Once we finish our meal, could you do me a favor and shower in the other room? The scent of your ex-boyfriend is still lingering on you, and it's making me feel queasy," he states.

"I haven't seen or been near him, Dominic. Why are you being so accusatory? You know that I would never intentionally cause you pain," she admits.

"Lies, lies, lies. All you bitches do is shit on the good guys in this world. We take you in, pour our hearts out to you, and promise you the world. And in return, you leave us for the ex that treats you like garbage.

"I want to trust you, Tiana, but your actions are making it complicated," he says, questioning why she didn't reach out while she was away.

"Gwendolyn threatened me, saying that if I reached out to you, she would have you killed. But I couldn't stop thinking about you the entire time I was away. Dominic, I know this isn't who you really are. If you trust me, we can find a way to make things right. Please listen with your heart instead of letting rage consume you."

"Rage," he laughs. "You haven't seen the depths of the wickedness I am capable of. I have the power to make the devil piss on himself when I tap into my most diabolical instincts.

"You should eat your eggs before they get cold. The longer you stay alive, the more I lose my appetite."

Tiana rises from her chair and forcefully overturns the table, sending food flying all over the floor. "I'm not some ordinary woman," she tells Dominic. "You can't talk to me however you want.

"I love you, but I'm not afraid of you," she continues. "Don't think for a second that I'll be an easy victim who will beg for mercy."

Dominic pauses, then claps his hands together. He looks at Tiana and says, "You're right about one thing - you're not just another victim. Because if you were, I'd have you on your hands and knees licking those eggs off the floor.

"I'm going to step into the other room," Dominic announces. "There's water for you to drink if you're thirsty. And don't try anything stupid while I'm gone. This place is monitored by cameras."

Tiana stands with her arms crossed, determination etched on her face. "And I'm not going back in that dark room either," she asserts.

He shrugs and walks away, ignoring the urge to look back. He mutters to himself, "Pull yourself together, Dominic. Tiana is no different than Jennifer - just another heartbreaker. Your life will be easier once you dispose of her. Stay focused - she deserves the same fate as all the others. Remember your purpose: to strike fear into those who dare to cheat in relationships."

He enters the room and opens his laptop, watching Tiana's every move on the screen. He sends a message to his hacker, asking for Michael's location. But the response is not what he wants to hear: the hacker doesn't have access to Michael at the moment.

Frustrated, he types a quick *WTF* and sends it back to the hacker. But the reply is still the same: *no access.*

Dominic scratches his head, staring at the message in disbelief. He picks up his laptop and throws it against the wall, shattering the lid and cracking the screen.

Growing angrier, he pulls out his phone and dials his brother's number, only to reach his voicemail. "You've been a thorn in my side for years!" he yells into the phone. "I know you're behind Michael's disappearance. If you want to play hero, let's settle this once and for all: Tiana's life for yours."

His frustration boils over as he realizes he can no longer live in Malakai's shadow. Despite his meticulous plan, his brother has taken another piece off the board.

His gaze fixates on the monitor, observing Tiana's restless figure pacing the room with rapid, agitated steps. She looks different now - her eyes, once bright, are now clouded with worry, and her shoulders are tense with stress. Why couldn't she remain the woman he first met? "Damn it, Tiana. We could have truly been happy together."

He yearns for her kisses, a final taste of her sweet and succulent pussy. His thoughts turn to sex, causing his dick to stir in his pants. He slaps it away and reprimands himself, determined not to be disloyal like everyone else in this world.

With a relentless stride, he leaves the room without so much as a glance in Tiana's direction. He reaches for a footlocker on the floor and unlocks it. Opening the box, he reveals a sleek and deadly Heckler & Koch submachine gun, along with several magazines and a bulletproof vest. He also retrieves other items from the trunk - mysterious objects that he knows will serve him well when his plan comes to fruition.

He slams the trunk shut with a forceful thud; his tense muscles visible as he loads one of the magazines into the machine gun. His eyes are steely and determined as he returns to the room with Tiana. "I suggest you find refuge in the other room," he says coldly. "It's bulletproof, and I'll even give you a flashlight this time."

"Go to hell, Dominic. Holding me hostage here is stupid. I never once cheated on you with Michael or anyone else while I was away." She spits out the words with venom, her voice filled with hurt and frustration.

He straps on his bulletproof vest to ensure it is snug and properly fastened. "Now it's a battle against my own flesh and blood. You can continue to scream at me, or you can seek shelter as I get ready to defend myself.

"Tiana, you were my ray of light in a world of darkness, and all I wanted was to spend every moment with you for the rest of my life."

"There is no need for anyone to lose their life tonight. What would Sasha think? What about her children who care for you?"

His fingers glide along the cold metal of the gun, taking in its power and weight. "The world doesn't care about me, but they will never forget The Relationship Killer. Maybe my brother can change my mind, and we can have a happy ending. However, I highly doubt it. Time is ticking away, and the game has begun." He smirks as he walks away from her.

CHAPTER 41

Malakai enters the building and is immediately greeted with a chaotic scene. Michael sits shirtless with jumping cable clamped to his nipples. As he approaches Michael, he hears Jaz shouting, "Get your badass over here!"

Graciana sprints through the room, wielding a tiny sledgehammer as Jaz chases after her. She comes to a sudden halt when she spots Malakai. The sledgehammer falls from her grasp and hits the ground with a loud clang. "Your little ass is in trouble now," Malakai warns, pointing at her. "Go sit your ass down before I lock you in the trunk."

Jaz arrives, out of breath. "You should really consider signing her up for track and field. I've been chasing her since our last phone conversation. Who's the white woman?"

"Gwendolyn Price, the leader of the recently busted hotel drug operation," Malakai states. "She's no longer a threat to us."

He gestures towards a seat and tells Gwendolyn, "Please sit down, and let's strategize together."

Malakai walks over to Michael and forcefully removes the clamps from his nipples. Michael's eyes widen in pain, and his chest is red and raw from where the clamps were attached. Gwendolyn stands nearby, observing the scene with fear and curiosity.

Michael grits his teeth, addressing them all. "You're all going to regret this, especially that little girl. Gwendolyn, are you siding with these people now?"

Sasha enters the building just as Gwendolyn is about to answer. "I'm here, and I followed your instructions to come alone."

"Thank you for understanding. I am pressed for time and have many tasks to juggle to save everyone, especially when my family is at risk. Our first priority is to ensure Michael becomes the Relationship Killer, effective immediately."

Jaz approaches the table next to Michael and grabs a pair of tweezers. She carefully plucks strands of hair from Michael's head, placing each strand into small envelopes. Next, she uses a syringe to extract some blood from his arm and transfers it to a test tube.

"Sasha, you are the only one who can access the case files. You have to find a way to place this evidence near the scene of the crimes in Alabama and Georgia. It doesn't matter how you do it. Just ensure that the local police get credit for finding it. They'll believe anything, and it will implicate Michael, and Charlotte's murders will be traced back to him as well.

"Furthermore, it is imperative that Gwendolyn remains unharmed and avoids any potential legal consequences. She can address the situation publicly and shift the blame onto one of her employees, if necessary."

"Hold up, wait a damn minute. Why shouldn't she suffer the consequences of her actions? The drugs, the killings, the abductions?" Sasha asks.

Malakai inhales deeply and focuses his gaze on Gwendolyn. "It took a great deal of investigation, and I had to verify my sources multiple times before confirming their validity.

"Gwendolyn is Dominic's biological mother." The room falls into stunned silence as everyone looks at each other, shocked by Malakai's revelations.

"Nearly three decades ago, she was impregnated by Theodore Price, her father's most trusted bodyguard," he explained. "Gwendolyn's father refused to pass his legacy on to a daughter who preferred men of color. He forced her to give up the baby and had our father killed."

Tears well up in Gwendolyn's eyes; her long lashes reflecting the light as they glisten. She can no longer hold back her emotions, and her face contorts with hurt and anguish. "I'm sorry," she sobs. "I always loved my son, but I could never find him, even with all the resources at my disposal."

"The only thing you did correctly in your life was suffocating your father while he slept and taking over his business. I'm grateful for that, as it shows you might have genuinely loved our father. However, he meant nothing to me. He abandoned my mother, leaving her to fend for herself. And I never even knew I had a brother until he attempted to kill me."

He smacks his hands together, signaling the end of his storytelling session. "It's time for me to face the rest of this night. Gwendolyn and Michael, you're both coming with me. Jaz, there's been a change in plans. You're coming along too. Sasha, you have a long drive back to Alabama and Georgia."

Graciana's hands wildly motion as she bounces up and down. "What about me, Papi?" she asks.

Malakai responds, "Sasha can take you with her and leave you at Catalina's. You'll be safe there."

Malakai grabs Michael's arm and forcefully pulls him out of the chair, leading him out of the building. The rope around Michael's wrists and ankles tightens as he shuffles along. A look of confusion and anger crosses Michael's face as he is dragged against his will.

Sasha charges towards him and strikes him in the mouth with the butt of her pistol. "That's for coming to my home and messing with my loved ones," she seethes as she spits at him. "I hope you don't make it through the night!" she screams angrily.

Malakai quickly switches vehicles and tosses Michael into the trunk, with Gwendolyn in the passenger seat and Jaz in the back. He turns on the ignition, and the sound of AC/DC's *Highway to Hell* fills the car.

Jaz chuckles, looking at Malakai with excitement in her eyes. "This is the perfect song for our journey," she exclaims. "Let's go save the world!"

CHAPTER 42

Malakai pulls his car up to the abandoned detention center where Dominic is holding Tiana captive. He parks, opens the trunk, and drags Michael out by his legs, unceremoniously dropping him on the ground.

"When this is all over, my crew will come for you," Michael threatens Malakai.

But instead of responding, Malakai simply balls up his fist and punches Michael in the mouth. "Shut up," he growls. "All your people are dead. They found your right-hand man hanging from the project window.

"I'll go in first to grab my brother's attention. Once he's distracted, you need to follow me inside. Jaz, make sure to take cover and protect Gwendolyn at all costs."

Malakai tightly grabs Michael's arm, using it as leverage to help him stand up. He then guides him towards the front entrance with a gentle shove. The entrance is adorned with bright red balloons, a stark contrast to the drab grey of the building. Above the entrance, a foreboding sign hangs with ominous words written in black against a white background: "WELCOME TO MY WEDDING... OR YOUR FUNERAL."

Malakai silently prays to God that he won't have to harm his own brother during their inevitable confrontation.

The doors slide open automatically, revealing a vast room approximately the size of half a football field. Doors line the walls of the far corners, and an upper level provides a perfect vantage point for ambushing unsuspecting enemies.

Malakai takes a deep breath and grabs Michael by the arm, pulling him into the building with a swift motion that triggers the motion sensors and illuminates the room. Malakai steps inside, his eyes scanning the space as each light flicks on one by one. A beam of light shines down from above, centering on a pole where Tiana is bound.

Dominic watches from his vantage point upstairs as Malakai moves towards Tiana, manipulating a control switch to dim the lights, except the spotlight focused on her. He then pulls out two smoke grenades and removes their pins before tossing them onto the floor. In one fluid motion, he runs to the other side of the room, pulls more pins, and hurls them over the railing into different areas of the room.

Malakai switches his handgun from safety to fire and cautiously approaches the corner of the room. He removes a handkerchief from his pocket and covers his mouth to block out the toxic fumes.

"Untie me, man! I'm going to suffocate in here!" Michael cries out, trying to escape the room's smoke and fumes.

As Jaz watches the toxic gases escape outside the entrance, she quickly retrieves two gas masks from the back seat. She puts one on Gwendolyn and secures it tightly, then puts on the second one herself. She gives a thumbs-up signal to Gwendolyn, who nods in response, indicating she is okay.

Malakai raises his gun and fires a shot into the air, signaling Jaz to enter and find shelter quickly. She rushes in and positions Gwendolyn behind a nearby desk, instructing her not to move.

As the smoke dissipates, they realize that the entrance doors have closed behind them, imprisoning them inside. Dominic watches their movements from within his night vision scope.

"Thanks for bringing more guests to our little get-together. I see the women and Tiana's bitch ass boyfriend."

Malakai directs his flashlight towards Michael, forcefully pushes him to the ground, and swiftly cuts the rope binding his ankles. "Listen, it would be wise for you to avoid any foolish actions, or else you may find a bullet in your head," he warns with intensity.

Michael's feet thunder on the ground as he sprints towards the door, his entire body quivering with each stride. From upstairs, Dominic takes a shot, and the bullet pierces through Michael's flesh, sending a surge of pain coursing through him like an electric shock.

With a cry of pain, Michael collapses onto the ground. "Shit! I'm sorry, please let me go!" he screams.

"You're not going anywhere until I say so!" Dominic shouts back.

"Malakai, I could have taken you down and everyone else the second you set foot in this building. But where's the challenge in that? Let's settle this like the old days. No weapons, just good old-fashioned hand-to-hand combat."

"Sounds good, little brother. Flip on the lights, and I'll be right there," he responds calmly.

Malakai reaches the final step and continues down the hall, spotting Dominic standing there with a seven-inch blade in his left hand. "Wait, I thought this was supposed to be hand-to-hand combat?" Malakai questions as he unloads the rounds from his gun and sets it on the floor.

"It's in my hand, and we are about to fight one-on-one. What's the issue?" Dominic taunts with a smirk.

"Dominic, as my brother, you should know that I don't usually justify killing someone. But this time is different. I'm here for Tiana because she holds significance for Asperilla and myself," Malakai explains.

"Significance? Ha! You probably want to have a threesome with her. Disgusting sex addicts," Dominic lunges at Malakai, his knife aimed directly at his face, snarling a retort as he strikes.

Malakai quickly ducks down, skillfully dodging the swipe of Dominic's blade. He then springs up with a powerful uppercut, delivering a sharp blow to Dominic's ribcage—staggering backwards, Dominic winces in agony.

"Please, Dominic, don't force me to harm you. I care for you deeply and I know the pain of losing something precious. Tiana's sister used to work for me, and her last request was for us to protect Tiana if she ever needed help. That's why I'm here, and so far, you haven't harmed her. I can tell you have feelings for her.

"Without me, you would have been in prison last year. The hacker you were working with betrayed you and planned to expose your true identity. I stepped in, took him out, and found someone more reliable to replace him."

Dominic relaxes his stance and takes a step back, carefully considering Malakai's words. "Alright, I believe you," he finally responds.

Malakai steps closer, urging, "Hand over the knife, and let's get out of here." But in his focus on the weapon, he misses the cunning grin spreading across Dominic's face. With a firm grip on the knife, Dominic slashes it across Malakai's chest in a swift motion, effortlessly cutting through his shirt.

A surge of pain jolts through Malakai's body as he feels the warm, sticky blood seeping into his shirt. Dominic's knee connects with his face, causing a sharp, throbbing sensation. As Dominic's left elbow repeatedly strikes Malakai's head, the pain intensifies.

"Fuck you, Malakai! I'm going to kill all you muthafuckers!" Dominic screams.

The air was heavy with unease as Dominic's hands clenched onto the handle of his knife, his gaze filled with hostility. Malakai's thoughts race with anxiety for the well-being of his loved ones and a steadfast determination to protect them at all costs as he frantically grabs at Dominic's wrists in their powerful scuffle, the sharp tip of the blade dangerously close to piercing Malakai's chest.

Malakai's jaw tightens as he leans in, sinking his teeth into Dominic's hand and drawing blood. His muscles strain as he exerts his energy to throw Dominic to the side. The adrenaline surges through Malakai's body, propelling him back to his feet.

"Get your ass up, Dominic!" he roars with determination.

Dominic's hands shake, his fingers unable to stay still with the surge of nervous energy coursing through him. He glares at the deep red imprint on his skin, his anger rising as he realizes he is not in control as he thought he was. "I'm going to make you feel this pain," he growls, tightening his grip on the blade in his other hand.

Renewed vigor surges through Dominic's body as he springs up and sprints towards Malakai. With precise movements, he lunges forward and drives his knife into Malakai's thigh, causing him to cry out in agony. Without hesitation, Dominic slips behind Malakai and encircles his arms around his neck, restricting his airflow with a powerful chokehold.

Jaz's heart is pounding in her chest as she quickly moves from her spot. She could feel the weight of Malakai's trust in her and the gun in her hand. Despite his plea for her not to harm his brother, she knew that one pull of the trigger would bring an abrupt end to everything. She takes a moment to collect herself and prays that Malakai has a plan.

She hurries to Tiana's side, untying her from the pole and supporting her as they make their way back to Gwendolyn.

Tiana pipes up, "Gwendolyn, why the fuck are you here?"

"Never mind that," Jaz interrupts. "What are we going to do about Malakai and Dominic?"

Malakai's elbow crashes into Dominic's ribs, causing a sharp and intense pain to radiate through his body. Then, Malakai forcefully slams the back of his head against Dominic's face. As a result, Dominic's vision blurs momentarily, and he stumbles backwards in a daze.

Malakai's expression is a mix of both pain and determination as he fights to remove the blade from his thigh. Dominic, on the other hand, approaches with pure rage etched on his face, his eyes fixed on Malakai's movements.

With a final burst of strength, Malakai wrenches the blade out of his leg and plunges it into Dominic's stomach. He deftly twists it to the left before swiftly retracting it.

He hurls the knife down the stairs and gets ready to fuck his little brother up. He begins to hobble towards Dominic, who clutches his stomach, but Malakai doesn't see his brother; he sees another adversary to defeat.

Dominic moves back, and in that moment, he experiences something new: fear and death seem to loom over him, emanating from his own actions.

Malakai swiftly lunges towards Dominic, delivering a hard elbow to his face. He then spins around and wraps his forearm tightly around Dominic's neck, cutting off his air supply. With ease, he lifts Dominic into the air while maintaining the chokehold.

Dominic struggles to break free, but it's futile as Malakai hurls him down the stairs. His body thrashes uncontrollably as he tumbles through the air before landing with a loud thud on the unforgiving ground below.

Malakai descends the stairs slowly, watching Dominic, who crawls along the ground. Despite his best efforts to stand up, Dominic's ankles give out, unable to support his weight due to a shattered bone.

With his muscles taut, Malakai moves closer to his brother, keeping his gaze fixed on his intended victim. He swiftly takes ahold of his brother's head and applies the guillotine choke, feeling the strain on his arm as he exerts pressure against his brother's resistance.

Dominic's face turns a deep shade of red as he struggles for breath, spitting off to the side. Jaz pulls out her gun and fires a shot into the air to warn Malaki, but he doesn't release his grip right away. Finally, Gwendolyn comes out from behind the table, pleading with tears in her eyes, "No, Malakai, that's your own brother. Please stop. I can't bear losing him again."

Malakai lets go of his hold and starts to move along the floor. Jaz hurries over to assist him while Gwendolyn rushes towards Dominic. Tiana is torn, not knowing who she should run to - the man who saved her life or her lover who wanted to end it.

Gwendolyn embraces Dominic tightly, tears streaming down her face. "I'm so sorry, baby. I should have been there for you. I should have searched harder to find you. Please forgive me." She vows to never let him go again.

Tiana storms over and shouts, "You want to fuck him too?"

Malakai informs Tiana that Gwendolyn is his biological mother. In a swift motion, Malakai removes his shirt and wraps it around his wounded leg as a makeshift bandage.

Michael smirks, finding the situation amusing. "This has got to be the most dysfunctional family reunion I've ever attended. Dominic, you're still a country boy," he taunts. "I've been fucking your mother and your girlfriend."

Tiana explodes in anger. "This is all your fault!"

"Whatever, girl. You were nothing but a stripper with half a brain before I came along," Michael retorts. "I made you into something."

Jaz hands Tiana a gun. "Sometimes, you just have to put dogs out of their misery."

Tiana gives a slight nod, indicating that she understands the assignment. However, she gestures for Jaz to wait a moment before proceeding. Tiana approaches the spot where the bloody knife is laying and picks it up. She then asks Jaz for the gun.

Walking over to Michael, Tiana aims the guns at his crotch and fires a single shot. Blood gushes from between his legs as he screams in agony, clutching his hands over his dick.

"I don't know what you're protecting," Tiana remarks coolly. "Your dick wasn't that impressive to begin with."

Throwing the gun aside, she climbs on top of him. Her features twisted in fury, her gaze intense and unrelenting. With a sharp glint of metal, she raises the knife above her head. As she repeatedly drives it into his chest, blood splatters onto her face and clothes, each stab propelling droplets of crimson through the air.

She lifts the knife for one final strike, driving the blade deep into his chest. As she walks back and over to the others, she checks to ensure they're all okay.

Tiana glances at Dominic, her expression wary. "Are you finished trying to kill me, or should I put you out of your misery, too?"

Dominic shakes his head and gasps, "I'm sorry, T." He struggles to catch his breath between sentences.

"Don't ever refer to me as Tiana again. That person is no longer strong enough. From now on, I am Mercedes Chanel," she declares as she wipes the blood off her face.

EPILOGUE

Malakai stands on his rooftop, the vibrant colors of the setting sun casting a warm glow over Tampa Bay as it glistens below. The silhouette of the city's skyline against the sky catches his eye, and he takes a moment to appreciate the beauty of it all. In this peaceful moment, he can't help but feel grateful for the life he still has, especially considering it has been almost two years since he nearly took his brother's life.

Malakai emphasized to his brother that his infamous reputation as The Relationship Killer had ended. The original purpose had been tainted, especially when Malakai found out that Dominic had fucked the plastic surgeon while he was carrying out his hit. He would never confess this secret, knowing that Mercedes would be furious if she ever found out.

Dominic and Malakai attended counseling to repair their relationship, which had a positive outcome. This also helped Dominic mend his relationship with Gwendolyn. Despite everything, Mercedes continues to love Dominic and forgave him after finding out Asperilla tried to kill Malakai more than once.

Malakai was about to recite a poem as the sun descended when he heard Graciana's voice. "Papi," she calls out, "Mami says the guests have arrived. She's still getting ready and asked if you could gather everyone outside before showing them to the dinner table."

He turns on his heel and strides towards Graciana, enfolding her in a warm embrace. She squirms under his tight hold and eventually punches him in the shoulder as he continues to squeeze her.

Graciana meets his gaze with a smile as she looks up at her Papi.

"Why are you grinning, Grace?" he asks curiously.

"Just wait and see," she replies with a mischievous twinkle in her eye. "Now let's go outside and meet the family," she says, pulling him by the hand.

They step outside through the grand entrance, their fingers intertwined. A sleek silver-and-black Mercedes Benz GLS glides up to the gates, its chrome wheels gleaming in the sunlight. The car moves smoothly up the long driveway. Malakai grins, knowing that when playing the game, only one man has more experience than him. The car parks, and a distinguished older gentleman steps out. Known as a father figure to Malakai, he carries the nickname "Kryptonite."

Malakai rushes over and embraces him, relief flooding his face as they reunite after years of being apart. Kryptonite opens the front passenger door, and Ms. Yu Yan gracefully steps out with her hair cascading down to her waist, flashing a dazzling smile that could blind you. Behind them, two of his favorite Asian Assassins, Mei and Meiying, step out from the back seat, with Meiying carrying a pickle jar with a dick floating inside.

"Absolutely not. Meiying, put that dick back in the car. I do not want that object anywhere near our food," Malakai firmly states.

The reunion was filled with joyful celebration as Malakai asks Grace to escort the guests into the dining room while he waits for the others to arrive. Everyone was thrilled to see how much Graciana had grown and remarked on how much she resembles her mother, Asperilla.

Devin and his wife Veronica "Vee" Williams were the next guests, followed by Jaz, Cherry, and Cherry's husband, Dennis. Susan Drummond, the DA, pulls into the driveway and was greeted with a hug from Malakai and a joke about Kryptonite's wife being inside the house, so they all better behave. She tells Malakai that her and Kryptonite's time has passed, and she will not return there again. She plants a kiss on Malakai's cheek before entering the house.

Malakai's excitement builds as he awaits his brother's arrival. It has been over a year since they last saw each other, and Malakai hasn't felt this thrilled since the birth of his daughter, Graciana.

Malakai rushes to the passenger side and opens the door, his eyes widening from the sight of Mercedes. "Are you going to help me up or just stand there, bro?" his sister-in-law asks, surprising him with her pregnancy.

Dominic emerges from the driver's side, joyfully shouting that he will be a father and Malakai an uncle. He held a box of Cuban cigars in his hand to celebrate the occasion. Malakai pulls Dominic in for a hug and kisses his cheek. "Wow, I'm going to be an uncle! This must be the surprise Graciana was so excited about."

Mercedes turns around and playfully scolds them. "Alright, guys, enough of the bromance." Then she turns to Dominic and adds, "Can you lend me a hand getting inside? I'm eating for two now."

More guests arrive: Isabella, Catalina, and Gwendolyn. Gwendolyn is the last to enter the house. She places her hand on Malakai's shoulders and speaks softly. "You remind me of your father in many ways, and he never stopped thinking about you or your mother. I know you have forgiven me, but please forgive him too. He was mixed up with dangerous people, and the only way to protect everyone he loved was to stay away. I care for you as if you were my own son, Malakai." She kisses him on the cheek before walking into the house.

And finally, there was the person responsible for planting all the evidence, connecting each murder to Michael. Sasha arrives with her family: her husband, Robert, and their children, Katrina and TJ.

Malakai embraces each person warmly and leads them into the house, guiding them to the dining room. The table is filled with an abundance of food, steam rising from each dish and filling the air with a tantalizing scent.

"Did you see your surprise, Papi?" Graciana asks eagerly, gesturing towards her Aunt Mercedes, who is pregnant with her first cousin.

Malakai expresses his gratitude and happiness, thanking everyone for spending the holidays with them. He encourages those unfamiliar to get to know one another, as they are all part of a family.

"Where's the lady of the house?" Kryptonite asks playfully.

"She's probably searching for the perfect outfit," Isabella adds with a laugh.

"I heard that shit," Asperilla's voice cuts through the air like a whip when she enters the room. Her attire exudes elegance, with a fitted dress and a brimmed hat elegantly perched on her head. Removing her hat gracefully, she clicks her heels and settles into her seat with poise and dignity. She gives her hat to Graciana, who models around the room, acting like a future mob boss.

Mercedes turns her eyes towards Asperilla. "My sister always spoke highly of you, saying you would do anything to protect the people you consider family. I regret that Ayanna could not live up to that standard; her betrayal is why she's not here with us today. Please know that I fully understand and I am committed to being loyal to Dominic and your family."

Asperilla nods, acknowledging Mercedes. "I'm sure you have many questions," she says. "We can talk more later if you'd like." She smiles warmly. "I also want to wish you a beautiful pregnancy, but are you both absolutely certain about the name Malakai?"

The table fills with joyful laughter. Malakai interrupts the happy moment by tapping his spoon against his wine glass, seeking everyone's attention. "Let's celebrate together," he says, "this is a moment to remember."

He continues, "Building a family of trust is essential for success. And looking around this table, I see future generations sitting with us." His tone turns serious as he adds, "We're not getting any younger, and I want to enjoy life as much as possible. I would go to war with and for anyone at this table."

With that declaration, he raises his glass to a toast. "Will you do the same for me?"

Everyone at the table agrees and responds with a resounding, "Salud!" as their glasses clink together.

"That's perfect because there's a storm brewing, and I can't split myself in two to handle it all," he says as he settles into his chair.

"Before we start eating, why did you have to drop that kind of news on us?" Isabella asks.

"Don't worry about that shit, girl. He's always having these premonitions and bad dreams. We are a strong team; anyone who messes with us will regret it. Now, let's enjoy this glorious Thanksgiving," Asperilla adds.

Jaz scans the room and takes note of the eclectic group gathered. "I propose we call ourselves the Justice League of Thieves!" she exclaims.

Malakai lets out a laugh. "I'm usually the one with poetic ideas, but today, that title belongs to you. I love it. Let's feast, celebrate life, and combine our individual strengths and weaknesses into a formidable force."

The group joins hands as Malakai leads them in a prayer of gratitude before they begin their meal. In his mind, he silently prays that they won't have to assemble the Justice League of Thieves anytime soon.

Meet Flenardo

Flenardo has gained acclaim as the John Wick of Erotica, captivating readers with his urban fiction that seamlessly blends steamy encounters with thrilling action and poignant emotions. His writing transports readers to the rough streets of city life, where he delves into the depths of human feelings and reveals hidden narratives.

When not writing, Flenardo channels his alter ego, Freknardo—a mesmerizing spoken word artist celebrated for his powerful poetry that resonates deeply with audiences. His performances are masterful symphonies of words, painting vivid imagery and evoking raw emotions through his carefully crafted language.

Together, Flenardo and Freknardo form a formidable team where creativity knows no limits, and the magic of words takes flight. Flenardo values connection, seeing every poem, story, or interaction as an opportunity for Verbal Intimacy with new friends, readers, and supporters.

https://freknardo.com/contact-me/

www.ingramcontent.com/pod-product-compliance
Lightning Source LLC
Chambersburg PA
CBHW070629260626
47161CB00007B/2641